Would I Lie to the Duke

THE UNION OF THE RAKES

WOULD I LIE
TO THE DUKE

EVA LEIGH

THORNDIKE PRESS
A part of Gale, a Cengage Company

LIBRARY OF CONGRESS CIP DATA ON FILE.
CATALOGUING IN PUBLICATION FOR THIS BOOK
IS AVAILABLE FROM THE LIBRARY OF CONGRESS.

ISBN-13: 978-1-4328-8841-1 (hardcover alk. paper)

Published in 2021 by arrangement with Avon Books, an imprint of HarperCollins Publishers

Printed in Mexico
Print Number: 01   Print Year: 2021

To Zack

To Zack

ACKNOWLEDGMENTS

This will be my twenty-seventh published romance and you'd think that the process gets easier with so much time and experience. It doesn't. But thanks to the efforts of some truly amazing people, you're currently reading an actual book and not a tear-stained scribbled note of apology.

To begin with, I want to thank Nicole Fischer, who very politely and kindly let me know that perhaps a *romance* and not a thinly veiled critique of capitalism was more what readers wanted. Thank you for guiding me through a rocky and challenging process, to create a book worthy of Rotherby and Jess.

Thank you to Kevan Lyon, who has championed my work for thirteen years, and Patricia Nelson, who keeps an eye on the details.

Thank you to Pamela Spengler-Jaffee, the hardest-working woman in publishing.

My sincerest gratitude and thanks to Rose Lerner, Theresa Romain, Megan Frampton, Sasha Strachan, Jen DeLuca (Hook gifs forever!), Sarah MacLean, Jenny Nordbak, Erin Ljungdahl (sorry Smith's *Wealth of Nations* didn't make it into the book), Farrah Rochon, Caroline Linden, Darcy Burke, and Tracey Livesay.

And thank you, dear reader, for going on this totally awesome '80s-inspired journey with me.

PROLOGUE
ETON COLLEGE, 1797

"This is bollocks," Noel Edwards, Lord Clair, muttered. "I shouldn't even *be* here."

He glanced at the four other E Block boys who, like him, had to spend the entire half holiday trapped in this infernal library as punishment for various misdeeds. Everyone sat at different tables scattered through the library, with sheets of foolscap spread in front of them.

Noel's gaze met the glowering eyes of Theodore Curtis.

"What the hell are you looking at?" Curtis demanded.

"It makes sense that *you're* stuck here," Noel fired back. "Not so sure about him, though." He jerked a thumb in the direction of Duncan McCameron, who leaned back in his chair with the perfect ease of an accomplished sportsman. "Or him," Noel added, nodding at Sebastian Holloway. The tall, bespectacled boy looked at him with alarm, as if terrified to be singled out.

"What about me?" William Rowe's voice was raspy, as if seldom used, and barely audible like it came from a great distance.

Noel turned his attention to Rowe. The pale, sharp-featured boy sat in the farthest corner of the library, either as a means of isolating himself or perhaps Rowe thought he might infect everyone with his peculiarity.

"I have no idea what you do with yourself all day," Noel answered candidly.

"But I know what you do," Rowe said with a strange little smile. "I know what *everyone* does. I'm a watcher. I watch *everything.*" He tapped his temple.

Well. With remarks like that, it was no wonder that everyone gave Rowe such a wide berth.

"What the deuce was Eddings thinking?" Noel grumbled. "Write an essay on who I believe myself to be? It's perfectly obvious who I am."

Curtis said with a sneer, "Oh, yes. We know. Everyone knows because you damn well shove it in our faces." He pitched his voice into an exaggerated aristocratic accent, and flapped his hands in the air. *"La, look at me, I'm a duke's heir."*

"I don't do that with my hands," Noel

shot back. "And that's not how I talk."

"Meaning's the same, though, innit?" Curtis drawled, then he slipped back into the caricature of genteel pronunciation. *"Be my friend, do. We'll have all sorts of jolly fun. Good-time Clair, that's me. Now, who's up for a round of Who Loves Me Best?"*

"Shut your goddamned gob." Noel curled his hands into fists.

"Easy," McCameron said, his voice rolling with a Scottish burr. "Curtis is only trying to rile you up."

"He's having me on," Noel said. "Right? I'm not like that." Of the boys being punished today, he and McCameron were the most alike, and though McCameron was merely an earl's second son, his athletic ability had earned him tremendous popularity at school.

But when Noel looked pointedly at him, McCameron only shrugged.

"I see all sorts of things," Rowe said in his crow's voice. "Like the chap in the middle of a circus — getting folk to do whatever you like. Dancing horses and trained bears, all of 'em, performing at your command."

Noel stared at the strange boy. "Just having a few laughs. No harm in that."

" 'Course not." Rowe smiled eerily at him. "But you're *here*, aren't you? Because of

11

what happened with Master Garlow."

Scowling, Noel jutted out his chin. "The prank didn't hurt anyone."

It *was* harmless. All Noel had done was convince a group of boys to splash ink on the teacher's garments in the clothespress whilst Noel distracted Garlow outside his rooms, using some nonsense questions about Latin verb declension.

When they'd been caught, it had come out that Noel had been the one to come up with the prank. The other boys had been flogged, but this special punishment had been given to Noel, who lost a half holiday to languish in this infernal library.

"Do you know how much togs cost, Clair?" McCameron asked.

Noel snorted, then — "I . . . don't, in truth."

"It's at least three months' wages." This astonishing statement came from the usually timid Holloway. A flush stained Holloway's cheeks, but he continued. "Master Garlow's clothes were already threadbare — I, uh, noticed his cuffs and collars are frayed."

"So it's a benefit the beak has to buy new things," Noel said, though uncertainty wound down his back. It was a new sensation, and he didn't care for it. "A few months' pay is a trifle."

"When a man's got almost nothing," Mc-Cameron said, "every ha'penny matters. I know this — second son, remember?" He tapped his chest. "That's why it's the army for me."

"Don't bother with your prattle," Curtis jeered at McCameron. "We're nothing to him. He won't remember a damned word we say. If it's not flattery, he's got wool in his ears."

It felt as though someone had hit the back of Noel's head with a shovel. Everyone, even his father and younger siblings, continually praised him.

Not these four boys.

"I don't understand." Noel got to his feet and looked at each of the boys in turn. "Why are you saying this to me? Don't you want to be my friends?" *Like everybody else?*

McCameron surprised Noel by grinning at him. "If you're looking for arse-lickers, seems like you won't find any here."

"Every society has a r-ruler," Holloway stammered. "And every ruler needs honest counsel."

"Or else he finds himself with a knife in his back." Curtis guffawed. "How about it, Clair? You going to take the batting out of your ears, or are you going to —" He mimed getting stabbed from behind, gurgled, and slumped over his desk.

Rowe snickered, and Noel got to his feet and looked at the boys.

He hadn't realized it when he'd walked into the library this morning, but perhaps these very different blokes might be precisely what he needed.

CHAPTER 1
WILTSHIRE, ENGLAND, 1817

Jessica McGale didn't *thrive* on chaos, but she certainly knew how to *manage* it.

"Be sure to let Powers know that her ladyship will overnight at the Three Graces Inn in Basingstoke," Jess said to Penny, Lady Catherton's maid, as they walked down the length of the portrait gallery. "And make certain that her ladyship doesn't order the roast pheasant. Pheasant never agrees with her."

"Yes, Miss McGale," Penny said breathlessly as she trotted next to Jess.

With an apologetic smile, Jess slowed her stride. She forgot, sometimes, that other people didn't move as quickly as she did, or with the same intensity of purpose.

"The stay in London will be brief," she continued without consulting the small notebook she kept in her apron's pocket. The notebook was merely insurance that she didn't forget anything important — but

15

Jess's memory was as reliable as an iron lockbox. It had to be. "We'll only need a dozen gowns."

"With the rest accompanying her on the Continent. Does that dozen include dresses for the daytime?"

Stepping into the corridor that led to the back chambers of the manor, Jess resisted the impulse to roll her eyes. Honestly, one would think that the lady's maid to a young and influential widow such as the Countess of Catherton would already know what her mistress required. Jess had been four months in her ladyship's employ, and was already considered, in the countess's words, "irreplaceable." Within two weeks of beginning her work for her ladyship, Jess advised the cook on what to prepare for meals, directed the gardeners' activities maintaining the estate's substantial grounds, and ensured that every moment of her ladyship's day was planned to the quarter of the hour. Focusing on Penny's anxious face, Jess said, "It doesn't. She'll need day and evening ensembles. I'll take them with me when I leave for London tomorrow. The rest will come with her a week later when she journeys to the city."

"Elegant gowns with you," Penny repeated, twisting her hands together, "and the rest with her ladyship." She nodded but didn't look particularly confident.

"Don't fret so. You'll be with her the whole time." Jess patted Penny's arm, even though she was impatient to move on to her next task. Lady Catherton had entrusted Jess with the preparation of her London town house in advance of her ladyship's arrival, and there was still so much to do before Jess departed the following morning. "I'm certain you can figure out whatever comes your way."

Jess had very little confidence in Penny, who often wore her cap inside out, yet for some reason, Lady Catherton seemed to entrust the maid with the appearance of her person.

"Yes, Miss McGale. Thank you, Miss McGale." Penny curtsied before rushing off.

There wasn't a single ha'penny of her salary that Jess didn't earn. Yet, in a particular way, she enjoyed being useful. Solving problems. Managing chaos.

She checked the timepiece pinned to the front of her dress and saw it was a quarter past the hour. Which meant she had an important appointment.

Jess went quickly to the back stairs and hurried up, up, up to her room just beneath the manor's roof. The door stood open, so

17

her visitor was already within.

Jess rushed into her room and threw her arms around the woman sitting on the edge of her bed.

"How bist, big sister?" Cynthia said, returning the embrace. Jess pulled back enough to gaze at her with golden-brown eyes that were the mirror image of Jess's own, as well as their late father's. She and Cynthia also had the same dark blonde hair and jawline — a legacy from their late mother. "I know we said to meet today, but if you're busy getting ready for the trip —"

"I've time for you. I always do." Jess stroked her hand down Cynthia's cheek. "Besides, I'm leaving tomorrow, and if I'm to get everything ready before Lady Catherton and I leave, it's got to be now. But do you mind if I pack whilst we talk?"

"Whilst?" Cynthia snorted. "Aye, now you're talking like a toff, too. The Wiltshire's gone from your voice." Cynthia's own words were spoken in the broad vowels of the West Country, the same accent Jess had heard and spoken most of her life.

"The more Wiltshire in my voice, the less I get paid." Jess had listened closely to the way in which Lady Catherton and her friends conversed, and had spent many nights practicing talking to herself in the

18

mirror, until only a hint of the West Country was left. "So . . . do you mind if I pack?"

"That's our Jess," her sister said with a fond smile. "Can't do only one thing at a time."

"There's just so much to do." After hugging her sister, Jess pulled her battered bag out from under her bed.

"Still reading the papers, too." Cynthia held up one of the half-dozen newspapers that were spread across Jess's bed. She peered at one sheet of newsprint. "Marking up the *Money Market* section, just like always."

"Lady Catherton gets them from London. No need to sneak them from the public house like I did back home." This was one of the advantages to working for a wealthy peer — access to daily newspapers that contained not only the latest goings-on politically and socially, but, most significantly for Jess, financially.

At the end of her day with Lady Catherton, after her employer had gone to bed, Jess would pore over the papers and dream of other things for herself and her family — bigger things.

She shook her head. Now was about staying a step ahead, not brooding over fantasies of what might be. She opened the minuscule clothespress that held her equally minuscule collection of garments, and deposited a stack of clean shifts into her bag.

"Soon," Cynthia said in wonderment, "you'll be living in Paris, and Berlin. Rome, too?"

"Possibly. Her ladyship said she wants to keep her dance card free to go wherever she pleases, whenever she pleases."

"Ah, the excitement of it! You don't seem glad about it, like."

Jess paused in her packing. "I'd be more pleased if I knew I was leaving the business in a better state. If only she'd given me more notice about this plan to live abroad." She clicked her tongue. "I'd have gotten Mc-Gale & McGale back on its feet."

"You, me, and Fred are *all* trying to do that." Cynthia's reproof was gentle.

"But I'm the eldest," Jess pointed out. "When Mother and Father passed, it fell to *me* to look after you and Fred. *Me,* to keep McGale & McGale going. And what a fine job I've done of it." She threw up her hands.

"Firstly," Cynthia said as she rose from the bed, "Fred and me weren't in cradle-hood when they died. It was but a year ago, and last I checked, we'd left our leading strings long behind us. So the burden's all of ours. Secondly," she continued, placing her hands on Jess's shoulders, "y[...] light that fire that turned a third of [...] to ash. None of us could have know[...] disaster."

Jess exhaled. Vivid memories of the blaze flashed, how she'd awakened with a sense of something profoundly wrong, and how out her bedroom window the flames had turned the night sky a sickly red. She'd sent Fred into the village to summon the fire engine, but by the time it had arrived, some of the farm's buildings had completely burned. The heat from the flames seemed permanently part of her now, no matter how cold the day or room might be.

In the wake of the calamity, the three McGale siblings had been forced to seek outside work, with the hope that they'd earn enough to rebuild.

Jess's employ as a lady's companion had been the most profitable. Then Lady Catherton suddenly decided to live on the Continent for the foreseeable future — taking Jess away from the family's efforts to make repairs. Jess could try to find another position, but the countess paid well, and it would be foolish to leave this one.

"We couldn't know, but now we do," Jess said darkly. "If we don't fix the farm up and soon, we'll lose everything. The business, and — our home. And without the farm and the house, you, me, and Fred become rootless. We'll drift apart like so many salsify seeds on the wind."

"We won't lose each other," Cynthia said, though her words were tinged with uncertainty.

"Without the house, where would we go? Off in separate directions to earn our bread, never united beneath a single roof." Jess rubbed her forehead. "How can I hie off to Paris when we're in such desperate straits? The task is *mine.* And I'll make everything right. I swear I will."

McGale & McGale had been part of the lifeblood of their family for a generation, when Jess's parents spent the months between growing seasons making and selling high-quality soap from their home. The soap itself used honey produced from the McGale beehives. For over two decades, the family enterprise had been limited by its size, selling in shops within a thirty-mile range.

"That bloody fire," Jess muttered. "I'd been right in the middle of formulating how to expand, thinking perhaps we could even sell in London and Manchester if we could meet the demand."

"Then the fire," Cynthia said glumly.

"It leveled all my plans." The family's dream of supplying luxury soap to Britain's hardest-working citizens was on the verge of collapse. "But we're not giving up. It's not over. I'll fix everything."

"How will you do that?" Cynthia asked. "Forgive me, Jess, but what we need is a miracle, and they're in short supply."

Jess took purposeful strides to the little cupboard that held her books and other essential items. She pulled out a stack of fragrant, paper-wrapped McGale & McGale Honey Soap, which she'd brought from home to use for her own toilette.

Holding up the soap bars, Jess declared, "Tomorrow, McGale & McGale conquers London. I'll pound on every Bond Street shopkeeper's door and introduce them to the wonders of our honey soap. I'll require an up-front deposit so we can make enough repairs to meet the initial demand. Then orders will come pouring in and we'll renovate the whole farm."

She never permitted herself the luxury of uncertainty. Even when her parents had been alive, Jess had been the one they turned to if something needed to be done. She balanced the ledgers, she negotiated the prices of crops and raw materials for soap production. She did whatever was required, and she did it well.

"Oh, Jess." Cynthia grasped her hands. "If anyone can make that happen, it's you."

"I keep my promises, Cyn."

Jess's plan *had* to work. Her family counted on her, and she couldn't let them down.

Chapter 2

LONDON

Over the years, Noel had learned a very important lesson: there was no better test of a friend's loyalty than a bout inside a boxing ring. Only members of his closest circle would ever attempt to punch him. The hangers-on, the lackeys, and the sycophants would never be so bold.

Noel ducked to avoid McCameron's right cross, but just barely. He countered with a hook to the body — which his friend blocked before quickly firing a counter jab to Noel's jaw. This time, the punch connected, and stars erupted.

"Go gentle on the bloke," Curtis called from beside the ring. "Dukes have porridge for muscles."

"Not . . . *this* . . . sodding duke," Noel managed to gasp as he struggled to keep his feet.

Blast him, McCameron was barely winded, but then he'd always had a ridiculous amount of athletic prowess, and while Noel sparred with his friend thrice weekly, McCameron would always be the better sportsman. It hardly seemed fair — except Noel was a duke with no fewer than eight homes, was a trusted confidant to Lord Liverpool, and possessed more wealth than three archbishops combined, while McCameron drew a second son's modest allowance along with a pension from years of service in His Majesty's army. So, there was a measure of balance.

Still, when Noel attempted to throw a left cross, the punch went wide.

McCameron took a step back and held up his wrapped hands. "You're fit to be knocked on your arse," he said in his burr. "Time for a rest. At the very least," he added when Noel began to argue, "it will give me a moment's pause so I can collect myself before you give me the drubbing I deserve."

"Don't . . . flatter me."

Yet Noel had to bend down and rest his hands on his thighs to make his head stop spinning.

"I'm not," McCameron replied easily. "You receive plenty of flattery from the droves that follow you hither and yon across London."

True enough. "Just ten minutes," Noel said. "Then we're back at it."

"Whatever you wish, Your Grace," Mc-Cameron said with a smirk.

"If I could move," Noel replied, "I'd make a very rude hand gesture right now."

"Like this?" Curtis demonstrated, throwing up two fingers, proving that when he wasn't in court, defending his clients, he was still as rowdy as he'd been back at Eton.

"The very one," Noel said.

He and McCameron climbed out of the ring to join Curtis, who offered them each a wet towel. Noel tugged the wrappings off his wrists, letting them fall to the ground, before taking the towel and running it across his forehead. He then draped it over his neck. Water seeped down Noel's back, but he barely noticed, with his loose shirt sticking to his sweat-slicked flesh.

"A glutton for punishment today." Mc-Cameron pulled off his wrappings to push his damp hair from his forehead. "You're usually in and out of the ring in three quarters of an hour, not two."

"Have to. It'll be at least a week before I can return here." Noel glanced around the pugilism academy, which at this hour of the day was full of gentlemen sparring with each other or else using weighted clubs to condition themselves. The air was sour with sweat, proving that even aristocrats stank. "I need to get my exercise in advance of what will be an almost motionless five days at the Bazaar."

Curtis tilted his head to one side. "What's this Bazaar?"

"I tell you every year," Noel said with exasperation.

"And every year I forget."

"This from the man who represents two dozen clients at a time." Noel shook his head. "The Bazaar is five days where select people of gentle birth and deep coffers gather at the Marquess of Trask's home to discuss investment opportunities. Trask brings in a highly curated group of ambitious men — and a few women — of business, who seek capital to fund the growth of their enterprises."

"Why go?" Curtis asked. "You can't need the blunt. You're rich as the sodding Pope."

"Only a portion of my wealth comes from my land," Noel answered. "The rest is tied up in investments, stocks, and futures. I like to keep an eye on the fiscal health of my title, and the nation. Don't snigger, Curtis," he added when his friend did just that.

"Can't help it. I doubt there's a bigger rake in all of London."

"Of course there isn't," Noel answered testily.

"And yet you're rubbing elbows with the country's sharpest financial players."

"I can be *both,* you know," Noel snapped. "And I'm not the sort to sit back and just watch my money pile up, regardless of its origin. The Bazaar tells me what I need to know, which enterprises are the most profitable, and which utilize unscrupulous practices. I'm a man of influence —"

"So you keep telling us," McCameron said drily.

"And other powerful people look to me for direction," Noel plowed on. "So I take what I learn at the Bazaar and pass it on to trusted colleagues."

"Here I thought *we* were your trusted colleagues," Curtis said. "Now we learn there are others you value more? Shameful." He appeared to sulk, but he spoiled the effect with a smirk.

"Don't be an ass," Noel retorted. "To you lot, I'll always be that spoilt boy in the Eton library."

"Not *entirely* a spoilt boy," McCameron said. "More like a spoilt nob."

"You are cordially invited to go fuck yourself," Noel said cheerfully.

McCameron made a rude noise. "Just the

same, you're going to the Bazaar, aren't you? Being the virtuous duke — to a point."

"Only moderately virtuous," Noel said. "And as Curtis so eloquently put it twenty years ago, everybody's got their noses up my arse. Might as well do some goddamned good with the power I've been given."

His friends had helped him learn that lesson at the age of fourteen, and he'd carried it with him in the two decades that had followed. When he'd become the Duke of Rotherby at the age of twenty-three, he had two intentions: enjoy the hell out of himself, and don't abuse his privilege.

He'd been remarkably good at both of those.

And in the midst of his whirlwind life, he had the friendship of four men — blokes who would never see him as a means to an end, never play him false, and, above all, be truthful to him and to each other. They kept him sane and anchored when the rest of his existence reeled as quickly as a spinning globe.

He'd never *say* as much, of course. Just the same, they knew how he felt about them, and their feelings for him.

"Now," he said with a grin, "it's time to get back in the ring and pummel each other. That's what friends do."

Energy hummed through Jess, echoed in the buzzing traffic all around. Stylish pedestrians crowded the pavement and the street itself was thick with glossy carriages and equally glossy horseflesh. It was a shame Cynthia could not be here to see this, for Cyn always had a love of fashion and the doings of Society.

Jess walked up Bond Street, keeping her stride even but brisk. Much as she wanted to linger in front of the shops' windows and marvel at the sparkling merchandise within, she had an objective here.

Each elegant person here represented Opportunity. And in her reticule, the bars of McGale & McGale soap represented the keys to that opportunity, and keeping her family together.

A sign painted in regal white letters over a navy background proclaimed DALEY'S EMPORIUM — she'd reached her first destination. Her heart thumped with a combination of excitement and nervousness as the bell on the shop door chimed upon her entrance.

Inside, glass-fronted cases held artfully arranged displays of products, including

31

bottles of toilet water, ceramic pots containing the most refined cosmetics, cunning scissors and blades for trimming hair and whiskers, and the complete equipage anyone might need to maintain their fingernails.

Carpet muffled Jess's steps as she moved deeper into the shop. A lone gentleman wearing the shiniest top hat she'd ever seen browsed the cases, while two women wearing shawls that must have come from India murmured to each other as they contemplated a hair-curling iron.

"Might I assist you, madam?"

She turned to face a gentleman with hair so pale as to be almost colorless. As expected, his dress was subdued and neat, precisely what a shop clerk catering to the elite would wear.

"I would like to speak to the individual responsible for selecting and purchasing stock for this emporium."

"That would be myself. Charles Daley, at your service." He bowed.

She held out her hand. "Miss Jessica McGale. A pleasure, Mr. Daley." When he shook her hand, she continued, her voice even but direct as she spoke. "When I came to London, I knew you were the first person I had to meet. You see, sir, I'm here to present you and your shop with a marvelous opportunity."

"What opportunity might that be?" He lifted an eyebrow.

"To be the first shop in all of London to supply its patrons with England's finest soap." From a small pack, she produced a wrapped bar. The scent of honey surrounded her and Mr. Daley as she lifted it up. "This, Mr. Daley, is McGale & McGale soap. Manufactured in Wiltshire, and of a quality so superior as to make French soap seem coarse in comparison."

She held the soap out to Mr. Daley, and he took it gingerly. "I've never heard of McGale & McGale."

"The scope of our operation has been limited," she said. "But we are known locally for the excellent quality of our product. Examine it for yourself, and you'll see I speak the truth. I invite you to experience its fragrance."

The shopkeeper brought the bar of soap to his nose and inhaled. His expression turned from wary to pleased. "Honey."

"Our soap is made using honey harvested from our own bees. Not only does it provide a delightful scent that both men and women can enjoy, honey also keeps the skin supple and soft, as well as helps to provide exceptional lathering ability." She pulled from her pack a flagon and a small bowl, which she set on top of a cabinet. "Will you permit me a minor liberty?"

She unwrapped the soap, then poured a splash of water into the bowl, then gestured for Mr. Daley to make use of them both.

His expression had turned dubious, but then, as he washed using the soap, he looked agreeably surprised. "It *does* lather nicely."

"And your hands will feel soft, not dry, after use. Observe." She tugged off her glove and held out her palm. "I wash with Mc-Gale & McGale soap, several times a day, and yet there's no roughness to my skin."

He peered closely at her hand. "Indeed, that's true. The cost?"

"We sell to you a ha'penny per bar."

"Reasonable."

"And as good as but less expensive than French soap."

He nodded, so she knew it was time to continue in her pitch. Though she dreaded the next part, she had to speak it. "I will be frank, Mr. Daley. There was a fire several months ago, and we're in need of repairs, but with a small outlay of capital, I've no doubt that not only will we be back to our original operational standards, we will outpace them. We can supply all the soap your customers will demand — and there *will* be a demand."

"Meaning, you'd require me to advance the money if you're to fill our orders."

She didn't like his wry tone, but kept her expression bright and open. "It won't require much —"

"I'm sorry, miss," he said. "That is simply not possible. Daley's Emporium is not in the habit of paying for products that have not yet been manufactured. This soap *is* exceptional, and I've no doubt that we would be able to sell a goodly amount, but 'tis not our policy to pay up front in the hope that our supplier might potentially meet our demand."

Before Jess could offer a counterargument, Mr. Daley went on. "Nearly all of the goods we sell here are recommended by some of the most esteemed individuals in England. The Earl of Blakemere exclusively uses shaving soap he purchases in my shop. The Countess of Pembroke sends her maid here monthly to obtain Mayfair Flower Essence perfume, which is only sold here."

"An aristocratic patron isn't a necessity for a successful product," Jess said calmly. On the inside, she felt herself grasping desperately for a handhold.

"True, but with an unknown manufacturer, such as yours, it would make a substantial difference." Mr. Daley sent her a sympathetic look as he handed her the bar of soap. "Again, my apologies. McGale & McGale soap is indeed exceptional, but until you can meet demand, and without a notable figure endorsing your product, we've nothing more to discuss."

"I see." She handed him a little towel to dry his hands, then wrapped the soap in the towel. Efficiently, she packed up the flagon and bowl, but heaviness sank in her chest. "Might I return if I can fulfill both of those requirements?"

"Of course. I look forward to it." He glanced toward the door.

It was time for her to leave. She gave him a curtsy. "Thank you for your time, Mr. Daley."

"Best of luck, Miss McGale."

She nodded, fixing a smile to her face, before stepping back out onto Bond Street.

This wasn't the outcome she'd hoped for, but it was unlikely that she'd secure a spot in one of London's most celebrated shops on her very first try. It was early in the day. With Lady Catherton still in the country, Jess could keep her attention focused on this task. She'd go into every single shop if that was what it took. She *would* find a way to salvage McGale & McGale.

36

Chapter 3

Hours later, the bell on yet another shop door chimed as it shut behind Jess, tolling the death of her hope. For a moment, she could only stand on the curb and stare blankly at the fashionable traffic parading up and down Bond Street.

No one here knew or cared that she'd spent the whole day walking this elegant stretch of road, trying to convince merchants that they ought to stock McGale & McGale Honey Soap for their esteemed customers — only to face rejection again and again.

What Mr. Daley had said was repeated to her by countless shop owners. No one would supply funds to help rebuild, and without elite customers or enough financial backing to make her soap a countrywide phenomenon, her family's business would wither and die.

Jess tried to take a steadying breath, but it

sounded like a shed rattling in a storm. She blinked rapidly, trying to force her tears back. She *would not* cry on Bond Street, not in view of the country's most wealthy and sophisticated citizens. But all the men's tall-crowned beaver hats and women's braid-trimmed spencers only reinforced how she would not, could not, ever succeed.

What would she say to Fred and Cynthia?

Someone on the street said in an insistent voice, "But, Your Grace —"

"A moment, Your Grace —"

Her thoughts broke apart as she became aware of a small crowd moving down the sidewalk, consisting of four more tastefully dressed men revolving like planets around the sun as they fought to gain the sun's attention.

Catching sight of the man at the center of their solar system, she understood why.

Some men possessed a quiet handsomeness that stole upon you gradually. It took a look and then another look before you could appreciate the angle of his jaw or the shape of his lips. You felt comfortable around a chap like that, as if easing into warm bathwater.

Not this man. There was nothing subtle about his looks. He was *spectacularly* handsome, so much so that Jess felt faintly annoyed, as if he'd made himself beautiful strictly to let everyone know how good life was to him.

He possessed a faultless jawline, and his lips were ripe as a summer fruit one *had* to bite. His nose was perfectly proportioned to his masculine face, and thick dark eyebrows arched above equally dark eyes that shone with intellect and a flash of wicked wit. He didn't have the height of a colossus, but he did have a long, lean body that surely made his tailor weep with gratitude to have such an impeccable canvas to display the exquisitely fitted clothing he wore now.

Energy and vitality radiated from him, along with the kind of health and polish that could only come from having whatever he desired whenever he desired it. This man had money. He had power. With every long stride he took — though his strides were hampered by the people crowding around him — he declared silently, *All of this belongs to me.*

It was strange, Jess realized, to desire someone whilst simultaneously resenting them.

"Excuse me," she said to a passing lady. "Who is that?"

The middle-aged woman in pearls sniffed as if offended that not only had Jess been importune enough to ask her a question, but also because Jess was ignorant of the spectacular man's identity.

"That," the woman said haughtily, "is His Grace, the Duke of Rotherby. Take a good eyeful, gel, because looking from a distance is as close as you'll ever get." Seemingly pleased with the set-down she'd given Jess, the lady walked away, trailed by her footman, who carried an armful of ribbon-tied boxes.

Jess was too astonished to care that she'd been insulted. Naturally, she knew who the Duke of Rotherby was. Or rather, she'd *read* about him for years in periodicals and newspapers. He was always mentioned in breathless prose, cutting a dashing figure through the *ton,* admired by all and sundry, and his presence at a social gathering ensured that it was declared a success. She had known that he'd inherited his dukedom at a relatively young age, but the fact that he was an extremely attractive man in his prime had never occurred to her.

The men circling the duke all clamored for his attention, their voices overlapping and creating a cacophony of well-bred syllables. He answered the questions, but that gleam of roguish — nay, *rakish* — humor in his eyes captivated Jess's attention. He seemed the possessor of some naughty secret, and damn if she didn't want to know what it was.

As he and his followers drew closer, she heard one of the men say, "Will you be at Viscount Marwood's ball tonight?"

"That depends," the duke answered, and *of course* he had a deliciously low voice that sounded like gravel on velvet. "We'll see if married life has dampened Marwood's wilder impulses."

"So, you'll go if he's tamed?"

The duke raised a brow. "God, no. Then again, if he's grown complacent in his married state, an intercession might be in order."

"What do you think of Buxton's silver plate manufactory, Your Grace? A sound investment, I believe."

She recognized the name Buxton from her daily perusals of the newspaper. He was a noted figure in manufacturing, and to ask the duke a question about the realm of industry was odd. Clearly, he was a man devoted to the pursuit of pleasure, and likely had no interest in finances and commerce.

"Not at present, it isn't," the duke said. "Production will be down and orders won't be fulfilled."

That was unexpected.

The man who'd asked the question made a scoffing noise. "Not so. Buxton himself said a fortnight ago that he'd hired men by the score to ensure demand's met."

"The duke is correct." Jess didn't realize she'd spoken the words aloud until the duke and his cronies all stopped midstride and turned toward her. *Hellfire.*

"Your pardon, miss," one of the acolytes said with a condescending smile, "but you speak of matters which a young person of middling means cannot understand."

"And which do not concern you," the first man added. "Certainly not a *woman.*"

"But you're wrong," she said.

Jess found her gaze locked with the duke's. Though a distance of several feet separated them, she sensed his awareness as if their bodies were snugly pressed together. It was not unlike being drawn into the dark, hot depths of a midnight lagoon. She might drown but never miss the lack of air.

He raised one of his eyebrows, his look subtly daring. "Go on, miss." Beneath his words, the message was clear. *You got yourself into this situation. Can you get yourself out?* "Tell us how I'm correct."

The hell with it. All day she'd listened to people telling her that she was wrong and her energies misguided. Now it suddenly became extremely important that Jess prove to him and to the men hovering around him that she knew exactly of what she spoke.

"The storm three days ago caused part of the roof to cave in at Buxton's other business," she said. "The furniture mill in Lambeth." As she spoke, the duke slowly nodded.

"We are speaking of his silver plate manufactory," the first man said as if she was a child. He added in a condescending tone, "Which is located in Croydon. The storm could not have harmed both establishments."

"And it did not." She spoke as calmly as possible, since any hint of feeling in her voice would immediately be seized upon by the men as proof that she was overly emotional. "But Buxton has pulled nearly half his laborers employed at the plate manufactory to work on repairing and rebuilding his furniture mill. With that many men absent from the plate manufactory, it will be impossible to deliver his goods by the promised date.

"Therefore," she concluded, "as the duke said, investing in Buxton's silver plate operation is not a sound decision. Not at the moment. But I would advise reconsidering the possibility by the end of summer, when buyers are beginning to think of entertaining their families for Christmas and Boxing Day."

It was as though all traffic had stopped on busy Bond Street. The silence that followed her pronouncements reverberated outward, so that even the hoofbeats of horses pulling carriages seemed muffled. The men surrounding the duke gaped at her, while the duke smiled.

It was a devastating smile. Brilliant and assured and ever so slightly carnal. Yet what made her breath catch was the genuine admiration in his eyes. He touched his fingers to the brim of his hat, which, given the disparity in their ranks, was astonishing.

A hot flare of desire sparked in her belly — something she hadn't felt in a long time. Not that long ago, she'd been engaged. She and Oliver had grown up together, gone to the same dame school, sat three pews apart at church. The attraction between them had been gradual, more like a warm blanket than a devastating conflagration. Even his lovemaking, after they'd agreed to marry, had been undemanding and gentle.

When he'd withdrawn his suit, she had barely missed him. Her body craved touch and release, but she'd barely gotten that with Oliver. So she'd resigned herself to a

44

life deprived of sensation. It wasn't what she wanted for herself, but there were things in life she had to accept.

Now, on this stretch of Bond Street, she was flushed and more fiercely aware of the duke than she'd ever been for any man.

"You are a veritable hawk amongst the doves, miss," he murmured.

She heard herself reply, "Meaning, Your Grace?"

"That you're an expert hunter, as opposed to this cote of prey." He made a flicking motion with one long, elegant finger toward the men surrounding him. "Have pity on them and try to eat only one or two."

A smile tugged at her lips. "I cannot help if they are so easily devoured. The meat would be too flavorless, though."

He laughed, the sound warm and husky. "A palpable hit."

Words sprang to her lips, but before she could speak them, the crowd around the duke surged back to life — and new men joined the swelling group of hangers-on.

"Your Grace," many voices cried out at once. "A moment of your time, Your Grace."

The crowd moved like a flood pouring down the pavement, carrying the duke along with it. He glanced back at her.

"Your Grace," she called after him. He

45

could have some advice for her, some insight as to how to crack the difficult London marketplace.

But she couldn't be heard above the countless other demands for his attention. And in a short moment, he was gone, swept up in the human tide.

She stood alone on the sidewalk, watching the space where he'd been.

Today on Bond Street had been a setback, yet she wouldn't admit defeat. She hadn't time for flirtations with a duke.

Perhaps, someday when she was old, she'd reminisce fondly about the time she flirted with a duke. Right now, however, she needed a dram of whiskey, and solitude.

The moment she stepped into the foyer of the rented town house, the butler appeared. "A letter arrived for you, Miss McGale."

She picked up the missive on the side table in the entryway. The thin cursive indicated that it was penned by Lady Catherton.

Jess carried the letter up to her room. Breaking its wafer, she frowned to discover a pound note folded within the missive. She read:

Miss McGale,
Due to an unfortunate incident getting

out of my carriage in the rain, I have sustained an injury to my ankle. The physician insists the only way to make a full recovery is through a strict program of non-activity. I am not to put any weight upon my ankle, nor jostle it, for no less time than a fortnight.

The entire situation is most irritating, and has curtailed my plans to come to Town before my departure for the Continent.

However, the property has already been leased in the city. It makes no sense for you to return here, since we will set off from the London docks. Thus, I have determined that I desire you to remain in the city. Doubtless, I shall join you at the end of the recuperative fortnight. I have enclosed a pound to cover any expenses you might incur during this time, but I urge frugality, and I anticipate receiving the remaining balance when I do finally arrive in London.

Yours, &c.

Lady C

Jess stared at the letter for a full minute to absorb its contents.

There was still time. Today had been a wash — with the exception of her quick interlude with the duke — but she could take advantage of her brief reprieve and come up with some way to secure McGale & McGale's future.

Her gaze fell on the newspaper that she'd left on her bedside table. She'd read it this morning, and a single line from the *Money Market* column had stood out to her.

In two days' time, the annual convocation of investors known to its intimates as the Bazaar will commence at the Marquess of Trask's London residence.

Picking up the paper, she ran her finger back and forth across the line of print announcing the Bazaar, until the ink smudged on her skin and the sentence turned illegible.

She was here in London at the same time as the Bazaar. If she could find some way to get inside, and pitch her family's business as a possible investment opportunity for England's most wealthy and influential, she might be able to save McGale & McGale. All it would take was one investor, one person to believe.

But it was notoriously difficult to exhibit one's business at the Bazaar. The process of applying could take years. She didn't have years — she had days.

In forty-eight hours, she'd go to the

Bazaar and finesse her way inside. It would be challenging, but she would use every bit of her persuasive abilities to gain entry. Once inside, she could give a presentation about her business to people predisposed to look for investment prospects.

She glanced down at her dress — it was clean and neat, but surely everyone expected someone to wear their finest garments at the Bazaar as a sign of prosperity, and respect. Unfortunately, these *were* Jess's finest garments.

Perhaps she could borrow one of Lady Catherton's gowns. Just for a few hours.

What was it the duke had called her? A hawk. He wasn't wrong, and she would use every ounce of her hunting ability at the Bazaar.

"Step lively, gents," Noel said over his shoulder. He crossed the threshold of the foyer to the gaming hell, already smiling. "If you dally, they might change their minds and turn you away."

"Might throw you out on your arse, too," Curtis noted as he kept pace.

Striding onward, Noel shot his friend a look of patent disbelief. "This is *me* we're discussing."

"Right," McCameron said drily. "Your

49

Sodding Grace."

"That's *Your Sodding Grace Who Got Me Into the Most Exclusive Gaming Hell in London,* thank you very much." He paused on the threshold to the main chamber of the gaming hell. The establishment was so de rigueur it didn't have a name. Even so, there had been a long queue outside its door.

He never had to wait in the queue, and made certain that he brought his friends in with him. Pleasure was always best shared.

The Bazaar began tomorrow, and though he looked forward to discovering new opportunities for ethical investments, he would have to abstain from his more riotous evening revels in order to stay alert during the day. Thus, here he was with his friends, gleaning pleasure from the night while he could.

The clock crept toward one o'clock in the morning, and yet, judging by the throngs within the main chamber, the sun could have been at its zenith. Men in their evening finery and women adorned in jewels stood cheek by jowl at the tables offering hazard, vingt-et-un, and faro.

He nodded at the ethereal blonde woman who managed the club, and she snapped her fingers to summon a server carrying a tray of flutes of sparkling wine. She took the tray from the staff member's hands and walked toward him.

"Cassandra," he said warmly as she approached. "My dear, how can you be more lovely than all the ladies' diamonds? You outshine them tenfold."

"Your Grace is always so complimentary." She handed him a glass before doing the same for Curtis, McCameron, and Rowe. "Planning on winning big tonight?"

"Haven't decided, but I know of a certain that I will show my friends a splendid time." He smirked at the trio drinking their phenomenally expensive wine. "Do try not to embarrass me, chaps."

"We'd never dream of it," Rowe answered.

"Not when you do such a marvelous job of it on your own," McCameron added.

Cassandra's eyebrows rose, no doubt shocked that a duke would permit anyone such liberties.

Noel only grinned. "Ingrates, the lot of you. I'm staking them tonight. There's no limit to the amount. No arguments," he added when all three of his friends made noises of objection. "It was my idea to come here, and it's my responsibility to ensure you enjoy yourselves. So button it."

"I'll bring the chips, Your Grace." Cas-

51

sandra dipped into a curtsy before striding away.

"Staking us isn't necessary," McCameron said.

"We've been friends for two decades, you oaf," Noel replied genially. "If I can't guarantee my closest comrades a good time, then I consider myself utterly useless. Curtis, Rowe," he said to the others. "Wend your way to the hazard table and stake unreasonable amounts. I need a few more of these" — he hefted his flute — "and then I'll join you."

Rowe and Curtis nodded, then moved toward the hazard table, where shouts of exultation mingled with groans of despair.

As he'd promised, Noel downed his sparkling wine in a few short swallows. The moment his glass was empty, a server appeared with a full one to replace it. Noel tucked a crown into the servant's pocket, and the man stammered his astonished thanks.

"You're burning as bright as Vauxhall fireworks tonight," McCameron murmured when the servant hurried away.

Noel grinned. "A night out with my friends necessitates a grand display."

"This display's noisier than most." McCameron studied him. "I'm not here to gamble, but I'd wager something's on your mind."

Curse McCameron for being an excellent soldier. Nothing escaped his notice.

At Noel's pause, McCameron said, "Out with it. Or I'll be forced to sing regimental songs at the top of my lungs and nobody wants to hear that."

"Nothing we need to discuss." When Mc-Cameron continued to bore into him with his gaze, he relented. "It's about a woman."

"Ah." An internal struggle waged behind McCameron's eyes, and Noel hated the shadows that lurked there, knowing they caused his friend pain. McCameron shook his head. "I can talk about women, you know. I'm not going to dissolve into a puddle of tears."

Noel almost wished McCameron *would* weep. Surely that had to be better, more productive, than forcibly ignoring past pain.

"I meant what I said about singing regimental ditties," McCameron said. "Unless you come clean and tell me about the woman that's lit all of your fuses."

There was no hope for it but to tell his friend everything. "I met a woman. She was . . ." How to explain the hawk of Bond Street?

The lady had possessed an angled jaw,

53

which revealed her dynamic personality as much as the words that came from her lips. Her slightly arched dark brows had lifted in silent defiance when he'd challenged her, and he'd been enthralled by the energy and intelligence in her tawny eyes.

She hadn't looked away. She hadn't retreated in deference. Every word from her lips had been like a perfectly cut gem. Blow for blow, she'd met him, and damn him if that didn't make her the most alluring person he'd encountered in a decade.

"I haven't been able to stop thinking about her," he admitted.

"Who was she?"

Noel snorted a laugh. "Hell if I know. I got dragged down the street by a swarm of sycophants before I could learn her name or anything about her."

"You're a ruddy *duke*," McCameron pointed out. "Surely you can find out who she is."

"I'm not certain I didn't imagine her. Though, she did manage to knock a few of my Bond Street grovelers on their metaphorical arses." He chuckled.

"If she was on Bond Street, she likely travels in lofty circles. You'll see her at some ball or some other gala you toffs throw to keep from dying of boredom."

"Aristo blood flows in your veins, too," Noel noted.

"*Scottish* aristo blood. That makes it stronger and thicker than English toff blood." McCameron clicked his tongue. "And if you don't meet her again, there's no harm in it. You've no shortage of female company. If I'm not mistaken, that brunette over there would be perfectly willing to help you forget any Bond Street beauty." He nodded in the direction of a woman who wore an enticing smile and not much else. "She'll grind you down to a nub, my friend."

"I need to save my strength for the Bazaar," Noel said. Odd, but he felt no pull toward the flirtatious brunette. Not when his mysterious lady continued to haunt him.

Damn it, he *was* a duke. He could have anything he wanted — surely he had some means at his disposal to learn her identity. As soon as the Bazaar was over, he would do just that.

A woman like that didn't come around very often. Like hell would he let her slip through his fingers. He would find her, charm her with his standard methodology, and, for a little while, make life very agreeable for both of them. As usual, he would make plain from the beginning that it would be a short-term arrangement. With a handful of exceptions, his lovers accepted these terms. Surely his Bond Street charmer would be the same.

Cheered by that thought, he hooked an arm around McCameron's shoulders. "Now it's time for us to show the rest of these English toffs how a few reprobates from Eton carouse."

CHAPTER 4

With her plan to gain entrance to the Bazaar firmly in place, Jess walked up Portland Place. She gave her stride the purposefulness that she needed to propel her through the next hour, deliberately ignoring all the voices in her head that told her she was mad. It wasn't easy, however. The voices were awfully loud.

She tugged on her gloves, making certain they were perfectly in place. As she had planned, the dress she wore today was borrowed from Lady Catherton's wardrobe. She pushed aside a stab of guilt over the unauthorized use of the garment. To succeed in business, one sometimes had to ignore the rules.

Looking her best was essential if she meant to talk her way into presenting for the attendees at the Bazaar. She'd brought her pack that contained more bars of Mc-Gale & McGale soap, along with the flagon of water and small bowl for demonstration, just as she'd done on Bond Street. Today, however, she *would* secure funding. The guests of the Bazaar were primed to look for investments, and she'd do her damnedest to see that at least one of them provided her the necessary capital.

As she neared Lord Trask's home, a man in the clothing of a marginally prosperous craftsman stepped to the home's entrance, a satchel in one hand. He kept licking his lips, and after he knocked smartly on the door, he wiped his hands down the front of his pantaloons. When the door opened, revealing a man wearing eyeglasses and a dark coat, he took a step back.

"Yes?" The bespectacled man infused this one syllable with hauteur.

Sweeping his hat off his head, the craftsman stammered in a thick Yorkshire accent, "I'm Farrow, of Farrow Ceramics and Tile. I'd . . . I'd like to present . . . to present my tile manufactory to the . . . the gentlemen of the Bazaar." He hefted the bag that, presumably, held samples of his goods.

The man in glasses held up a sheaf of paper. "Farrow Ceramics and Tile is not on my list of approved presenters, and if you are not on this list, then you are not authorized for entrance."

"I've come such a long way," Farrow said desperately. "From Sprotbrough —"

"That is obvious," the door-minder intoned. "And the distance you've traveled is not my concern. I suggest that if you do seek to present at the Bazaar, you go through the standard channels and apply to Lord Trask's man of business."

"I have." Farrow clutched his hat to his chest. "For years."

"Sir," the bespectacled man said wearily, "you must clear the way. I wish you good morning." He pointed to the street.

The Yorkshireman's shoulders slumped, then he dejectedly dragged himself off the stoop and down the street.

Jess stood, stunned at what she'd just witnessed. Clearly, her plan to talk her way into the Bazaar wasn't going to work. She had to come up with an alternative means of getting inside, and her mind frantically spun as she worked out a new strategy.

One thing was certain: she couldn't turn back now.

The man in glasses turned his attention to her, and her stomach dropped. "Miss?"

She stepped to the door, her pulse a hard, insistent beat in her ears, and fixed a wide smile to her face that she hoped looked charming rather than desperate.

From inside the house came the sounds of many people talking — the Bazaar was already underway.

"May I assist you?" The man in the spectacles peered at her.

She tipped up her chin. "I'm a guest of the Bazaar."

"I have accounted for all our female guests," he replied.

"Likely you didn't know that I would be in attendance this year." That sounded logical enough.

"Stapleton?" a voice sounded behind the man in glasses. "Is aught amiss?" An older gentleman with substantial white whiskers and a broad torso emerged, wearing the look of a man completely in his domain. Lord Trask.

The Bazaar's mastermind stood in front of her, his eyes sharp as he regarded her. This man could be McGale & McGale's making. Or he could allow it to wither and die.

"My lord," the man — Stapleton — said deferentially, "this young woman says she is a guest of the Bazaar."

"Dallying, Trask?" a deep and faintly familiar voice asked. "If I'm not mistaken, you promised us a breakfast with some of those buns your cook makes, so we oughtn't dawdle."

The Duke of Rotherby appeared behind Lord Trask. He glanced in her direction before turning his attention to the marquess. A moment later, his gaze was back on her and he smiled at Jess with recognition and pleasure, as if he'd been given an unexpected gift.

"Well, well," he said. "If it isn't Lady Hawk of Bond Street."

"And if it isn't His Grace, the wolf," she returned.

"How am I a wolf?"

"One hunter recognizes another."

"A fine pair we are." He shouldered the butler aside to lean against the door frame, his arms folded over his chest, one booted foot crossed over the other. "A hawk and a wolf roaming London. Sounds quite star-crossed. And yet it's the poor people of this town I pity more — to have a duo such as us unleashed on the populace."

"We predators have a reputation to uphold."

Jess never spoke this freely with people of higher ranks, but somehow the road to intimacy between her and His Grace had been paved from their first meeting.

"Beg pardon, Your Grace," Lord Trask said, poking his head around the duke's

61

long body. "Who is this lady?"

"The brightest mind on Bond Street." His gaze held hers and a hot bolt of awareness shot through her. It was as though she felt him in every corner of the labyrinth of her being. "Saw it in action myself."

"Is that so?" Lord Trask raised his eyebrow and considered her, his eyes not especially compassionate.

"You were dressed in slightly more casual garments at the time." The duke glanced at her borrowed finery.

Words flew from her lips. "That was my traveling ensemble. I'd just come to Town from my country estate and didn't want to sully something finer with dust from the road."

"Sensible." The duke nodded.

"Forgive me, madam," Stapleton said, frowning in puzzlement. "You are?"

Her gaze swept over the foyer she glimpsed behind the trio of men. A painting of idealized farmers in an idealized field of wheat caught her eye. "Lady Whitfield," she blurted. "My husband, that is, my *late* husband was the baronet Sir Brantley Whitfield."

She smiled at Lord Trask as if he should recognize the name. Which of course he couldn't as she'd literally just made it up.

So, naturally when Lord Trask could only frown at her confusedly, she supplied in a helpful tone, "Sir Brantley went to Cambridge with your cousin . . ." She'd spent many nights at Lady Catherton's country estate carefully reading and memorizing *Debrett's*. It was important to keep apace of the aristocracy's unions and deaths, since such information often came in handy when reading the *Money Market* column.

She searched her memory for Lord Trask's page in *Debrett's*. "Mr. Edward Melrose."

"Edward is something of a rapscallion," Lord Trask said with a hint of exasperation.

"The very word to describe Mr. Melrose, but not all of his intimates are of the same stripe." She trilled a laugh, and felt the duke's warm interest on her. "In any event, your cousin had enjoined Sir Brantley to attend the Bazaar almost three years ago. My late husband was especially fascinated by the realm of finance, and unfortunately his final illness came on before he could request entrée." She fumbled in her pack and was relieved to find a handkerchief, which she used to dab at her eyes.

"My condolences on your loss," the duke said somberly.

"Thank you." She tucked the square of cambric back in her pack. "But I'll not speak of grim matters." Jess smiled again. "My mourning is over and at last I'm able to attend in my husband's stead. I realize that there is a more formal procedure for securing a place at the Bazaar —"

"We can bypass that," the duke said in a voice that was both commanding and convivial. "Can't we, Trask."

It did not escape Jess's notice that this last statement was not a question.

God bless this man, Jess thought, *and his gorgeous face and even more gorgeous confidence.*

"I . . ." Lord Trask looked back and forth between Jess and the duke. She gazed at him sunnily, and the duke's expression held such assurance that she could not imagine anyone denying him anything.

"We already have two ladies as guests of the Bazaar," Lord Trask said.

"Aside from yourself, unless His Grace is the only other male guest," Jess said with a polite smile, "you need not concern yourself that women might outnumber the men. You have more than three men as part of the Bazaar, yes?"

It was always a good idea to ask someone a question to which they would have to reply in the affirmative — thus making them predisposed to be agreeable.

64

"Well . . . yes," Lord Trask said slowly.

"Then it's settled," the duke pronounced. His glance toward her made it clear that he was well aware of her strategy.

With a small grumble, Lord Trask stepped back to make room. "Do come in, Lady Whitfield. It's a pleasure to welcome you to the Bazaar."

"Indeed, a pleasure." A flare of heat in the duke's eyes scorched her. "Looking forward to seeing you hunt."

"Be cautious," she replied. "I cannot be held responsible for the devastation I wreak if you step into my path."

He gave her an endearingly lopsided smile, which he implemented with all the skill of a seasoned rake. "But I will die happy."

Oh, he was trouble. But then, so was she.

Jess stepped across the threshold.

As she climbed the stairs in Lord Trask's stylish home, she made certain to keep her back straight and her steps confident.

Pretend to be a lady for the next three days. Mingle with England's elite. Steer them toward financing McGale & McGale, but it must be done subtly. She could do this.

"You are enjoying your time in Town, Lady Whitfield?" the duke asked behind her.

"I am now," she said — which was true. She'd pull off this coup and then, when Lady Catherton healed, they'd be off to the Continent. Jess need not worry about seeing the duke, or anyone else from the Bazaar, again. In the interim, she'd at last have the chance to do what she'd always desired: to be a viable player in the game of business.

"As for myself," he said, "I consider London suddenly quite delightful."

"I'm certain you find everywhere delightful." She reached the landing and waited for him to join her.

"Well, everywhere finds *me* delightful." He reached the landing, and while he kept a respectful distance, her head spun at having him so near, without the protective span of a Bond Street sidewalk between them. "People are inclined to become excessively agreeable in my presence."

He was spectacularly attractive, and his eyes managed to be both flirtatious and insightful, so astute that she wouldn't be surprised if he could see her all the way down to her shift and drawers.

"An understandable reaction to a duke."

He lifted an eyebrow. "Madam, are you suggesting that it's my title that makes me so welcome wherever I go, and not the

66

excellence of my person?"

"Your Grace likely receives bounteous flattery from all and sundry. Surely you can't be so desperate for a compliment that you thirst for mine."

A laugh burst from him, intimate and velvety, and heat unfurled within her.

"But you do have my thanks," she murmured. "It was kind of you to gain me entrance to the Bazaar."

"Nothing to thank me for." He waved his hand dismissively. It was a rather beautiful hand, large and veined and masculine, and she had a quick image of that hand stroking up her back. "The Bazaar will benefit from your presence. We need sharp minds. And I'm nothing if not motivated by pure self-interest. *I* wanted you here."

A small explosion of pleasure went off in her chest, though it was dangerous to feel it. "Again," she said, "you are excessively kind."

"I'm not excessively anything." He shrugged, but the movement was sleek and drew attention to his superbly tailored coat, and the shoulders that filled it.

"That is untrue, and we both know it. You are the definition of excess."

He laughed again, and the world narrowed so that it contained only them. "You are

67

indeed a hawk. No one but a bird of prey can strike with such cutting accuracy."

"And wolves take particular delight in the hunt." She was freed from the cage that being a hired companion had locked around her. And he seemed to enjoy her own pleasure in being unchained. "I do agree with you that adding me to the Bazaar will benefit it."

"A bold claim. Some of the country's most esteemed financial minds are within that room."

"They don't know what I know." She tapped a finger to her temple.

"I do not doubt that." His gaze was equal parts sensuality and intelligence. And entirely admiring. "My lady." He bowed and then moved into the drawing room.

There was a knock from downstairs. From her vantage on the landing, she could observe the butler opening the door. A man with slicked hair stood on the step, a portfolio beneath his arm. She couldn't quite hear what the man said, but the tone of the butler's response made it plain that his presence wasn't welcome. The door closed firmly as the man on the step protested piteously for entrance.

"Damn importunate rascals," Lord Trask muttered beside her. "Every year, they turn up, hands out, begging for entrance, and every year, I have them turned away."

"How unfortunate," Jess said. *For them,* she added silently. Minutes earlier, she'd been one of their number.

"One came in as a guest," the marquess continued, his expression grim. "Pretended as if he was here to take part in the Bazaar. But he gave himself away."

"Gave himself away?" Cold trepidation inched up her back.

"In truth, what he was actually here to do was drum up investors in his own scheme." Lord Trask scowled. "Thought he was so clever, slipping hints, ingratiating himself, and then, 'Oh, I happen to have a venture in need of funding,' " he said in a nasal voice. "Bah! I had Stapleton show him the door as soon as I rooted him out. A blackguard and conniver."

"Indeed," Jess murmured. "What a dreadful person."

She made herself smile serenely. Inside, however, she felt as though she stood on the edge of a cliff, waving her arms to keep herself from plummeting down.

She needed a new strategy — one that was so subtle, so carefully deployed, that not even the highly sensitized Lord Trask would be aware of her maneuvering.

"Suppose I ought to introduce you to the others." Lord Trask held out his arm.

She placed her hand on the marquess's sleeve. Not but a few days ago, she was fetching Lady Catherton's hat and making certain that her mistress's luncheon was appropriately hot when it was served, and now here she was, walking on the arm of one of England's most significant people.

"What did His Grace mean about Bond Street?" Lord Trask asked. "I gather you encountered him there and made something of an impression."

She made an offhand gesture. "He was receiving poor counsel from some hangers-on — I simply offered better advice."

The marquess lowered his voice. "A bit of a comet, the duke. Dazzling as he streaks across the firmament."

"Who attracts his fair share of satellites." On Bond Street, he'd been trailed by hangers-on, and was clearly used to being the center of attention.

How he *felt* about being the center of attention, that was a matter of greater study. It was as though he did enjoy being the most important man within a mile radius, and also found it a bit tiresome.

"They all revolve around him," Lord Trask

said, "but they never stay in orbit for long."
He lowered his voice. "Don't know much
about how astronomy works, but the duke
possesses his own physics, and he's got a
way of loosening his gravity whenever his
interest wanes." Lord Trask gave Jess a look
fraught with meaning.

"There's no danger of that," she replied.
"I've my own arc to trace across the firmament, and can't be distracted by a bit of
celestial dazzle."

She and Lord Trask stepped into the
drawing room. Her gaze moved over the
score of gentlemen and ladies milling
around the chamber. She wasn't precisely
awed by the genteel company — Lady Catherton often entertained members of the
aristocracy and gentry — but never before
had she been amongst them as an equal.

Her gaze touched on the men — and two
lone women — in the chamber as she
worked to formulate a new plan. The first
thing she needed to do was determine who
would be the most responsive to the possibility of investing in her business. She had
too little time to try to sway anyone unwill-
ing or, worse, hostile.

For the next quarter of an hour, Jess met
people whose names she'd read about in
the financial and gossip sections of her

newspapers. She did her best to keep her outward appearance calm and even, but there was so much opportunity in this one room she practically vibrated with interest.

"Lord Hunsdon," the marquess said as he guided her toward a thin-framed man with papery fair skin, "this is Lady Whitfield. She's joining us this year. Lady Whitfield, the Viscount Hunsdon."

"My lord," Jess said.

The viscount coolly nodded at her, barely interested in her presence as he turned his attention to Lord Trask. "We're starting soon, aren't we?"

"We are," the marquess said. He glanced at Jess. "Lord Hunsdon is one of the Bazaar's returning guests. Been coming here for over a decade."

"You must enjoy the prospect of finding new enterprises," Jess said. "Exciting, isn't it?"

"Only when they're sizable," Viscount Hunsdon said sourly. "Those small, trifling schemes are worthless to me."

So much for Lord Hunsdon, she told herself.

From the corner of her vision, she caught sight of the Duke of Rotherby as he listened politely to a stooped, elderly gentleman. The frailty of the older man highlighted the duke's robust vitality.

Awareness bloomed in her stomach. If she was wise, she'd give him a wide berth. She had a purpose here, and it wasn't flirting with an outrageously handsome duke. Oh, but she liked it, though. Liked *him*.

What were the layers beneath his polish? It would be an adventure to find out. And, given what the marquess had said about the duke's easygoing attitude toward his amours, His Grace would never ask for anything substantive.

"Lady Farris," her host said as they approached a handsome woman with streaks of gray in her dark brown hair. "This is Lady Whitfield. I believe this will be the first year both of you have attended the Bazaar."

Lady Farris's eyes brightened. "Oh, thank goodness I'm not the only virgin here."

Lord Trask coughed into his fist, but Jess laughed.

"I promise I will make our first time gentle and respectful," Jess said.

"Not *too* gentle and respectful, I hope. Or else I may find myself nodding off."

Their host looked slightly scandalized. "Ladies! This is a serious gathering."

"Absolutely correct, Lord Trask." Lady Farris gave his sleeve a consoling pat. "Your pardon. I'm only just out of mourning and

I forget myself. I will endeavor to be on my best behavior." But she shot a wink in Jess's direction before drifting away.

"She used to be so decorous," Lord Trask murmured. He shook his head.

"Ho, there, Trask," the duke said from across the chamber. "Are we to mill about like so many geese in need of herding, or shall we commence?"

"Presently," the marquess said. "I'm escorting Lady Whitfield to a seat."

Lord Trask guided her to a place on one of the numerous sofas arranged in the room. As she sat, a gentleman hurried to take the place beside her. Jess gave the man a polite smile, all the while assessing whether or not he would make for a good investor in McGale & McGale.

"Ilsington." The duke stood in front of the sofa and aimed a dry look at the man seated beside Jess. He nodded toward a chair on the periphery of the room. "You'll be more comfortable over there. Good, fresh breeze from the open window keeps the mind clear."

"How right you are, Your Grace." The man leapt to his feet, bowed at Jess, then quickly made his way to the indicated chair by the window.

The duke folded his long body onto the

74

sofa, his movements sure and smooth. He glanced at Jess, a small smile notched in the corner of his mouth. "Do you mind if we share the sofa? I'm terrifically old and my hearing isn't quite what it was. This seat offers the most advantageous position."

"And if I said that I did mind," Jess replied, holding back a scandalized laugh, "especially your presumption that I *wouldn't*, might you then find somewhere else to sit?"

"Of course," he said at once. He did seem slightly puzzled that she might object to his company. Likely, almost no one ever did. "Er, do you?"

"As you're already seated," she said airily, "and I'd hate to tax your very aged body by requesting you do change seats, you may sit beside me. *This* time."

He inclined his head. "My thanks, Lady Hawk."

"You are welcome, Your Wolfish Grace." She said this with as much of a regal manner as she could muster, which was a surprisingly large amount, especially in relation to talking with a *duke*.

The sofa was not very big, and while she'd met men of larger stature than His Grace, he exuded an animal energy that seemed to fill the space between them. He radiated heat, and within moments of being seated

75

beside him, she was warm and acutely aware of her own body. The seat shifted beneath her, and she could feel every scrap of linen between her gown and her skin.

"Ah, Trask." The duke waved the marquess forward. "Shall we begin?" With those three words, all conversation in the chamber ceased. Everyone looked toward Lord Trask, who now stood in the middle of the room.

"My servants are distributing the agenda for the next five days," Lord Trask explained. Liveried footmen circulated through the chamber, and Jess took one of the offered sheets of paper. The schedule appeared quite full.

Their host explained, "Today we'll have a light repast, and then meet again early tomorrow morning for the first of our juries, wherein sundry individuals present their prospective businesses to us. We will take that time to question and investigate them as much as we desire, and then determine which of these businesses shall enjoy the benefit of our investiture. We will also take outside excursions."

"We're to be wrung out like so much laundry through a box mangle," the duke said, but there was no annoyance in his voice.

"Fear not," Lord Trask answered. "We've

determined certain hours for leisure. I'm not without compassion."

"That's not what they say at the billiards tables," a gentleman in a floral waistcoat said, and chuckled.

The duke laughed. "Indeed, no, and you still owe me thirty quid, Prowse. Plus another bob for offending the company with your waistcoat."

Amused chuckles floated up from the company.

"Are we quite finished?" a silver-haired woman clipped. "If you keep nattering on, I may perish of hunger on this sofa."

"We are indeed finished, Lady Haighe," Lord Trask said with a bow. He strode to the bellpull and tugged on it. Within moments, footmen entered carrying silver trays laden with sandwiches, buns, and other edible dainties, to which the guests helped themselves.

Now was the time for her to gather more information.

Jess stood and moved toward Lady Farris. "If we're the two newcomers to the Bazaar," she said warmly, "we can help each other navigate. Are you at all nervous?"

People loved talking about themselves, and the more you asked them about themselves, the more agreeable they found you.

"I've raised three children into adulthood." The countess patted Jess's arm. "Nothing inured me to life's vicissitudes like waking up to find a child covered in vomit standing beside my bed. Multiple times."

"At least *you* weren't covered in vomit."

"Believe me, I have been."

"Surely then you'll find investing a relatively tame experience. Have you much proficiency in it?"

"None, and I'm looking forward to a new experience." Lady Farris's expression grew serious. "After my husband passed away, my eldest son and I did a thorough accounting of the title's coffers. We discovered some appalling things — sugar plantations, and the like. I made certain we divested from those holdings."

"Understandable."

Lady Farris was eager to try something new, which could mean she would be eager to explore the world of a small business. She also cared about the ethics of her investments.

Some people didn't think about the origins of their wealth. They only wanted to increase their fortune, regardless of its source. How many Bazaar guests held the same attitude? *They* might have deep pockets, but did Jess want to work with *them*?

She glanced toward the duke on the other side of the room, surrounded by people. The Duke of Rotherby was never alone. How . . . exhausting. Surely he would prize a moment to himself from time to time.

Two of the men vying for the duke's attention seemed satisfied with the conversation, and bowed before retreating to another part of the chamber. One man, however — Lord Hunsdon — continued to hover close.

The wisest thing would be to steer clear of the duke and spend her time learning more about her fellow Bazaar guests.

And yet she walked purposefully in his direction — as if she could not stop herself. As if she was ruled not by her mind, but something far wilder and entirely unpredictable.

CHAPTER 5

Noel barely listened to Viscount Hunsdon's words as, without moving his head, he tracked Lady Whitfield walking toward him.

She brightened the atmosphere of Trask's drawing room. Their brief conversation on the doorstep and then on the landing had reverberated over and over in his mind, drowning out Trask's usual introductory remarks.

It had not been a very long exchange, but damn him if it hadn't been the most stimulating conversation he'd had in years. Outside of the four men he considered his closest friends, he couldn't remember meeting anyone who had been able to meet him verbal blow for verbal blow.

As he'd sat beside her on the sofa, there had been a palpable vibrancy to her, as though, like the hawk he'd likened her to, she could spread her wings and take flight at any moment to wheel through the sky.

Anticipation coursed through him — he looked forward to a delicious pursuit.

"It's rudimentary knowledge that English agrarian systems are infinitely superior to those which are practiced on the Continent," Hunsdon droned on. "I was saying to Liverpool the other day — we're quite intimate, you know, the prime minister and I — that what English farmers do best is . . ."

Noel drew straight as Lady Whitfield came to stand nearby. A warm, sweet scent teased him, and brought his body to full attention.

"I beg your forgiveness for interrupting," she said in a husky voice. Her gaze slid past Noel and she smiled as she looked at Hunsdon.

"My lord," she said, "I believe that your opinion on crop rotation is being solicited by the gentlemen over there." She nodded toward Trask and three other men engaged in serious discussion.

"Oh, indeed?" Hunsdon's eyebrows rose in surprise, then he quickly assumed an expression of jaded superiority. "Naturally. There's few who know as much about turnips as I do. Excuse me, Your Grace, Lady Whitfield."

He bowed, then strode across the room to the other group. Before any of the men could speak, Hunsdon launched into a considerable lecture, with the words *Pliny the Elder* and *taproot* being repeated several times. His audience could only listen dazedly.

"That makes us even, I believe," Lady Whitfield murmured.

"Madam?"

"You gained me entrance to the Bazaar, and I liberated you from your agriculturally minded friend's verbose company." She glanced at Noel, her lips quirking. "Unless I was presumptuous. It did look as though you were moments away from throwing Lord Hunsdon out a window."

"You've no idea how often I entertain that thought."

She nodded, her expression serious. "I imagine the streets of Mayfair would be covered with unconscious noblemen."

Oh, but he liked her, and the fact that she was entirely unexpected made her even more delightful. "Makes it difficult to drive one's phaeton."

"Let's not be hasty," she said pertly. "It might add some zest to the experience — a living obstacle course that will try the skill of anyone who claims to be an expert at the ribbons."

Her eyes were the color of dark honey,

82

and the mind behind them fascinated him. It was rare for him to converse with someone and not know what they were going to say next. He felt slightly off balance, a shade uncertain, and the most shocking thing was the pleasure that sensation gave him.

"I . . ." He searched his mind for something to talk about. "Are you long out of mourning?"

Very nice, you ass. Perhaps next you could splash lemon juice in her eyes.

"I'd rather not discuss it," she said.

"My apologies if I've been indelicate with your feelings, or if I've upset you."

To his surprise, she gave a soft laugh. "Fear not, Your Grace. I'm made of sturdier stuff, and it takes more than a handful of words to cause me injury. Now, if you promise me a pint of bitters but give me pale ale instead, then, perhaps, I might take offense."

"I will never wrong you thusly, madam." A lick of heat traveled along his spine as they shared a smile. "I am disappointed in myself, however."

"That is highly unlikely."

A startled laugh leapt from him. She had no fear, certainly not of him, and his heart thudded in his chest to be so clearly seen beyond the glossy veneer of his title.

"But I am," he insisted. "I can remember, for example, what I saw at the Imperial Theatre last February — an excellent burletta, incidentally, written by Lady Marwood — and I can remember that my younger sister's favorite flower is the harebell. So I have considerable faith in my memory, but," he went on, holding her gaze with his, "I cannot remember meeting you before the other day on Bond Street."

"No," she said, her voice soft. A hint of pink crept into her cheeks, enthralling him. "You wouldn't."

Yet she didn't explain herself or offer a reason why she, a woman of sufficient rank to marry a baronet, would have never crossed Noel's path until two days earlier. He knew *everybody,* but he didn't know her.

Now he did, however. And it didn't matter so much as to where she'd been, but that she was here with him at this very moment.

"What of you, Your Grace? How did you come to be so invested in the world of investing?"

He waved his hand dismissively. "Perhaps I find it amusing."

"I see." A look of disappointment flashed across her face.

It was clear that she had hoped for a more thoughtful response. His usual repartee would not suffice. And, in truth, he'd had too many conversations with too many women — too many people — where all that had been offered were pretty blandishments and shallow observations.

"The world is changing," he said after a moment. "The country's changing. It's not the fixed, unmoving castle on a hill, with England above it all. We have to open our eyes and see that our actions have repercussions."

Her gaze was bright. It seemed she appreciated the fact that he'd gone beneath the surface, and actually spoke from his heart. "An unusual position."

"It shouldn't be."

"Your Grace." A Black man approached, removing the spectacles perched on his nose as he did so. He had gray hair and the look of a man who knew exactly how to get what he wanted out of life. Noel had been introduced to him that day, and recalled that his name was Mr. Victor Walditch. He'd made himself a fortune through supplying materials to the hundreds of building and improvement projects throughout the country. "Is there a particular presenter that you're looking forward to seeing at the Bazaar?"

"Isabel Catton, of course," Noel said without hesitation. "Best cakes in London, if not the world. I have a fervent, nay, unseemly amount of hope that we're to sample her shop's wares."

"I must agree," Mr. Walditch added.

"Intriguing," Lady Whitfield said, "that she alone is the head of her operation. There's no male figurehead."

"Why should that matter?" Mr. Walditch asked. "I should hope that the soundness of a business is entirely dependent on the individual, regardless of their gender."

Lady Whitfield nodded, and the corners of her mouth lifted, as if Mr. Walditch's answer pleased her.

Noel turned to the woman beside him. "Lady Whitfield, you've met Mr. Walditch?"

"Only this morning," she said, "and we hadn't much time to get acquainted. Perhaps later we might discuss McAdam's road-building proposals."

Noel learned something every day. Today, for instance, he learned that hearing a woman discussing transit routes aroused him. No, not hearing *a* woman discussing pavement and transit routes. *This* woman.

"You've a wide range of interests, Lady Whitfield," Noel said.

"Always." She added after a moment's pause, "Not everything, in truth. For example, I know very little about reptiles."

"I know a woman who would be most eager to illuminate you on the subject."

"Ah, it's kind of you to suggest that, but natural philosophy is a subject that will never be my main point of focus."

"And what might that be?" Noel asked.

"To be candid," she said, "it's money. Finance. The world of business." Her expression brightening, she continued. "All of it is as fascinating as any scientific discipline. Dynamic, too. Never the same from day to day as the world changes so quickly. These concepts such as capital and demand are so abstract, but also grounded in the reality of people's lives. I cannot help but think —"

She abruptly went silent, and in the quiet, Noel suddenly craved the sound of her voice, and the passion in her words.

"Tell me," he urged. "What do you think?"

"Yes, do," Mr. Walditch added.

She shot them both a cautious glance. "You truly want to know?"

"Why shouldn't we?" Noel demanded.

"Because women aren't to speak of such things. It's crass and beneath us, soiling our purity with the grime of commerce." She grimaced.

"Prevailing wisdom can go hang," he said. "Many mouths speaking the same words doesn't make it true. Besides," he added, "sex doesn't determine one's intellectual ability any more than one's preference for eel pie."

Mr. Walditch shuddered. "Speak no more of eel pie. Even the smell sends me to my bed."

"There, you see." Noel nodded at the magnate. "He's far more intelligent than I am, and cares not for eel pie."

Lady Whitfield chuckled. "Then I count myself fortunate to be amongst friends. *New* friends."

"You and I first met the other day," he noted, "so we are old friends." He plucked a glass of sparkling wine from a servant's tray, then handed it to her. Noel also took a glass for Mr. Walditch and for himself.

Once he'd received his wine, Mr. Walditch bowed and excused himself, leaving Noel alone again with Lady Whitfield.

She took a sip. "I would think you have no shortage of friends — one more might be excessive."

An easy quip rose to his lips, something charming but without substance. But that wouldn't be enough. Not for *her*.

"I've no shortage of people eager to tell me, *Yes, Your Grace,*" he said, his words dry. "And I have an abundance of others that attempt to inveigle me to sponsor a bill, or finance their schemes."

She narrowed her eyes. "I cannot fathom you."

"Madam?"

"I *do* read the papers," she said wryly. "Accounts of your enjoyment are plentiful. By this point, I'd wager Oxford could ask you to lecture on what it means to be a rake."

Noel had once spent three days at a house party where he and a lovely, experienced opera singer had circled each other, their conversation ripe with blatant innuendo, her every look in his direction calculated to seduce and enflame him. When they had at last gone to bed together, it had been explosive.

These few minutes with Lady Whitfield enticed him far more.

"Rakes are very learned fellows," he said.

"But infrequent in their attendance at gatherings such as the Bazaar, where there may not be many opportunities for debauchery." She tilted her head, regarding him, and the depth of her perceptiveness scoured him. He felt raw, exposed.

The sensation wasn't unpleasant. It was . . . delicious.

"Which are you, then?" she asked after a moment. "The rake, or the man who carefully considers the basis of his wealth?"

He debated for a moment. With how much of himself could he trust her?

Other than his friends from Eton, he trusted few others. Yet in the short time he'd come to know Lady Whitfield, he found that he *wanted* to trust her. Her cutting brilliance beguiled him and her warm, sweet scent reminded him of sunlit fields and long summer nights. A scent that was hers alone.

"I will tell you something," he finally said. "Something few know about me."

Her brows rose, as if she understood how significant it was that he would consider disclosing a truth to her. She moved her head, presenting him with her ear. "You may whisper it."

Noel studied the scroll of her ear. They were useful and ordinary things, ears, but hers were beguiling. She wore no earbobs, which was unusual for a genteel woman, and so there were no glittering gems or creamy pearls to snare his attention.

He wanted to be the recipient of her confidences, too, so they both held precious pieces of each other.

"Rakehood is diverting," he murmured, leaning close. Her sweet fragrance enfolded him. "But it doesn't nourish my soul."

"Is that what you seek?" she asked lowly.

"I haven't formulated the question," he admitted. "So I cannot know the answer." He laughed softly. "This isn't easy — confessing my own uncertainty."

"When the world knows you as a man of singular influence." She moved back slightly. "You do burn brightly, but there's more to you than a merely dazzling gleam in the darkness."

His breath left him, and for a moment, he was utterly without words — a rarity. He managed to collect himself enough to drawl, "Unjust, madam."

"Am I?"

He leaned in slightly, shortening the distance between them even more. Her pupils widened, her lips parted — yet not with fear. He did see caution in her gaze, but there was curiosity, too, and the stirrings of attraction.

There was a relief in knowing that he unsettled her as she did him.

"To strip me bare, here, in mixed company, when you keep yourself fully armored." He took another step closer, and her honeyed scent nearly made him sink to his knees. "I look forward to the next five days, and discovering just who you are beneath your defenses."

She stared at him as though taking his

91

measure, just as he assessed her. His breath came quickly, as did hers, while they both subtly, silently, and motionlessly pushed against each other's wills, determining their tolerances — who would give, and who would take.

"I do appreciate that you have been so frank," she said at last. "I will honor that. I imagine very little is denied you. But Your Grace must understand that, with me, ultimately, you will be disappointed." She finished the last of her wine before setting the glass on a nearby table and striding away.

Noel watched her go, hearing the excited beat of his heart. It was as though he woke from a long dream.

CHAPTER 6

It had not been easy to walk away from the duke — especially after he had revealed so much of himself to her — but he was a distraction she could not afford. She'd left him because she'd had to, telling herself that it was for his protection as much as her own.

She'd spent another hour talking with the other guests, learning who would be worthwhile to subtly approach regarding investing in her business, and who she ought to steer clear of. At least she had a foundation of a plan, and could move forward with it.

She now sat on a stone bench that stood at the edge of the yard behind Lady Catherton's town house. She lifted a small glass of sherry to her lips and sipped. It wasn't quite strong enough, but it was the only spirit she could take from the house without arousing the staff's suspicion. The servants came with the rental, and so they had little loyalty to whomever occupied it. But gossip was always a prized commodity, thus she had to be careful.

"Afternoon, miss."

She nodded at Lady Catherton's coachman as he approached. He was short in stature but barrel-chested, fair skinned, and the remaining hair he had was streaked with silver.

"Lynch, is it?" He had driven her from Wiltshire to London.

"At your service, miss." He eyed the glass in her hand. "Sherry, is it?"

"Alas, yes." She sighed.

"If you wait but a moment, I've some whiskey we can share."

"Here I thought I didn't believe in angels."

He chuckled before trotting toward the stables. A few moments later, he returned with a bottle and two dented metal mugs. He poured a healthy amount of whiskey into both vessels, then handed her one.

"Your health," she said, lifting her mug.

"And yours, miss." They tapped the rims of their cups together.

She took a swallow of the liquor and it agreeably burned its way down her throat to settle warmly in her belly. "God bless you, Mr. Lynch." She nodded at the seat beside her. "Join me?"

"My thanks." With a soft groan, he lowered himself down on the bench.

They sat together in companionable silence, drinking whiskey and listening to the muffled sounds of traffic that traveled down the mews. For the first time in hours, Jess permitted herself a slow, deep exhale.

"That's a sound," Lynch said with a shake of his head.

"The day has been long." Which was an extremely abbreviated way of saying that she'd spent her last few hours dancing madly atop slippery ice — made all the more precarious by the presence of one exceedingly handsome, witty, and wicked duke. Who seemed intrigued by her. Attracted. There had been no denying the spark of interest in his eyes, or how she'd fought to keep her head level with poor success. Even now, she was tight and hot and aware of him throughout her body.

The duke was a complication she could not afford. And yet he was irresistible. She hadn't flirted with anyone for years, not since the early days of Oliver's courtship.

She'd been forced to shut the door on any lingering feelings she might have once had for him. He'd shown his true self to her, the one that had resented her dedication to keeping McGale & McGale going. She was well rid of him.

There hadn't been time or room for other men. She'd kept her head down, focusing solely on the task of preserving the family business. Certainly when she'd appeared at the Bazaar this morning, bantering with a duke had not even merited a place on her mental list of things that might occur.

Yet she'd done it. And couldn't quite bring herself to regret a moment.

"I suppose," Lynch said, breaking the silence, "I'm not supposed to notice you wearing her ladyship's rigging."

Her mouth hitched into a small, rueful smile. "Plausible deniability if things fall to bits."

Lynch waved his hand. "If the cat's away, there's no harm running loose in the larder."

"Your forbearance is appreciated." She sipped at her whiskey. It was coarse and rough drinking, but it reminded her of home, and helped firm her resolve. "Truth is, I'm attempting something that's more than a little mad."

"You're young enough," he said easily. "Exactly the time of life when we can be mad."

"I'm young," she said grimly, "but some days I feel so old. They're counting on me."

"Who is?"

"My brother and sister." She rubbed her

thumb along the rim of her cup, a small movement, and the only one she felt capable of just then. Weariness lay heavy along her limbs. "I'm the eldest, and it's up to me to take care of them. I thought I had a means to do so. But that plan was scuttled and I'm fighting to get another off the ground. There's a methodology to it, yet I have to make everything up as I go."

She dropped her head and used her free hand to rub her forehead.

Lynch whistled. "Carrying a full load, that's for certain. What's the next step?"

"Plant some seeds," she said. "Drop hints. Be subtle as hell. The trick is to make the other person believe it's *their* idea, and then praise them to the heavens for coming up with such a brilliant notion."

"Wily," Lynch said, but there was admiration in his voice. "Obstacles?"

"Many. And a distraction, too. A very handsome, seductive distraction." She had to keep away from the duke, but the trouble was that she didn't want to. Not when he had revealed a hidden part of himself to her, showing her that he was far more complex than anyone believed.

With Fred and Cynthia counting on her, and their mother's words hanging over Jess's head, she could not allow herself to be led astray by dark, alluring eyes.

Get the job done. Play her part. That was what she had to do. But in order to act the role of lady, there were things that needed addressing.

"I'm certain you know London better than I," she said. "Where might I go to hire myself an abigail? Temporarily, of course." She had the money that Lady Catherton had sent to her, and from that she could draw a maid's fee. Today, she'd found one of her employer's more simple gowns, but if she was to attend the Bazaar for four more days as a baronet's widow, she would have to dip into Lady Catherton's wardrobe, and wearing those garments required assistance.

"There's a hiring agency near Finsbury Square that'll set you up nice and proper. Give me ten minutes to hitch up the cattle and take you there."

"It's not an easy thing for me to ask for help," Jess said sincerely. "So I thank you for yours." She placed a hand on his ropy forearm.

He covered her hand with his own. "There now, miss. Us folk who earn our coin the hard way, we've got to see after each other. If we don't, nobody will. Not them upstairs, that's for certain."

"Not them upstairs." As thrilling as it had

98

been to flirt with the duke, the hard truth of it was that she needed to keep her attention firmly fixed to her objective. Tomorrow, she would continue her campaign to find investors for McGale & McGale.

She would gently prod the guests to find who would be most interested in funding the business's rebuilding and expansion. She had not been able to speak to all of them today, and she had to make certain she didn't make any critical errors moving forward.

It might be easy to approach the duke about securing financing from him — but the pull between them made it impossible. She would not use their attraction in that way.

A shame. The duke was gorgeous and, under other circumstances, she would have relished the chance to flirt with him.

Her family, both living and dead, counted on her. The duke was an indulgence and temptation, and she could not yield to either — but, damn, how she wished otherwise.

Noel had never walked up the stairs to Lord Trask's drawing room with as much energy as he did this morning.

That energy dimmed slightly as he stepped into the chamber and scanned the guests —

only to find that Lady Whitfield was not there. It merely meant that she hadn't yet arrived, but her absence hit him with an unreasonable disappointment.

"Looks like you could use some motivation," Mr. Walditch said as he approached. "We've been helping ourselves to coffee and tea and something to eat." He waved toward a table at the side of the room that contained refreshments suitable for the morning.

Noel tipped his head and went to pour himself some coffee. "At this hour, I cannot fathom why I have bestirred myself."

"From what I've heard, there's a new enlivening presence." Walditch winked. "You threw Lord Ilsington off the sofa to sit beside her."

"I *practically* threw him, but did not, in point of fact, *actually* throw him off the sofa. You would know if I did."

Still, the display of territoriality was unusual — he never made claims on women's attentions. It was just good manners to permit a woman to make up her own mind as to with whom she wanted to spend time. He wasn't some oaf, imposing his slavering attendance on someone.

Yet he'd been impelled to be near Lady Whitfield, to fall into the depths of her perceptive golden eyes and even more

100

perceptive thoughts.

Hell, there was no reason why he couldn't follow the attraction crackling to life between them.

A moment later, she walked into the drawing room, her stride purposeful, her chin high. "Good morning, my lords, my ladies. Your Grace," she added, turning to Noel.

When her gaze met his, an exquisite flare of nascent arousal crackled up his spine. He watched, fascinated, as the tip of her tongue wet her bottom lip.

He wasn't mistaken. As intrigued as he was by her, she was equally enthralled by him.

Yes — this year's Bazaar was far more interesting.

"Welcome back, my lady," Lord Trask said.

Noel grabbed one of the small plates on the table, and quickly arranged some pastries atop it. He stepped forward and held it out to Lady Whitfield.

"You'll want to fuel yourself for the morning ahead," he said.

She gave him a polite smile. "Thank you, Your Grace, but I've had my breakfast already."

He bit back a wry laugh. She likely had no idea that until that moment Noel had never waited on *anyone.* And yet his attention had been spurned. How novel.

"As you please," he said affably as he handed the plate to a footman. "But when you're nodding off and we're hours from luncheon, you'll regret that decision."

"It wouldn't be the first regret I've lived with. Nor the last."

"We're to begin in a moment, if you'd care to have a seat." He waved toward the same sofa they'd occupied the day before. "And if you should feel faint from hunger, I will be right beside you, offering a manly shoulder to lean upon."

"I'd thought that gallantry had gone the way of King Arthur," she said, lowering herself down onto the sofa, "disappeared into the mists of time."

"Aren't you pleased to discover that you're wrong?" He sat beside her, catching her fragrance of sunlit sweetness and breathing it in deeply.

"If you're looking for a maiden in a tower to rescue, I must disappoint you. There is a shortage of castle turrets in Mayfair. And," she added, her lips curving into a beguiling smile, "I am no maiden."

"What a relief. Neither am I."

Her laugh was liquid as it trickled warmly through his body.

Lord Trask coughed pointedly, and Noel reluctantly nodded his agreement that it was time to get to work.

He pulled out his notebook and pencil, then observed her tugging off her gloves before pulling a writing tablet and a piece of graphite from her reticule. There were no baubles on her fingers, not even a mourning ring. What would it feel like to have her trail one of her naked fingers across his shoulders?

"We've a full agenda today," Lord Trask announced, "so let us begin at once. Our first presenter is Mr. Mitchell Hart, from West Bolton Mills."

Noel braced himself for what he suspected was about to happen. His instinct proved correct when Hart commenced speaking at length about his cotton-milling establishment near Manchester. He talked of the speed with which his mill could produce muslin, aided in its pace by the scores of workers operating the equipment. Illustrations on placards depicted the layout and machinery.

Noel was careful to keep his expression neutral as he wrote *No respite for workers* in his notebook.

"From whence do you source your raw cotton?" Lady Farris asked from her place across the room. "Egypt? India?"

"I secure excellent cotton at minimal cost from suppliers who grow their cotton in the American South — predominantly in Georgia and Alabama." Hart beamed. "American cotton is much less expensive than Asian, and of finer quality."

An unsurprising revelation, but it cemented Noel's decision to never invest in Hart's mill.

Finally, the presentation ended, and Hart bowed before exiting the drawing room.

Lady Whitfield turned to Mr. Walditch, seated nearby. "Are you all right, sir? The cotton's origins —" She shook her head, and did not conceal the disgust in her expression.

Walditch offered her a weary look. "It is a fact of life, my lady, that men such as Hart profit from slaves. He will not receive a penny from me."

Nor, if Noel had any say in the matter, would Hart be given money from anyone in Noel's wide sphere of influence.

"Tell me you aren't going to invest in that mill," Lady Whitfield whispered to him.

"Good God, no."

Though the movement was slight, he saw her shoulders loosen with what seemed like relief. "Good. That's good."

He looked at the line of her profile as she bent over her notebook. Though he would not permit himself to read what she wrote, he did see that her handwriting was much more bold, and far less tidy, than most ladies' penmanship.

Like her, it defied expectation.

CHAPTER 7

Jess assessed her reflection in the mirror of
the ladies' retiring room. She tucked a
wayward curl back into its arrangement —
which had been provided by the abigail
she'd hired yesterday. Indeed, the whole of
Jess's stylish appearance today was courtesy
of her temporary maid, and a good thing,
too. She needed to appear as elegant and
worldly as possible when learning more
about the remaining Bazaar guests.

Already, she knew that the two other
women could be possible investors, and Mr.
Walditch had shown that he would support
a business helmed by a woman. Viscount
Hunsdon was out. The other men, however,
were less-known quantities.

She'd find the opportune time, but she
needed to be strategic. In all things.

The time on the gilt clock showed that
she had just two minutes left before the next
presentation was to begin. After smoothing

her hand down her skirts, she headed toward the drawing room.

Even though he did not speak loudly, she heard the duke's voice out in the corridor. Its deep tones stroked along the bare skin above the neckline of her gown, and she fought a shiver. She paused outside the drawing room, collecting herself before facing him once more.

Yielding to the temptation he offered was unwise. She had to remember that.

Jess stepped into the drawing room and her gaze immediately searched for him.

His back was to her, so she had a brief moment where she could openly admire the span of his shoulders, and the athletic ease with which he held himself.

As if sensing her attention on him, he turned, catching her in the act of ogling him.

He smiled devilishly. And no matter how much she told herself that an involvement with him was dangerous, it didn't stop her pulse from hammering. The knowing look he gave her was pure sensuality — she would have to work very hard indeed to keep away from him.

The deuce of it was, she didn't *want* to put distance between them.

Following logic rather than instinct, she approached a red-cheeked man who had been introduced to her as Lord Sundon.

Minutes later, she had learned two things. The first was that Lord Sundon was uninterested in conversing with the female guests of the Bazaar. The second was that no matter how she attempted to approach him regarding McGale & McGale, he would never listen to her as a matter of principle, since, in his words, "ladies are too flighty to understand figures and finance."

Correction — she had learned three things. The third was that she had far more control over her temper than she'd believed. After all, she hadn't hit Lord Sundon over the head with a vase.

"My lords and ladies," Lord Trask announced, "Mrs. Catton's presentation will commence. Please take your seats."

"Correction," the duke said. "We are going to Isabel Catton's bakery, where we'll not only hear her presentation, but we are to have a private tasting of her most popular items."

Jess resisted the impulse to clap her hands together, but she *was* excited. Isabel Catton's bakery and sweetshop was one of the most popular of its kind in London, possessing an unparalleled reputation for excellence.

Jess had hoped to visit Catton's during

her brief time in the city. She wanted to taste the country's finest pastries, and surely there would be lessons to learn at the shop as to the successful management of a thriving business — with a woman as proprietor.

"At this moment," the duke said, "a caravan of carriages awaits us downstairs. The servants have collected our hats and coats, and if we move quickly, we can be at Catton's within half an hour. You *will* want to move quickly before the best iced cakes in London are devoured, or else you'll witness the disgraceful spectacle of a duke's public tantrum." He gestured impatiently toward the door. "What are you waiting for? Do you want to see me scream and turn purple?"

Chuckling, murmuring, the guests made their way out of the drawing room. Jess was about to join them, but she heard Trask clucking at the duke.

"Might have warned me, Your Grace," the marquess said, sounding slightly wounded.

"You would have presented me with a litany of reasons why we shouldn't go," His Grace said. "Head on downstairs. I shall meet you in a moment."

The marquess muttered, but did as the duke instructed. A moment later, Jess and His Grace were alone.

"There's another reason for creating such upheaval, isn't there?" Jess asked him.

"No sense confining ourselves to a drawing room and slowly suffocating to death. The room is pleasant enough, but there's a whole city out there, just waiting to be overrun by a bunch of monied toffs."

"And . . . ?" she pressed.

"And . . . Catton's is a delightful place. I thought it would make you smile to go there."

She looked at him steadily. "It's flattering that you would go to such lengths to please me."

"I sense a *however* hovering nearby."

"However," she went on, "you made a decision without asking my opinion, and you didn't bother to tell Lord Trask, either. You simply acted. It was very ducal."

The brightness of his expression dimmed. "In your mouth, the word *ducal* doesn't sound entirely complimentary." He scowled. "Hell. I was being rather autocratic, wasn't I?"

"Rather."

"Admitting fault is not something I've practiced. Today, I'll amend that." He exhaled. "My apologies, my lady. Moving forward, I'll try not to be such an overbearing ass." He glanced at her. "You could voice some objection to my use of the term *overbearing ass.*"

"I could, but I shan't." She offered him a wry smile as he scowled deeper. "No need to brood about it. We'll proceed with the day and enjoy our time at Mrs. Catton's shop. And, Your Grace?"

"Yes?"

"Thank you." Smiling to herself, Jess went down the stairs and collected her coat and bonnet. She met the other guests as they filed out of Lord Trask's home.

Lady Farris looped her arm through Jess's. "The female contingent of the Bazaar can ride together. Can't we, Lady Haighe?" she asked the older woman.

"Only if you promise not to talk about men," Lady Haighe fired back.

"Gracious, no," Lady Farris said. "There are so many more interesting things to discuss. What do you think, Lady Whitfield?"

"My early years were quite rustic," Jess said, "and experience has taught me to prefer the company of goats over a carriage full of men."

"Less bleating with the goats." Lady Farris winked at Jess when one of the male Bazaar guests harrumphed.

As a footman handed Jess into a waiting

vehicle, she caught sight of the duke emerging from the house. He was in midstride as he donned his tall-crowned hat, and he moved sleekly, with virile grace.

She was partly pleased that he'd arranged the visit to Catton's for her pleasure — and annoyed. At the least, he'd apologized for being so arrogant.

Blast it, she didn't want to *like* him.

"We *can* make an exception," Lady Farris said from the opposite seat, "if you're inclined to discuss His Grace."

"Did you know that goats belch?" Jess asked.

Lady Farris smirked. "Very well. We'll stick to more bovine topics."

The duke's face appeared in the carriage window. He favored all of them with a blinding smile. "You have wisely chosen to segregate yourselves, ladies. Hopefully, no one will notice if I borrow a bonnet and pretend to be one of your sex so I may join you on the ride to Catton's."

"Go on with you, rascal." Lady Haighe sniffed. "No one would mistake you for a woman. You've got half a day's beard growth and smell of tobacco."

"So does my great-aunt Lucretia," he said.

Jess pretended to cough to hide her laugh.

"Begone!" Lady Haighe thumped her

walking stick on the floor of the carriage.

"Ladies." He winked at Lady Haighe, then touched his fingertips to the brim of his hat before disappearing from the carriage window.

"We're not discussing men," Lady Farris said, "but if we *were*, I'd say that it's fortunate that His Grace is a duke. Men like him without the benefit of a title usually wind up as women's hired lovers."

"But their clients are always satisfied," Jess noted.

"*That* is a certainty."

The carriage lurched into motion, and they were underway. As the vehicle rolled through the streets of Mayfair, Jess said to her companions, "Lord Trask seems to have a policy to only invite widows to be guests of the Bazaar."

"Not *widows*, plural," Lady Haighe said. "Widow, singular. For years it was only myself. What a collection of sausages that drawing room was. This year," she continued with a glint in her eyes, "I harangued and harassed Trask into inviting Lady Farris. I wanted married women and spinsters, too, but he immediately rejected the idea. Spinsters, he said, hadn't enough capital to be of significance."

"And with married women, it must have

been the usual nonsense about a wife's opinion being the same as her husband's." Jess rolled her eyes.

"Ha," Lady Haighe barked. "In life, my husband knew better. He left all important decisions to the wisest one." The lift of her chin clearly indicated that in her marriage, *she* had been the most sagacious.

"An exceptional circumstance," Lady Farris said. "Certainly *not* the rule." She considered Jess. "What of you, Lady Whitfield? Are you finding widowhood to be a delight or a torment?"

"I categorically enjoy being on my own," Jess said, which was true enough. Early in their courtship, she and Oliver had gotten along well. So well, in fact, that they had even slept together after they'd promised to marry. But after her parents had died, and Jess had taken over the responsibility of managing McGale & McGale, he'd grown sulky and resentful, demanding her attention for himself. Either she could put all of her focus on him, making herself into a good and subservient wife, or he would not wed her.

She had not been sorry to see their engagement end.

"There, now," Lady Farris said, sitting back against the cushions. "I knew I liked you for a reason."

A short while later, the carriage came to a stop on a busy street. The footman opened the door and handed all the passengers down from the vehicle.

They gathered in front of a bustling shop, and Jess noted a queue of well-dressed people snaking out of the door. The painted sign across the front of the shop read CAT-TON's, and a smaller sign advertised, "All goods made with East India sugar." People bearing light blue boxes tied with brown satin ribbons left the shop with a triumphant air, as if they'd secured their portion of a dragon's treasure.

A woman stood beside the door, her posture upright and full of confidence, her expression proprietary. Surely she had to be Mrs. Isabel Catton herself.

The duke approached her and they spoke quietly. A moment later, Mrs. Catton went inside, and the duke motioned for everyone to follow.

They made their way through the bustling shop, moving through the room full of crowded tables. Though there were some men seated there, the customers largely seemed to be women enjoying a pot of tea and plates of sweets whilst exchanging the latest gossip.

Mrs. Catton led the procession through the main chamber and then down a corridor. She drew aside a velvet curtain to reveal a parlor with nearly a dozen tables arranged around the perimeter.

Jess's attention shot to the silver platters in the center of each table. "Are those — ?"

"Samples," the duke said from behind her. "Oh, yes." He rubbed his hands together, looking very much like a pirate on the verge of plundering.

Despite the shop's aromas of sugar and butter, having the duke so close by filled her senses with his delicious scent — bergamot, apple, with just a hint of moss-covered oak. Her awareness was the unfortunate byproduct of years she'd spent cultivating a discerning nose. She always tested the fragrance of McGale & McGale soap to ensure it wasn't too overpowering or too faint. The proof that she'd done her job well was on her own skin.

But all fragrance altered depending on who wore it. There was something within a person's particular composition that changed a scent, and whatever musky charm the duke exuded from his pores combined with his eau de toilette to make her lightheaded as she walked ahead of him.

She wanted to lick him.

"I'm looking forward to it."

Her gaze snapped to him. Was mind reading another of his ducal gifts? "Pardon?"

"The presentation. And sampling an array of Mrs. Catton's delicacies."

The Bazaar guests seated themselves, three to four people per table. At Jess's table was a wealthy brewer by the name of Mr. Parley, as well as a man she'd been introduced to as Baron Mentmore. She hadn't had the chance to determine whether or not they would be good prospects, but their response to Mrs. Catton would surely help in that area.

The duke also sat at her table. But he did not sit right beside her, which was slightly disappointing, even as she knew that a little distance between them was for the best.

She pulled from her reticule a stick of graphite to take down notes when Mrs. Catton took her place in the middle of the room.

"Good afternoon, my ladies. My lords." She dipped in a quick curtsy. "I shall be brief and direct."

Much as Jess wanted to pay attention to the presentation, her gaze was riveted by the sight of the duke's ungloved hand resting on the table. Though it didn't have the calluses or cuts of a working man's hand, it seemed quite capable and strong.

Would it be delicate or rough against her skin?

A shame you'll never *discover the answer to that,* she mentally snarled at herself.

"It is my intention," Mrs. Catton said, "to build Catton's shops in other major English cities. To do so, I require investment capital. Which brings you here to my business," she added with a small smile.

"What would be the return?" the duke asked. "I assume you mean we are providing capital for loans, not ownership stakes."

Jess sat up straighter at his unexpected — but astute — comment.

"The return would be twelve percent," Mrs. Catton answered.

Here was a good lesson for Jess — she would have to emphasize the return on her potential investors' money.

"Perhaps you might question why you ought to invest in my proposed scheme. Why should my shop be any different from any other in Manchester or Liverpool? To answer that, I invite you to try the cakes on your tables."

Jess peered at the confections. They were little squares of cakes, with pale pink icing topped with a minuscule sugar flower.

"It looks too adorable to eat," she murmured.

"Nothing is too adorable to eat," the duke answered.

Heat pulsed through her as their gazes held. She could not look away, not even if Lord Trask pointed a blunderbuss at her and called her a fraud.

"Please," Mrs. Catton urged, "have a taste for yourselves."

Jess ripped her attention away from the duke. She plucked up one of the cakes and popped it into her mouth. The confection was a symphony of texture and flavor, a delicately crumbed cake perfumed with rose water with a slightly crunchy sugar icing that had been flavored with strawberries. She wished she hadn't jammed it into her mouth rather than relishing it, bite by bite.

As the duke was doing. He took a bite, chewed it contemplatively, and then took another. Thoughts and impressions flickered across his face and she could see how deeply he appreciated Mrs. Catton's craft.

She was so fascinated by watching him that when he gazed at her, she didn't look away in time to disguise her interest. All she could do was stare at him and chew.

"You've . . ." He reached for her.

She held very still. His hand brushed the

corner of her mouth. She felt the texture of his skin, its heat, the softness of her own flesh against his.

Turn your head, her body demanded. *Just a little so you can draw his finger into your mouth. He'll taste of green earth and sugar. And he'll be warm. So warm.*

But he drew his hand back before she could act on her mad impulse. A tiny fleck of icing clung to his fingertip.

He licked his finger.

She was not the sort of person who swooned. Yet watching the duke lick the very place on his finger that had touched her mouth . . .

"Judging by your silence, my lords and ladies," Mrs. Catton said, dragging Jess back into the room, "you appreciate the fruits of my shop's labors."

Jess came to attention. She had provided a sample for the Bond Street shops, and she had learned from Mrs. Catton's presentation that having a sample of her product was essential in gathering interest. But she couldn't just march into Lord Trask's drawing room with a bar of soap in her hand.

She *did* have one of the wrappers in her reticule.

Mrs. Catton continued, "*This* is why I believe expanding the range of Catton's is a plan destined to flourish. The potential for success far outweighs any incurred risks."

There was more talk, more analysis of operating costs and the means by which the satellite shops would be constructed, and discussion regarding staffing, which would affect the quality of the baked goods produced.

Jess had gleaned valuable knowledge today, but she fought to stay focused on her goal. She'd make use of the soap wrapper — the trick was figuring out how and when.

And her mind kept circling back to the duke. She could thoroughly describe the shape of the duke's lips, and speculate on the feel of his tongue against her flesh. Tonight, she knew, she would dream of those lips, and then, just as now, she would struggle to think of a reason why she shouldn't kiss them.

It came as no surprise at all to Jess that the duke had made arrangements for a special private luncheon at an exclusive club in Belgravia, a short caravan's ride from Catton's.

"This is a gentlemen's club," Jess noted as she and the other guests climbed the short flight of stairs to the front door. She'd heard of the club through her careful perusal of newspapers, and that many significant financial and political understandings had been negotiated in its rarified atmosphere. "We don't belong here."

"You suggest that I am no gentleman?" The duke looked affronted, then a corner of his mouth hitched into a half smile. "Correct, madam. Only by breeding, but not behavior."

"She means we ladies do not belong here." Lady Haighe sniffed.

"Typically, women are not permitted entrance." The duke stood back to allow the three females to cross the threshold. Once inside, Jess noted the foyer and the entire interior were paneled in dark wood with accents of blue-and-white porcelain here and there. "But it took very little persuading for the proprietors to change their minds about their policy. For the next two hours, in any event."

A man in livery gestured for everyone to move toward a large parlor, which they did.

"Surely the request coming from a duke had nothing to do with it." Jess stepped into the room. Long banquet tables had been arranged in a horseshoe shape, draped with snowy-white linen tablecloths. Sparkling silver and gilt-edged china had already been laid out in anticipation of the Bazaar guests.

"It was merely my oratory skills that

persuaded them," the duke said. "And the tureens full of money. And, Lady Whitfield," he added in a lower voice, "once again I must ask for your forgiveness."

"This was all organized before you realized the error of your ways," she said wryly.

"The error of *one* of my ways. I'm rather fond of my others."

She shook her head. Blast the man for being so bloody charming.

The gentlemen waited to take their seats until after the women had done so. Fortunately, several people sat between Jess and the duke, with Baron Mentmore beside her. After being thoroughly distracted by the duke at Catton's, she needed all of her attention and concentration for this luncheon.

She could not wait any longer. It was time to act, or else her presence here at the Bazaar would be for nothing.

"Where is my handkerchief?" she murmured, rifling through her reticule. "I could have sworn I brought it with me, and — Oh, I beg your pardon!" Her exclamation came as the soap wrapper tumbled out, directly into the lap of the baron.

"What's this?" the gentleman asked, holding it up.

"It's nothing, truly. Just some paper that

was wrapped around a bar of soap a friend of mine gave me. How dreadfully embarrassing! I do apologize."

Baron Mentmore handed her the wrapper. "It has a lovely fragrance. Is that honey?"

"I believe so? I'd saved the paper because it smelled so delightful."

"That's it." The duke snapped his fingers. "That's what you smell like." He gave her a roguish smile.

Her stomach leapt in response. To distract herself, she studied the paper, though she knew precisely what it said because she had been the one to write up the description on the packaging. "It says it's made in Wiltshire, Baron Mentmore. That's where my friend bought it, I believe, if you were thinking of purchasing some for yourself or your wife."

The baron's eyebrows lifted. "Yes, my wife would enjoy that."

"A marvelous idea, my lord," Jess said. "It would be a simple matter to send a footman to Bond Street to obtain some for you. Here, you can keep this." She tucked the paper into his hand before turning her attention to the meal before her. "This soup is delicious, don't you think?"

Conversation continued, with the luncheon progressing smoothly.

She glanced at the duke. He conversed with Lord Trask, seated beside him. And though he did not break off in the middle of their exchange, his gaze — full of searing awareness — met hers.

Her belly fluttered. Yet she did not break the connection between them, and his eyes darkened.

Lord Trask said something to the duke, and he turned his attention back to the marquess.

Jess took a sip of wine, but it did little to cool her. Having finally made her first move, introducing McGale & McGale soap to the Bazaar, the wisest thing to do would be to steer clear of the duke. She did not want him to believe she'd used targeted flirtation to secure his investment or interest in her family's business. That would be beyond unforgivable.

Staying away from him was best.

That didn't stop her from wishing. Wishing, and wanting.

Chapter 8

With the meal concluded, and the members of the Bazaar making their way back to the waiting carriages outside, Noel acted.

He strode to Lady Whitfield, standing on her own as she adjusted her shawl in preparation for going outside.

She looked up at him, short curled lashes framing golden, perceptive eyes. Her ripe, sweet scent teased him. The whole of the day had been an exercise in delicious anticipation, and being this close to her, his body tightened in expectancy of more. More of her incisive intelligence, more of her wicked, barbed wit. More of her.

"Behold, madam," he said, "within the course of a day I am a changed man."

Her assessing gaze swept across him. "It must be an internal change, Your Grace, for you appear much the same this afternoon as you did this morning."

"Indeed, it is something that could not be

detected by the naked eye." He didn't miss the way her breath caught at the word *naked*. "Earlier today, it had been my intention to insist that you have dinner with me tonight."

The column of her throat worked as she swallowed, and he saw there the flutter of her pulse. "But now you have another intention?"

"Now I *ask* you to have dinner with me tonight."

"Funny, I didn't hear any such question. Only another command."

He chuckled lowly. "Habits are difficult beasts to break. *Please* will you dine with me tonight? Just the two of us. I crave your company away from the Bazaar."

"Prettily phrased, Your Grace." Her cutting words were underscored by breathlessness. "I take it you have considerable experience proposing trysts."

"I also have considerable experience with what happens during trysts, and make certain that everyone receives the benefits of my practice."

A pink flush stained her cheeks, but she didn't look away. "Receiving rejection must be unusual for you."

"That's what this is?" He tried to keep his voice light. "A rejection?"

Her lips quirked. "How shocked you sound."

"Forgive me my impertinence. I find you fascinating, and I flattered myself in thinking I wasn't alone in this attraction."

"You aren't." Her cheeks went even more rosy, a delightful contrast to the coolness in her tone. "A word of advice about me, Your Grace. I prefer to do things in my own time, and at the urging of my own inclination. When *I* decide I want you in my bed, I will let you know."

"When," he said. "Not *if.*"

"Indeed." She tapped him once in the center of his chest, and though she'd donned her gloves, and despite the layers of his waistcoat and shirt, he felt that tap like summer lightning. "A more sagacious woman than I would tell you no. In this, however, I am not so sage. *I* will lead in this dance. *I* will tell you when I'm ready for more. Until then . . ."

"Go slowly," he said.

"*Very* slowly."

He felt himself smiling. "Where you lead, I will follow. I'll have you know, not being in command will be a first for me."

"And here I thought you'd left your virginity behind long ago." She looked pointedly at his arm. "Now you may escort me outside to the carriage."

He snapped to attention, offering her his arm. It felt like the greatest blessing a man could receive — and one of the most erotic experiences he could remember — to have her rest her fingers gently on his sleeve.

"Your servant, madam," he murmured before guiding her toward the front door.

Careful to keep from splashing himself, Noel held the three pints over his head as he eased through the crowd gathered at the bar.

"Steady on, my lord," a man in the clothes of a laborer said. "Or you'll get a soaking and reek of ale."

"I've smelled worse." Noel threaded his way toward his companions ensconced at a settle.

The chophouse's rowdy atmosphere sharply contrasted with the Bazaar's sedate mood. Men crowded around small tables, jostling and jabbering at top volume as they hacked at pieces of beef and knocked tankards together. There were more fashionable chophouses, places where well-to-do men dined with informal dignity, but that was precisely why Noel had selected the Flea and Firkin for tonight.

The tavern owner sidled up beside him,

frowning with worry. "Certain I can't help you with those, my lord?"

"Almost there," Noel said easily. "Besides, this way I look the hero to my friends."

He left the tavern owner behind and finally reached the settle, then thunked the tankards down onto the table. "Refreshments, miscreants."

McCameron grabbed his drink, and Holloway — wearing the annoyingly pleased countenance of a man newly married — did the same.

Noel dropped to his seat, his limbs loosening. "Now we can get to the business of revelry." He drank deeply from his tankard. He needed this, to be out with his friends, so he could keep himself from brooding over Lady Whitfield's rejection. It wasn't *precisely* a rebuff, but here he was, with his friends, rather than warming her bed.

He had to think of something else besides Lady Whitfield lying abed. "Meant to tell you, Holloway, your benefactor, Lady Farris, is at the Bazaar."

"Grace and I were ridiculously fortunate in finding a patron as progressive as she," Holloway said, then added gravely, "So I expect you to see to her comfort and security."

"Put your lance down, Sir Readsalot. The

lady attends to herself, and quite admirably. Same applies to all the women of the Bazaar."

"Look at the way he lights up whenever he mentions women." McCameron nudged Holloway with his elbow. "Rotherby, you made us think you attended that thing out of the pure goodness of your ducal heart."

"I'll never tell anyone to think *less* of me. Besides, there's only three ladies, so that hardly constitutes me running rampant at a girls' finishing school."

"Who are the ladies at the Bazaar?" Holloway asked.

"Lady Farris, Lady Haighe, and Lady Whitfield." His heart thumped as he said her name.

"Whitfield?" McCameron lifted a brow. "I've not heard of her."

"Nor I," Holloway said, and added meditatively, "though if she doesn't haunt the scientific library and hasn't authored a monograph on societal structures, it's unlikely that I'd hear of her."

"A widow. Youngish. Her late husband was a baronet. Sir Brantley Whitfield. Turns out she's the woman I saw on Bond Street."

McCameron stared at Noel, his gaze incisive. "Hm."

"Have a care with your elbow," Holloway

exclaimed when McCameron nudged him again.

"What?" Noel demanded. "What does that *hm* mean? And stop prodding Holloway in the pancreas."

"I'm no physician, but I think he's hitting my liver," Holloway murmured.

"You're never laconic when describing women," McCameron said. "And the way you talked about your unknown Bond Street beauty, you sounded partway besotted with her. Now you're just barking out terse descriptors, which leads me to believe she's truly got you infatuated."

"For God's sake, McCameron, we're not at Eton anymore." Noel rolled his eyes.

"Hold a moment — did she *refuse* you?" McCameron sounded half horrified, half delighted. At Noel's silence, McCameron exclaimed, "Oho! The impossible has happened. You asked a woman to go to bed with you and she actually said no."

"Is that how it's done in the *ton*? You simply request sex from a potential partner?" Holloway pulled a notebook from his pocket and frowned as he wrote in it. "You never mentioned anything like that when you were teaching me how to be a rake."

Noel grunted. "Because that's not how it works. There's such a thing as wooing. Like the way you pretended to woo Lady Grace."

"I was *actually* wooing her." Holloway grinned. "But you're prevaricating. You asked this Lady Whitfield to have sex with you."

"I didn't amble over to her, waggle my eyebrows, and point at my crotch."

"But you *did* proposition her," McCameron said doggedly. "And we can infer from your presence at the Flea and Firkin at" — he glanced at his timepiece — "eleven twenty-seven in the evening that she declined your proposition. Else you would be enjoying each other's company at this very moment."

"She didn't say *no.* She said *go slow.* Two very different meanings. So . . . I'm going slowly." It *was* novel for him, but there was a kind of delight in this back-and-forth with Lady Whitfield. It filled his body with hot, eager energy. In a short time, he'd come to adore the strength of her will — she'd given him a justifiable setting down only that morning when he'd unilaterally decided everyone would go to Catton's, and she refused to heap him with flattery, or accept his practiced flirtation.

It was like stroking a fingertip across a knife, taking a chance that he might be cut, and welcoming the wound.

"And you agreed to her terms," Holloway said thoughtfully.

"Contrary to certain people's opinions," Noel replied, "I'm not a slavering beast, roaming the countryside in search of damsels to defile." He smiled to himself, thinking of how she had called him "Your Grace, the wolf." He was hungry for her, like a wolf. "I will give her as much time as she needs. And if she ultimately decides she doesn't want me, so be it."

McCameron braced his arms on the table, his expression turning serious. "You'll survive. I have it on good authority."

Noel and Holloway shared a quick look. Two years had passed since McCameron had received word on the eve of Waterloo that the woman waiting for him back home had married someone else. McCameron had returned from war with several visible scars and, Noel suspected, an invisible one on his heart.

"I will," Noel said. "No man ever died from blue bollocks."

"Actually," Holloway threw in, riffling through the pages of his notebook, "there are several cultures that believe lack of sexual congress saps a warrior's powers, which might lead to his defeat on the battlefield. In fact, I have notations here —"

"Fortunate for you, I'm wearing my favorite boots," McCameron said, "else I'd chuck one at you."

"My feet are bigger," Holloway retorted. "I'll brain you with my shoe."

"Enough talk." Noel pointed at McCameron and then at Holloway. "You two. Arm wrestle. It's the only way to settle this."

McCameron shrugged, then planted his elbow on the table. Holloway pushed up his sleeve and clasped McCameron's hand, revealing a muscled forearm. Though Holloway was a scholar of anthropology, he kept himself physically fit. "I accept the challenge."

The two began to wrestle in earnest. As they did, Noel got to his feet.

"All right, blokes," he announced to the room, "we're now accepting wagers. Decorated veteran versus acclaimed but oddly robust scholar." The other patrons of the chophouse couldn't resist a contest, and soon the table was ringed with cheering men.

Chuckling, Noel folded his arms across his chest as he watched Holloway and McCameron turn red from exertion. Thank God for them, these ridiculous buffoons he loved so dearly.

CHAPTER 9

"Ah, Lady Whitfield."

Jess turned as Lord Prowse approached her, Baron Mentmore trailing after him. The morning presentations had yet to begin, and nearly everyone had assembled in Lord Trask's drawing room.

The duke was not in attendance.

Which was perfectly fine. She didn't need to keep looking toward the door, or strain for the sound of his distinctively solid but assured tread on the stairs. When he arrived, he arrived, and she would not notice each minute he was absent.

"Your insight is welcome," Lord Prowse said. "If you'd be so kind."

"My lords, I would be happy to assist you." She regarded both noblemen, who looked at her eagerly. "Please tell me what requires my expertise."

"It's only that Mentmore thinks grain is a poor investment, and I am positive there is always money to be made in agriculture. Which of us is correct?"

"The answer isn't so easy. Taking into consideration the poor harvests from last year . . ." As she talked, mentally Jess gave a wry smile. As Jessica McGale, hired companion, these men would never have pressed her for an opinion on anything, let alone something as weighty as finances, and yet, believing her to be Lady Whitfield, her thoughts had weight and meaning.

Being listened to, being truly *heard* — she could easily get used to it.

While she spoke, Baron Mentmore and Lord Prowse nodded. The baron actually wrote in a notebook, his hand moving quickly across the page as it appeared he transcribed what she said.

It was a topic on which she could speak at length, and with considerable enthusiasm.

Quick but strong footsteps came up the stairs, and then she *felt* him enter the room. He spoke in a low voice to Lord Trask.

"And when factoring in the need for . . . for . . . grain abroad, you . . ." She shook her head. "Forgive me, my lords. My thoughts have suddenly scattered."

"Good morning, my lords. Lady Whitfield." The duke's voice came from just behind her. "You're looking very studious,

Mentmore."

The baron held up his notebook. "Lady Whitfield was kind enough to oblige us with her thoughts on the growth and exportation of grain."

There was no help for it. She *had* to face him, if only to see that astonishingly handsome face of his. The warm appreciation in his eyes was her reward for doing so. He had a way of looking at her as though the rest of the world had dropped away into shadow.

"I should hope you *do* consult her," he said. "I'd think you very foolish not to. She'll rule us all one day."

"Rule England?" she asked. "Or the world?"

"Whichever pleases you best. We'll be grateful subjects, regardless of the size of your realm." He bowed, but his gaze stayed on hers, and suddenly the room felt especially hot.

She hauled her attention to the other men. "Did your wife enjoy the gift, Baron?"

"The gift . . . ?" He blinked.

"The soap," she said, smiling. "The one that smells of honey. You were going to gift your wife with it, I believe."

"Yes! Indeed. Do you know," Baron Mentmore said in disbelief, "my footman visited nearly every establishment, *none* of the shops carry it. It must be available for purchase only in Wiltshire."

"Shame," Jess said. "A quality product like that would surely be popular if it was obtainable in London."

"England is rife with small businesses," Lord Prowse said sullenly. "Not *all* of their goods can be sold here."

"Very true," she said mildly. "We couldn't flood the market with products from hither and yon, and if an operation is very small, they wouldn't be able to meet demand. Although —" She shook her head. "Never mind. A passing fancy."

"Go on, Lady Whitfield," the duke said. "Your *passing fancies* outweigh most people's most deliberate and careful thoughts."

"I was merely thinking that the right small-scale business, with sufficient capital from outside sources, could potentially do very well here in London."

"Such as a soap manufacturer?" Baron Mentmore asked.

"Soap?" Lord Prowse made a scoffing noise. "Hardly worth anyone's attention."

"Consider Beau Brummell," Jess said. At the puzzled looks she received, she went on in an assured voice. "A man of influence, Brummell. Well, he was, until he fled to the

139

Continent."

"He was vocal about the importance of bathing," the duke said.

"To do it daily," Baron Mentmore added. "Use hot water over the entire body."

"Who has time for that?" Lord Prowse exclaimed.

"Many people, I assure you," the duke responded drily.

"Brummell's power can't be overestimated," Jess said. "Look at how many of the gentlemen of our company are dressed."

More than half the men sported light-colored pantaloons, a white waistcoat, white neckcloth, and dark coat. Even the duke's ensemble followed this principle — though he wore his with an artful insouciance that could only come from not caring what other people thought.

"What of it?" Mr. Walditch asked, coming over to join the group, with Lady Farris at his side.

"Brummell's opinions have filtered down to all levels of society," Jess said. "From neckcloths to bathing. I wouldn't be surprised if people took more baths because of him."

"More bathing means more soap." Baron Mentmore's eyes widened. "Gracious."

"You may be onto something, my lord,"

Jess said to the baron. She nodded, and Baron Mentmore nodded right along with her. Within moments, half the assembled people were also nodding — though the duke wasn't of their number.

Lord Prowse looked sullen. "It's nonsense."

"It isn't," Baron Mentmore said in an injured tone. Defiantly, he continued, "I'm going to have my man of business look into the people who make that honey soap. Could be an opportunity there."

"Do let us know what you discover," Jess said, calm and collected, but inside she danced. The seeds had been planted, and, even better, she'd steered the conversation in such a way to make the others believe it had been *their* idea.

The baron would learn more about McGale & McGale, including the fire. But Jess and her siblings had been transparent about the catastrophe, so there would be no chance of being accused of deceit. If Baron Mentmore's man of business was worth his wages, he'd see that there would be a ripe investment opportunity for his employer. And if that man didn't recognize it, tomorrow, Jess would make certain that the baron, and sympathetic others at the Bazaar, knew it.

Lord Trask appeared at the duke's side.

She held her breath, worried that the marquess might castigate her for bringing in a business in search of capital — exactly what he'd grumbled about when she'd first gained entrance to the Bazaar.

"Time to begin," he said.

She exhaled. Safe, for now.

Jess moved to perch on a delicate chair, careful to keep from staring too long at the duke. Instead of sitting, he stood toward the back, his arms folded across his chest. Moments later, a man entered carrying a covered birdcage. Soft avian sounds came from beneath the cover.

"My lords and my ladies," the man said, "I am Bartholomew Pine, and I present to you today the solution to rapid communication in major cities."

He tugged the covering off the cage, revealing a tiny sparrow.

"This solution will be far less expensive than using footmen or hired boys to deliver messages," Mr. Pine said tremulously. "Trained sparrows will take brief communications from your home to a central hub. You can *chirp* at someone with your short message. The hub is where the sparrows will feed, so if someone wants to see if they have received a message, they can check the *feed,* as I call it."

Confused mutterings rose up from the guests.

"Does that mean we'll have to continuously hover around the feed to see if anyone has a message for us?" Viscount Hunsdon asked.

"Obviously, you cannot spend all day at the feed," Mr. Pine stammered.

"That would be a spectacular waste of time," Baron Mentmore said irritably.

While Jess pitied Mr. Pine for receiving such a poor reception, his idea seemed ludicrous. She shared a look with the duke, and his expression revealed that he felt the same.

She also pitied the poor bird, who hopped around its cage, unable to spread its wings and fly.

"Why not use pigeons?" someone demanded.

"Sparrows are quite tractable, with the right training. I will demonstrate."

He opened the cage door and reached for the sparrow. The bird immediately flew past his hand and out into the room.

Chaos reigned as everyone leapt to their feet and exclaimed in horror, amusement, or a little of both. Some took cover from the bird's frantic fluttering. Grown men hid behind furniture and shrieked in alarm as if they were being set upon by bloodthirsty monsters. Their fearful cries made the sparrow carom through the chamber at a blinding speed.

"Take cover, Lady Whitfield," Lord Trask cried.

"I grew up in the country," she answered calmly. "Birds don't frighten me."

When the sparrow landed upon a tall cabinet, Jess grabbed a nearby chair and brought it over. She climbed up onto the chair, her movements deliberately slow.

"Pretty bird," she crooned. She gently held out her hand. "Here's a good bird."

The sparrow tilted its head and regarded her with its shiny black eye. Her hand inched closer and closer. A little bit more, and she could grab hold of it.

"God help us!" someone screamed.

Alarmed, the bird flew straight toward Jess's face. She pulled back sharply. The chair beneath her tottered, and she fell —

Into the duke's arms. He caught her and held her firmly. A gasp escaped her lips as she flung her arms around his neck, but whether it came from her close call or the feel of his solid body against hers, she didn't know.

All she *did* know was that she clung to

him, while he had a firm grip on the dip of her waist, and their mouths were quite, quite close.

His gaze skimmed down to her lips. She was suddenly dizzy, and startled excitement made her inhalations come even faster. As he lowered her gently so she could stand, she slid down the length of his torso, her thighs brushing against his.

She barely felt her feet when they touched the ground.

If he lowered his head just a tiny bit more, if she rose up on her toes a fraction . . . they would kiss.

She needed to learn his taste, as much as she needed to draw another breath. In minute increments, they drew closer, and closer still . . .

"It's getting away!" somebody yelled.

The spell between her and the duke broke, and they stepped apart. Twin stains of color stood out on his cheeks, his chest rising and falling.

And then the sparrow took flight from a ledge, out the open window, and into freedom.

She exhaled shakily. *At least one of us is getting what we want.*

Once everyone had collected themselves, it

was time for the next presentation, which was to be held in a dockside warehouse.

Noel brought up the rear of the company as the Bazaar guests filed into the building. The scent of the river lay heavy and dank outside, and within the structure itself, there was a charred scent, as though something had recently been on fire.

Lady Whitfield took several steps back, as though pushed by something unseen. In the dim light within the warehouse, she appeared pale.

He was beside her in an instant. "Are you well, madam?"

"It's nothing." She gave him what was likely an attempt at a reassuring smile, but it frayed at the edges. "My sense of smell is sensitive, which can prove inconvenient at times."

"Fortunate that I decided not to douse myself in sardines and vinegar this morning."

His jest, weak as it was, had the desired effect. She chuckled softly, and color returned to her cheeks. A darker pink had dusted her face when he'd caught her earlier. He'd seen the way she'd looked at his mouth, too, and she'd been silken and lush against him. Since then, he'd been edgy and aroused, and he was grateful for the

146

opportunity to leave Trask's drawing room behind for an outing to see another presentation.

"What a remarkable place." Her gaze roamed through the building, and while most of it was empty, a giant metal tank occupied part of the space. From it came a series of lead pipes that snaked through the warehouse, with what appeared to be hand pumps set at intervals, and hoses attached to the pumps.

A Black man in a beautiful ink-blue jacket and mahogany silk waistcoat stood beside the giant tank, while a Black woman in a neat gown with a heavy canvas apron adjusted a few pipe fittings.

"Have we all assembled?" the man asked crisply. "Very good. I am Dionysus Graves. This is my wife, Judith."

She nodded at her cue, and said, "We present to you our fire-suppression system to be implemented in mills and factories."

For the next twenty minutes, the Graveses explained that by the time a fire brigade could arrive at a mill, the conflagration would have likely decimated most of the structure and could have cost many lives. Their system could be installed directly in a mill to be used by the workers themselves, and while it might not completely douse a fire, it could curtail the damage and danger considerably. The engineering of the Graveses' contraption was something to behold, and though Noel had fared relatively well with his education in physics, he marveled at the adroitness of the couple's minds.

Mrs. Graves said, "Distinguished lords and ladies, we will now demonstrate the effectiveness of our system." She nodded at her husband, who approached a sizable pile of splintered wood.

Mr. Graves struck a flint, creating sparks. The sparks flew onto the wood, and within a moment, the pile of wood caught fire. It was a significant blaze, throwing tremendous heat.

A soft gasp sounded beside him. Lady Whitfield shook — not from cold. Her eyes went wide, the lurid light from the fire turning them glassy. Her fear was a palpable thing.

It was the fire that terrified her.

At once, he placed his body between her and the blaze. He wrapped his arms around her trembling shoulders and guided her quickly toward the exit. "A few more steps," he murmured, "and then we'll be well away from it. I'm here. You're safe."

"Th-thank you."

Hearing her stammer in terror shot straight to his heart. She never showed fear.

As he led her to the door, he looked back over his shoulder. Mr. Graves worked one of the pumps whilst his wife held the hose, directing a robust stream of water onto the fire.

Trask sent a questioning look in Noel's direction. He responded with a hand gesture to indicate that everything was under control, and for Trask to stay with the others.

Once outside, Noel escorted Lady Whitfield toward the waterfront. "The river isn't the most delightful fragrance, but it should take the smell of smoke away."

"Again, I'm grateful." Her voice, he was relieved to hear, was even, but she continued to shiver.

Noel pulled off his greatcoat and settled it over her shoulders. It engulfed her, and she objected, "I'm dragging it on the ground. It will get dirty."

"My valet, Beale, is entirely too conceited. Cleaning mud off my coat will set him down a peg." They came to the edge of the river, and he carefully seated her on a crate. "Better?"

She drew in a breath, then made a face. "I understand what you mean about the river's scent. Yet it is better." For a moment, she was quiet, then asked, "Do you think anyone noticed?"

"Trask saw us leave, but he was the only one. You needn't worry. He's not the sort to gossip."

She kept her gaze trained on the water, watching the comings and goings of ships and boats and all manner of other water-faring vessels. "It's not gossip that concerns me. I don't —"

"Don't what?" he urged gently.

"I don't like to be seen as vulnerable," she blurted, then clamped her lips together as if embarrassed by her outburst.

He felt his brows lift. "But you're human. Of course that means that sometimes you must be vulnerable."

"Doesn't mean I like it," she muttered.

"I don't like it, either." He clicked his tongue. "What if people realize that the Duke of Rotherby is only a godlike being, and not actually a god?"

"They never will believe that," she said drily.

He sobered. "A wise lady reminded me that being a dictatorial boor isn't appreciated by others. And that sometimes there's a benefit to be had in delving beneath the surface."

"And do *you* think that?"

150

He shrugged as he watched a man on a skiff navigate between huge tall-masted ships. "She's shown me that life is an ongoing education. There's always something new to learn, some new experience to have. For example, here we are, beside one of the busiest rivers in the world, full of ships going all over the globe, the heartbeat of the nation, and all I can think about is the curve of the back of your neck."

She brought her hand up to gently touch her nape. The gesture was so tender, so *vulnerable,* it nearly brought him to his knees.

"Apologies," he said gruffly. "You asked me to go slow —"

"Slow," she said, turning to look up at him, her eyes bright, "not *stop.* "

He curled his hands into fists to keep from reaching for her. "As you wish, Lady Whitfield."

"My name is Jessica, but my friends and family call me Jess." She bit her lip, then offered, "You may, as well. If you like."

"I would," he answered readily. It was a gift, her name, and he held it tightly. "The names my friends call me aren't suitable for mixed company, but I'd be honored if you would call me Noel."

"Noel," she repeated. The single syllable

had never held such music before as it did coming from her lips.

They were silent together, though the noise from traffic along the river made the moment anything but quiet. He held himself very still, as though by remaining motionless, he could preserve this span of time, stretch it out into an infinite realm that contained him and her alone.

She exhaled. "I . . . had an experience with fire. I wasn't hurt, but . . . it was frightening. I can still feel it, sometimes. Its heat. And I don't care for sitting too close to the fireplace."

"Understandable that the Graveses' demonstration might elicit feelings of fear. You know," he added, "I myself have a secret fear. I . . ." He cleared his throat. "I don't like rodents."

"Rats and mice and such?"

"The same," he said stiffly. "When I was young, I found a mouse living in my mattress. My nurse took it outside and set it free, but I hated the thought that I was lying unconscious on its home. It might have even crawled on me when I was sleeping." He suppressed a tremor of revulsion.

She rose to her feet. "In that case, let us head back to the others. And whatever you do, don't look down."

152

"Why?"

"Because there's a terrier-sized rat eating its luncheon about five feet away."

It was remarkable how vanity could change one's behavior. He knew with absolute certainty that if she hadn't been there, he would have gagged and in general made an ass of himself in front of the entire London docks.

Instead, he flexed his hands in an attempt to calm himself. The rodent didn't worry him half as much as what he intended to do next. "Would you accompany me to Vauxhall tonight?"

"Ah, you *asked*." A smile bloomed across her face, but the happiness it gave Noel dimmed when she added, "I am not certain that's a wise idea."

"What if we weren't alone?"

"Depends on the company."

He inclined his head. "The other Bazaar guests." His breath held as he awaited her answer. She couldn't know how difficult it was for him to offer himself up in this way, and he didn't *want* her to know. All he desired was for her to exercise her free will in choosing him. That was what mattered. Her choice.

A long moment went by, and she was silent. Then, just as he was on the verge of begging her for an answer, she said, "I should like that."

He said, "I suspect that, if I tried, at the moment I could literally walk across the surface of the Thames from sheer happiness."

"Your Grace —"

"Noel," he reminded her.

"It's *my* suspicion that you are mainly pleased by my agreeing to go with you because you're unused to women refusing you anything."

"Like a child denied a toy." He scowled as anger flared. "I am *not* a child. This is no tantrum."

She inclined her head. "You're right. You deserve better than I have given. My apologies. It's only . . ." She glanced down. "You're so very *much,* and I'm more than a little afraid of what I feel when I'm with you."

His anger burned away, replaced by something he had little experience with: humility. Here again, she transformed him. "We shall venture forth together, and take each moment as it presents itself."

"A wise course of action."

He offered her his arm. "Shall we?"

"One thing first." She pulled off his coat and handed it back to him. "Thank you for

154

the loan, Noel. And for trusting me with your fear."

"Ever the gallant." He donned the garment, and his head fogged. Her honeyed fragrance surrounded him — trapped within the garment's fibers — and as he led her back toward the warehouse, he vowed that Beale would never, *never* clean his coat.

CHAPTER 10

As the gentleman giving the final presentation left the room, Noel immediately surged to his feet.

"A small treat tonight," he said to the guests. "I've arranged private tables in supper boxes at Vauxhall. Nothing more revivifying than arrack and pyrotechnics." He added, "That is, I ask you all to join me, if you will."

Everyone murmured their appreciation and excitement over the prospect, and Jess couldn't keep from smiling. It was for *her* that he did this, and her head was full of stars. Even as she knew his secrets and vulnerabilities, he dazzled.

It was arranged that the Bazaar participants would meet at nine o'clock at Lord Trask's home, and then caravan to minimize traffic congestion. When Noel acted, he acted decisively, with no detail omitted. She couldn't help but be impressed by such thoroughness.

Nerves and excitement accompanied her home. She feared she would reveal herself to be a gauche country girl, gawking at the sophisticated pleasure garden. But how she longed to see it, and be there with Noel.

Tonight would be a night of making memories. None of this could last, and she would hold everything as tightly as she could.

Once at home, she and Lynch stood together in the stable yard and nursed whiskeys.

"Have you ever been to Vauxhall?" Jess asked him. "I've read about it. Tried to picture what the gardens might look like at night, lit up by thousands of lanterns."

"Can't say as I've gone there." He scratched his fingers across his shining head. "It's three shillings sixpence to get in, so I save my coin for a fine meal or some of Catton's cakes."

"Is it a dangerous place?" She lifted her shoulders. "There's the Dark Walk. A place for assignations. But I'd heard its shadows hide cutpurses and men lurking there to prey upon unaccompanied women."

"Might be. But all of London's dangerous. Wallop anyone who tries anything. Better to give a lad a punch than have his groping paws all over you." He shrugged. "His bruises and broken bones will heal. Or maybe the wounds will putrefy and he'll rot from the inside out. Serve him right, won't it?"

"A sensible attitude." She lifted her hand, coiled into a fist. "I've knocked a few blokes onto their arses when they warranted it."

He tapped her fist with his fingers. "Good lass."

"Anything else I might need to know about the gardens?"

"Only that you ought to enjoy yourself."

A quick nap — which involved mostly lying on her bed and staring at the ceiling — followed by a bath revived her for the night ahead. Her abigail attired her in a diaphanous gown of saffron-hued silk and secured pearl pins in her hair. A white satin wrap draped around her shoulders to protect her from an evening chill.

Jess examined her reflection in the pier glass. She tried to resist the impulse to run her hands over the fabric, though it wasn't easy. Never again in her life would she have the opportunity to wear such fine clothing, and she wanted to savor it, even as she felt a sting of resentment that, with the people of the Bazaar, she could not fully be herself.

With Noel, she felt more *herself* than she

had in a long, long while. She wasn't the eldest sibling responsible for everything. She wasn't the deferential paid companion. She did not have to curb her tongue or wear a smothering cloak of humility.

But even that was predicated on a lie.

"Awful pretty, my lady," Nell said admiringly.

Naturally, an abigail would praise her mistress, but Jess hoped Nell was sincere. Jess wanted to look her best tonight. It was only natural, all part of her plan. It had nothing to do with a duke who gave her his coat when she shivered, and possessed impossibly dark eyes.

Fortunately, the night was fine, making her walk to Lord Trask's pleasant enough. Each step wound her excitement higher and higher — her first time at Vauxhall, her first evening with Noel.

Pleasures to savor.

She entered the downstairs parlor, where everyone had convened. Looking around, she searched for Noel. Then she froze when she saw him.

His simple, elegant evening clothes only reaffirmed how exquisitely his garments — and he — were made. He looked at her from across the chamber, and she was bolted to the spot.

Briefly, he looked stunned, as though witnessing something extraordinary, something beautiful.

Her. He looked at her as though she was beautiful.

His gaze heated. Then he smiled, a true smile, wide and white and dazzling. She took a step toward him, drawn forward by the insistent need to be closer.

Someone said something to him, and the moment between her and Noel broke apart. But not completely, because he shot her one more glance that clearly said, *This isn't finished between us.*

After a quick exchange with Lord Trask, Noel clapped his hands together. "We're all here. Shall we venture forth, my friends?"

There was a chorus of agreement. Noel strode forward and offered Jess his arm. He started when someone tapped a fan on his shoulder.

"You have *two* arms, you know," Lady Haighe said pointedly.

"Horrendously remiss in not offering it to you." Noel extended his free arm to her. She glanced at it as though debating whether or not to grant him her favor, and then, with a sly smile, she rested her fingers on his sleeve. Noel murmured, "You honor me."

"Don't I, though?" The older woman sniffed.

Jess couldn't stop herself from smiling. Men far outnumbered the women of the Bazaar — there was no shortage of other gentlemen to escort Lady Haighe. Yet how could Jess begrudge Lady Haighe her desire for Noel's attention?

Mr. Walditch attended Lady Farris, and with all the company accounted for, they went down to a row of waiting carriages. Jess, Lady Haighe, and Mr. Parley climbed into Noel's coach. Then they were off.

Other than her walk to Lord Trask's, she hadn't been out after dark in London. Nights at the family farm or in her village were long and quiet, and she had often taken solitary rambles through the darkened countryside.

In London, she had to return to the town house and spend the evening with a solitary meal and her stack of newspapers. When she'd walked tonight, she had been too preoccupied with thoughts of the coming evening, and being with Noel again. Now it was all she could do to keep from hanging her head out of the carriage window and watching the city at night. There were people, so many people, parading up and down the lamp-lit streets as though it was

161

high noon. Shop windows were also illuminated like glowing jewel boxes, and orange sellers and piemen cried their wares.

"It's a risk for me to show my face at Vauxhall," Noel said, snaring her attention. "Last time I was there, I caused something of a disturbance."

"Surely not," Lady Haighe insisted. "A man of your rank."

"The management was a trifle displeased when I borrowed three carts full of colored lanterns. And the singers. And the orchestra. And the cooks, and —"

"Essentially, you stole Vauxhall," Jess said, fighting a smile.

"*Borrowed,* madam. It was my intention to return it. Eventually."

"God preserve us from overindulged men." Lady Haighe sniffed.

"We are a blight," Noel said solemnly. "Yet I trust tonight that between yourself and Lady Whitfield, you will curb my more profligate tendencies."

"If I had a frigate every time a man made a woman responsible for his actions" — Jess snorted — "I'd have an armada."

"A woman in command?" Mr. Parley seemed slightly appalled.

"Why not?" Noel lifted a brow. "Queen Elizabeth commanded one and look how well that turned out for the nation."

"Really, Your Grace," Jess said, attempting to sound vexed. "If you insist on saying such things, I will have no choice but to like you."

His gaze gleamed in the half-light of the carriage. "*Like* is a lukewarm emotion. Better to inspire something with a little more heat. Hate me if you must, but I'd rather that than passionless *liking*."

Jess pressed her lips together. There was no danger of anything passionless — not where he was concerned.

They crossed Vauxhall Bridge, and the caravan came to a stop. Footmen helped the ladies out, and Jess admired the gates to the pleasure garden as the others assembled.

"Everyone's admission is already paid," Noel said, every inch the magnanimous host. "Please, go in. And above all, enjoy yourselves."

"My lady," Mr. Parley said, presenting her with his arm.

It was better to have the brewer escort her than to show a particular preference, so she took his arm with a grateful nod. She couldn't stop herself from looking over her shoulder toward Noel. Lady Haighe had commandeered him.

Good. That was good. Because the way the lights shone in his eyes, he was temptation incarnate, and once inside the pleasure garden, she would be in his world.

Vauxhall was a place where anything could happen, where the world turned on its head, and farmers' daughters could flirt with dukes.

She didn't know if, on the other side of the pleasure garden's gate, she could trust herself to behave. And she didn't know if she wanted to.

CHAPTER 11

Jess could count on one hand the number of times she'd been drunk. Certainly, she'd never partaken of opium.

Walking the grounds of Vauxhall was like imbibing several bottles of spirits *and* eating opium.

Colored lanterns dazzled from strings and were suspended from tree branches. Acrobats and dancers spun in colorful configurations, a fire-breather shot flames from her mouth, and a magician performed sleight of hand with silk scarves. Strolling musicians seemed to compete with each other as to who could play louder.

Then there were the patrons — men and women of every color, every class, crowding the walkways, jostling and shouting and laughing.

It was fantastic. It was almost too much.

"This way, good children," Noel called to the Bazaar guests. "To the supper boxes."

As he led the group, Jess kept her gaze fixed on Noel's broad back rather than the spectacle around her. His presence anchored her, keeping her from flying off into the cosmos.

More than once, he looked back. At her. Every time he did, her heart beat a little faster.

They moved past a large pavilion housing an orchestra, past tables set up beneath the trees' canopy, and on toward a long colonnade that housed the supper boxes. The boxes themselves were closed on three sides, and the open front enabled the diners to see and be seen. Unlike the rest of the pleasure garden, these boxes contained what appeared to be the elite. The men and women within them wore finery so elegant they fairly reeked of wealth. They preened before the people walking by, as though they knew they were as much a part of the spectacle as the acrobats.

"No need for shyness," Noel said, ushering her and the others into a trio of empty boxes. "Sit, eat, drink. Partake of everything Vauxhall has to offer."

Jess found herself seated at the center of one table, Mr. Walditch on one side of her, Noel on the other. In the jeweled light of the lanterns, his face was preternaturally

166

handsome, but it was his expression of easy confidence that made her palms damp. He inhabited his body and the world with assurance, as though he never questioned himself.

He caught her looking at him. The smile he gave her was slow and hot.

A server came around to fill their glasses. Seeking to cool herself, Jess took a long swallow of her drink. It was sweet and spiced and so delicious she quickly downed more.

"Have a care," Noel murmured. "The arrack punch here is notorious for making people forget themselves. I've seen more than a few arrack-fueled brawls."

"I'm far tougher than I appear."

"Then you must be Heracles's daughter because I've never met someone so strong." He took a handful of grapes from a salver and placed them onto her plate. "Don't think I haven't noticed."

"Noticed what?" Apprehension tightened along her neck, but she feigned nonchalance by popping a grape into her mouth.

She'd been careful to keep all of her comments about McGale & McGale couched in the language of merely an interested investor. She should have known that someone as observant and insightful as Noel had caught on to her.

"Many at the Bazaar seek your counsel," he said. "With good cause — you're damned insightful, and when it comes to financial matters, you're bloody brilliant."

"I fail to see the problem with that." She'd been called pretty, and clever, but never brilliant. And that this praise came from *him* . . . But worry undercut her pleasure. Had he perceived her secret agenda?

"*You* were the one urging Sir Brantley to attend the Bazaar," he continued. "It was your idea the whole time. Your being here is not happenstance."

She exhaled a laugh as relief coursed through her. "Not happenstance at all."

"I knew it." Noel slapped his hand on the table.

A server presented a platter of what had to be the thinnest slices of ham Jess had ever beheld. With great ceremony, the server set the platter down and backed away.

"May I serve you?" Noel asked, his voice low and dark. "I'd enjoy it very much."

"Yes, please," she answered breathlessly.

As if from a great distance away, she heard Mr. Walditch talking with Lord Sundon. Neither of them seemed to be aware of the conversation happening beside them. Or they did notice, and opted not to involve themselves.

"You're a star attraction." She glanced toward a trio of perambulators, two women and a man. All three of them sent Noel clear looks of longing. And they weren't the only passersby that showed him interest.

Yet Noel's attention remained fixed on her. As he leaned back in his chair, his gaze didn't waver from her face. "Tell me your favorite book."

"Why?"

"I'm collecting pieces of you, like a beachcomber looking for polished stones and beautiful shells. Later, when they're home, far inland, they can look at those stones and shells and remember."

She pressed a hand to the pulse fluttering in her neck. "I'd no idea dukes were poetical."

"When suitably motivated."

"The answer depends," she said. "Sometimes it's Smith's *Wealth of Nations*. It isn't my favorite, per se, but I can read it over and over again and find something new every time." Her copy of the book was much battered, several of the pages loose in the binding. She had to secure the whole thing with twine.

He gave her a lopsided smile. "And what about when you're not in the mood for

169

economic theory?"

She'd made use of Lady Catherton's library, and had inhaled the works of Shakespeare. "*As You Like It.* I know it's a play and not exactly a book, but I've never had the chance to see it performed, so I only know it from reading."

"It's Rosalind's story," he said with a nod. "Everyone else is just a plaything for her to toy with. She deserves better than Orlando."

She propped her chin in her hand. "Does anyone truly deserve her?"

"No," he said thoughtfully, "but they can try." His look scorched her. "There's certainly pleasure in the attempt."

She tipped up her chin, a wordless dare. "And *your* favorite book?"

"Here, now," Mr. Walditch interjected. "If you're both going to discuss books in the middle of Vauxhall, I'm going to have the bully boys throw you out."

Jess laughed, delightfully scandalized by Mr. Walditch's threat to a duke.

Noel chuckled and held up his palms. "Fair enough. Tonight's for pleasure, and I'm determined Lady Whitfield will have more than her share of it."

Oh, help.

Mr. Walditch shook his head before dividing his attention between his plate of cold meat and conversation with Lord Sundon.

Jess turned her attention to the people walking past the supper boxes. She easily spotted the companions. Here and there in the crowd, there were women in plainer dress, trailing behind women in elegant silk, their gazes trained on the ladies they were paid to serve. The in-between women, neither fully servant nor part of the family. They were required only because others found them useful, but their own wishes, their own desires, those were covered in holland cloth and forgotten in dusty rooms.

Wanting Noel — and she did want him — was wrong. It was selfish to put her needs before her family's. And yet, and yet . . .

Wasn't there one thing for herself? Not forever, not even for a day, but perhaps just a single hour that belonged to her alone? Couldn't she have that?

"I can tell when you're thinking because the smallest crease appears between your brows," he murmured. "Just here." He moved to touch his fingertip to that same spot, but caught himself and dropped his hand.

"Gentlemen do not point out women's wrinkles." Her words were censorious, but her tone was playful.

"I don't consider them wrinkles. They're

171

lines on your map, leading me to all your mysterious territory."

Her heart thudded, but she said, "Recall what maps used to say — *here be dragons.* You don't know what my dragons might be, or if you can slay them."

"I don't want to slay your dragons. I want to feed them apples and make friends with them."

"Dragons aren't horses," she felt obliged to point out. "They don't eat apples."

"Then I'll feed them sheep or virginal lads, or whatever it is dragons eat. Though, I imagine that virginal lads don't taste very good. Ropy and chewy and green."

Giddy, deliciously freed from *should* and *should not,* she regarded him. "You said it would please you to serve me."

"So it would." His voice was deep as dreams.

"I would like you to" — she held his gaze with hers — "escort me to view the fireworks display."

It should have been wrong or strange to issue commands to him. The difference in their true stations was impossibly wide, never to be breached. But having him serve her felt *right,* in a profound sense that even now she was coming to understand. Because he yielded his power to her, trusting her with it, and even as that yielding filled her with humility, she was emboldened, too.

He believed in her. He recognized her power.

His smile was wide and heart-stopping. "My lady," he said, dark eyes shining in the light of torches and lanterns, "nothing would give me greater pleasure."

When he rose, she also stood and took his offered arm. "Tonight is about pleasure, after all."

They joined the crowds milling through the gardens. Noel used his size and natural authority to guide her safely through the throng. He was in all ways attentive, his gaze almost never immobile as he navigated the crowded paths. When his hand came to rest on the small of her back, she wanted to close her eyes and lean into the sensation. Thank God her garments were lightweight — they permitted her the indulgence of his touch upon her body. Perhaps it was for the best that there were a few layers of silk and linen between them, because if he did touch her bare skin, she would go up in flames.

"Where are you taking me?" she asked above the din.

"The best spot for viewing the fireworks. Few know of it."

"You do."

He leveled his gaze at her. "I know so many things."

"So you say," she replied airily, "but many men make claims without offering an ounce of proof."

He stopped abruptly to face her. "You're playing a dangerous game."

"I know," she confessed. "I cannot seem to stop myself. It's just . . . when I'm with you . . . I feel . . ."

"You feel . . . ?"

She stared up at him. "Like myself."

For a moment, neither moved or spoke. Then, "This way," he said, guiding them off one of the main paths. There were people here, too, but far fewer. Their numbers grew more and more scarce, until Jess found herself completely alone with him beside a tiny pond. Little jewellike fish swam beneath the surface of the water.

"Oh, but it's charming." Jess pressed her fingertips to her mouth as she took in the enchanted scene. She glanced down and saw a strip of shiny fabric near the toe of her shoe. She used a fallen twig to pick up the object.

It was a garter.

She lifted one of her brows. "Is this why you brought me here?"

"You've found me out," he said drily. "I'm

a trophy hunter, collecting garters and drawers. I keep them in a locked cabinet beside my bed, and late at night, I take them out and groan delightedly as I throw them into the air like raked leaves."

She snorted, then, with a flick of the twig, sent the garter spinning off into the darkness. "I've little desire to touch a stranger's underclothes."

"Then you deny yourself one of life's greatest enjoyments." He rested his hands on her shoulders, and her heart leapt like it had been let out of a cage. Instead of pulling her closer, he turned her so that her back was to his front.

"What are you — Ah!" The first burst of fireworks exploded. He had positioned her so that she'd see the pyrotechnic display.

Yet she'd seen such things before. Granted, the fireworks that a traveling circus troupe had used had been on a much smaller scale, but they'd impressed her. Now she had to force herself to look up at the sky and the adorning bursts of light and color. The noise was terrific, jolting her down to her marrow.

It was Noel, however, that captivated her. She tilted her head back to see him. She could watch the colors sculpt the angles of his face for hours. No doubt he'd seen the

Vauxhall fireworks many times, but his expression was one of appreciation — even joy. He had every reason to be jaded by life. In some ways, he was. And yet he allowed himself the simple delight that came from watching pyrotechnics. As though he still held out hope that the world contained delightful surprises.

"Noel," she whispered urgently.

Despite the noise from the fireworks, he seemed to hear her. "Jess?"

"I said I wanted to move slowly."

"I remember."

She took a breath. "I very much want to kiss you. And I hope you very much want to kiss me."

He moved to face her, his expression intent on her alone. "I do not *very much* want to kiss you."

"Oh." She didn't often give in to tears, but at that moment, as his rejection cut deeply, her vision swam. Embarrassment choked her as she tried to calculate how to escape the group and get herself home immediately, without money or a carriage.

"I *need* to kiss you."

CHAPTER 12

Noel looked down at Jess, her face illuminated by the fireworks. Sharp hunger tore into him, the desire in her eyes stoking his need higher, until he was certain he could flare like one of the rockets overhead — exploding into light and color.

"You do?" She didn't speak above a whisper, yet even with the noise of the fireworks so terrific, he heard her.

He stepped closer, so that there was barely any space between them. Her warmth encircled him.

"It's all I think about," he growled. "Going slowly has been an exercise in exquisite torture." His voice was rough as gravel as he spoke. "I keep looking at your mouth and wondering if your taste will be sweet or spiced, or perhaps a bit of both."

"I don't know how I taste," she breathed. "I want you to find out."

She tipped her face up as he stroked his

thumb along her cheek. Her gaze went heavy lidded as he swept his thumb across her lips. He caught the floral scent of arrack on her breath, heard how her breath came in shallow rasps, saw the desire cut into her features.

They swayed into each other, until they pressed close. He growled at the feel of her, soft and feminine, against his taut body.

He cupped the back of her head with his hand, overwhelmed with a heady mixture of desire and tenderness — the need to claim, the need to protect.

He angled her so that their lips aligned. Her breath came faster, and faster still.

"Tell me you want this," he rumbled. "Tell me you want this as much as I do."

"And if I don't?"

"Then I'll stop."

He started to move away, but she gripped his shoulders. "Don't. Don't stop. I want this. For *me.*"

She lifted up onto her toes as he lowered his head and their lips touched, softly. They took small, exploratory sips of each other, discovering what it meant to finally yield to the desire that had built and built until it could no longer be denied.

The kiss deepened. She opened to him and his answering hunger surged. The stroke of her tongue against his coursed through his entire body, lighting torches in his muscles, his cock.

He was afire as she clung to him. Her breasts pressed snug to his chest, and his free hand cupped her waist to urge her closer.

She gasped in response as he dragged his lips from hers to scratch his teeth along her neck. He would devour her. She dug her nails into his back, stoking his hunger even higher and hotter.

"Yes," she breathed. "More."

"Goddamn it, Jess." He bit her hard just where her neck curved to her shoulder, then soothed the sting with his tongue.

He slid his hand higher up, skimming over her waist and along her back, until it rested just beneath the curve of her breast. Yet he did not go farther, a silent question as to whether or not she wanted more. She angled her body, fitting her breast into his palm, and he snarled in approval. His hand covered her, stroking her. He brought his fingertips to her nipple and rubbed it into a tight point.

She gave another pleasured gasp.

"Wanted this," he said in a voice so low it was subterranean. "You. In my arms. Wanted to feel you writhe against me, hear

179

you moan." He lightly pinched her nipple and she rewarded him with the moan he'd desired.

She felt delicious, a gorgeous collection of curves swathed in silk. He'd been struck by the color of her gown tonight, as golden as the sun, and with her just as dazzling within it. Now he wished the fabric would melt away beneath his hands, leaving her bare.

A man and woman's laughter sounded close by.

She tore herself from his embrace. He needed her back in his arms, her mouth against his, but he had to respect the distance she'd put between them.

"We can't . . ." She seemed to fight to get her breathing under control. "We can't do this here." She touched her fingers to her overheated cheeks. "I want to, though. God, how I want to."

"You destroy me — piece by piece. And I welcome it."

Her eyes were wide, her face flushed. He'd kissed her lips into overripe temptation. He felt a muscle work in his jaw as he struggled to calm himself.

Still, he glanced toward the deeper shadows, calculating the distance it would take to hide them both in the darkness and give in to their aching need.

180

Her gaze skimmed down his body, and her eyes widened to see the length of his cock pressed snug in his breeches.

A hint of a smile tugged at the corner of his mouth. "No elegant or witty words from me now. I want you."

Need was written in her face — the finest text he'd ever read — yet a battle was fought behind her gaze. He held himself still. This was her choice to make.

"We ought to get back," she said regretfully. "The others might be looking for us."

Much as he wanted to protest, he nodded. Working quickly, he smoothed out his waistcoat and adjusted his neckcloth. She had almost completely untied it.

She tugged on her bodice and shook out her skirts, then patted her hair. "My coiffure must look like a windblown hayfield."

"Let me." He stepped close, and their fingers tangled as they both worked to put her hair in order. She sighed when he stroked his hands along her scalp and down the nape of her neck.

"How do you know so much about ladies' hair arrangements? Do you help your lovers reassemble themselves when they rise from your bed?"

He did not want to speak of any other lover. He would never be so crass as to judge one woman against another, but more than that, he wanted to honor what he felt with Jess. There would be no comparisons. "I have two sisters and was frequently impressed into service dressing their hair."

"They had no maid of their own?"

"At that age, they had a nurse who spent too much time flirting with an under-groom. So the task of making them into tiny ladies fell to me." Fondness warmed his words. His sisters had been the bane of his existence when he'd been a boy, and he'd missed them terribly when he'd been sent to Eton. Now he saw them and their families every Christmas, and he enjoyed his role as indulgent uncle. "Have a look in the pond and see if I did your coiffure justice."

She did so, peering at her reflection in the water. "Excellent. If you ever decide to relinquish your claim to the dukedom, you've a bright future in women's hairdressing."

"Tempting."

She turned to him and smiled — then realized he wasn't speaking entirely in jest. Disbelief in her voice, she said, "You'd give up countless country estates —"

"Four. No, six. Damn, at the moment I can't recall." His first realization that not every boy stood to inherit half a dozen estates had come at Eton. Granted, most of the boys there had come from the ranks of the elite, with their own sizable inheritances, but almost none of the other students could claim the level of wealth and holdings that he had.

"Half the country's wealth, and the ear of Lord Liverpool himself?" Her look was puzzled.

He gazed skyward. "It's the height of churlishness to complain about everything I have. I live the best life a man can have. That's undeniable."

At first at school, he'd been so proud of himself, smug in his superiority. But then he'd met four boys in the library who'd taught him that a person's value wasn't predicated on their coffers or land.

Thanks to them, he felt the responsibility of tending to his estates and tenants. It was a privilege to have as much — but damn if it didn't also sometimes weigh heavily on him.

"And yet . . . ?"

"And yet . . ." He exhaled. "I've good friends, men for whom I'd do anything. Beyond them . . ." It struck him now, the facts of his world, and a sudden hollowness resounded within him, at odds with the lingering heat from kissing Jess. "I'm often alone."

"You're seldom alone," she said gently.

"The throngs you'd find surrounding an animal trained to entertain. There are my four friends — but to most others, I'm a well-dressed ladder. A means to climb higher." His smile for her was small, but genuine, and the locked cabinet of his innermost heart opened. But it didn't frighten him. He leaned into it, testing what it was to be so truthful with another. "It's different with you. I'm not a dancing bear or a way to get anywhere. I'm a man."

There was no disgust or fear in her eyes, no calculation as to how to exploit the knowledge he'd given her. All he saw was her warmth, and his smile widened. "When I'm near you, I'm very aware I'm a man."

She looked stricken, then glanced away. "We really do need to return to the others."

The heaviness in her voice alarmed him, sending prickling concern across his shoulders. "I've pushed you too far, made you do things you didn't want to do."

"You must not know me at all," she said softly, "if you believe anyone could make me do something I didn't want for myself."

He inclined his head as gratitude and relief surged. "Point taken."

"I'm merely tired. The day has been long."
Appreciation shone in her gaze. "This
morning, you stepped between me and a
conflagration."

"Was that today?" He snorted in disbelief.
"Can't be. It feels as though —"

"As though?"

Noel hesitated. He'd taken a few steps in
baring himself to her, but could he take
more? Each revelation left him more and
more exposed. She could use anything to
her advantage. Certainly others in her position might.

But Jess wasn't like that. He believed that
completely.

"No point in prevaricating. Games are
things to be played with other people,
people I don't care about." He drew a
breath, loosening his hold on his apprehension. "The truth is, it feels as though I've
known you forever."

The column of her throat worked. "It's
mutual, that feeling."

Just then, he did feel like a human fire-
work, brilliant as it exploded across the sky.
He'd given her a piece of himself, and she
had treated it with care and respect, not
because she wanted something from him,
but because to her, it seemed as though he
was fully flesh, as vulnerable as anything

185

that walked the earth.

Before he could take her in his arms again, she said with regret, "It's time to go back."

There was disappointment that this idyll couldn't last forever, but he wasn't a lad any longer. He knew what the responsibilities of the world entailed, including leaving this place, when all he wanted was to stay and stay and stay.

"Of course." He offered her his arm, and when she took it, he led her back down the winding path. They joined up with the more populated walkways.

She looked skyward. "The fireworks have stopped."

"For now."

CHAPTER 13

Jess took the measure of the drawing room on the final full day of the Bazaar. They'd already seen two presentations and were taking a pause before the last push.

Noel had been drawn into conversation with Lord Trask the moment the prior presentation had ended. She resented the marquess's presence, as much as she required him to act as a bulwark between herself and her desire for Noel.

They had kept apart today, as if things between them were too hot, too sensitive, to be handled for very long.

Now he seemed to sense her looking at him — he had a way of finding her wherever she was, as though they were magnets forever drawn to each other — and his eyes were dark, almost as dark as they had been last night at Vauxhall.

She broke away from his gaze, busying herself with pouring a cup of tea from the refreshment table.

She had a task to complete, a reason for her dissembling that brought her to the Bazaar. Noel wasn't that reason and it was important for her to remember that.

Guilt needled her. Over the past few days, she'd come to think of some of the guests as friends, and it did not feel right to manipulate them. If there had been a choice, some other way of salvaging her family's business — and her family itself — she would have gladly done it.

But there was no choice. She had to do this now, and face her guilt later.

After taking a sip of tea, she approached a gathering of Bazaar guests that included Mr. Walditch, Ladies Farris and Haighe, and Baron Mentmore.

"But is it sound, to invest?" Mr. Walditch said, clearly adding to an ongoing conversation. "If a business fails once, it could again."

"Depends on the circumstances of the failure," Jess said. "Acts of God, and so forth."

"I had nothing to do with it," Noel said, joining the group. "Whatever *it* was."

Jess pushed down against a rise of excitement and pleasure, but now she knew what it was like to be kissed by his lips, to feel his hands on her body. The same body that demanded more of him.

She did *not* want to include Noel in her plans for McGale & McGale, but she couldn't deliberately exclude him from the conversation. There was no hope for it.

Lady Haighe snorted. "The vanity of today's bucks."

"Is but a paltry ember compared to the conflagration of the previous generation's conceit," he said with a smile. "Besides, I seem to recall my mother whispering an anecdote that involved you, forty years ago, having your portrait painted *dénudé,* and throwing a ball with that painting prominently displayed for everyone to see."

Though Jess didn't speak French, she had a fair idea what that last word meant, judging by the knowing chuckles of the others — and Lady Haighe's surprising blush.

"It was a different time," she said gruffly, before lifting her chin. "And I was *stunning.*"

"Don't know if God was involved with that soap operation," Baron Mentmore said, his face slightly red, "but it was rotten luck, and that's for certain." He turned to Jess. "My man of business looked into the people who make that honey soap, my lady. What was it called? McGill? McShale?"

189

"I think it was . . . McGale." Knowing full well what he would say, acutely aware that she had to very carefully navigate the discussion, she asked, "And what did he learn?"

"A fire wiped out a major part of their production facilities. They're on their last legs." He shook his head mournfully. "Bad situation all around. One I wouldn't involve myself in."

As calmly as she could, she said, "True, but I've been thinking about what you said about Brummell. A soap manufacturer seems like a good investment."

"Not *that* manufacturer," Mr. Walditch countered.

"Consider, though," she said thoughtfully, "with the McGale operation, there would be ample opportunity for expansion and modernization. It *was* bad luck that there was a fire —" She fought a wave of memories, trying to douse the flames of the past with a few measured breaths. "However, if the product's good, then what better situation to rise up from the literal ashes?"

Seeing the looks of doubt on the listeners' faces, she recalled the demonstration of the Graveses' fire-suppression system. "The latest technology could be implemented to ensure that such a disaster wouldn't happen again." She tilted her head, as if considering something. "Many of the people presenting to us claim that their businesses are prospering. Indeed, they all assert such splendid profitability for themselves, I marvel that they even need us at all."

"I had not considered that," Mr. Walditch murmured thoughtfully. "But would they approach us if their enterprises struggled?"

"Or," Lady Farris said, "they *are* struggling and choose not to inform us."

"Surely they would have to disclose that." Mr. Walditch removed his spectacles and polished them with a cambric square before setting them back on his nose.

Tread carefully, Jess reminded herself. "Then we would have to decide whether or not it's sound to put capital into an operation fighting to survive. We'd need to know what made a particular business have difficulties. If it was mismanagement, then there's no inducement to tie my financial future to theirs. But I would think differently about an enterprise that had suffered from an external obstacle, such as the Mc-Gale operation."

She continued, "If a business had suffered some catastrophe — a poor harvest from bad weather, for example, or a storm causing a ship to sink with its cargo — I'd be

191

more agreeable to considering them as an investment possibility. So long as they were transparent about the source of their misfortune."

"Makes sense," Noel said. "We're none of us beyond the touch of misfortune. It has no rhyme nor reason. No need to punish someone for something beyond their control. If the soap interests you, Mentmore, pursue it."

"I am sending one of my servants to Wiltshire today on an errand, and they are to change horses and return immediately," Jess said. "I could write to the soap makers and ask for more information from them directly, rather than rely on hearsay. It might be worth a closer look — and we'd have answers before the end of the Bazaar tomorrow."

"A lot of trouble for you, isn't it?" Baron Mentmore asked.

"It's the work of but a moment," she answered. "And, who knows, perhaps we'll discover something worthwhile."

She mentally exhaled when the others nodded their heads in agreement. Perhaps this mad venture could work, after all.

"Walditch," Lady Haighe said, "what do you think of the proposal for the canal expansion?"

As conversation continued, Jess decided it was wisest to quit the field whilst things were still in her favor. She murmured something noncommittal and walked to where refreshments were laid out.

She sensed him beside her, and lost her taste for cakes. *His* taste was what she wanted, spiced and rich and drugging.

"Tell me your plans for after the Bazaar," he said.

"After tomorrow?"

"The Season's still at its height, which means a surfeit of assemblies and social gatherings. They're not tremendously exciting, unless you happen to enjoy middling punch and too many people attempting to be amusing. But there are other pleasures to be had in London. You'll stay for those, surely." He made a soft scoffing noise. "Listen to me. I've seen anglers in the River Spey fish with greater subtlety. But I don't give a damn." He stepped closer. "I just want you."

Her face — her whole being — heated. Desire the likes of which she'd never known wrapped around her like enchanted vines, and she didn't want to be freed from them.

But, as the stories said, all enchanted things had to come to an end.

"I am leaving the country," she said softly.

"Going to the Continent."

He blinked. "Will you be there long?"

"I cannot say." Pain radiated from her to speak the words. At the very least, they were the truth.

His brow furrowed. "Then there isn't much time left. For you and I."

"Not much at all," she murmured.

She had to face the terrible truth — if she could not secure investors at the Bazaar, then McGale & McGale would cease to exist. The farm itself would be lost, her family fractured.

With an influx of funding, she could leave her position as a hired companion and focus all of her attention and efforts on the business.

But if she could not save it, she would be a hired companion again.

In either case, there could be no Noel. She told herself that was how it had to be. She had to be a clear-eyed realist — this fantasy would end. But damn her if it would be over far too soon.

That evening, a dinner was held in Lord Trask's home. Jess had just enough time to go home, bathe and change, and then return.

With a glass of cordial in her hand, she

circled the parlor, where she and the other guests had gathered once the meal concluded. The mood was light, conversation flowed readily. Lord Trask beamed from his place by the fire, basking in the glow of a host who had created an exceptional evening.

It had been impossible not to stare at Noel throughout the course of the night. He'd sat in the position of honor at the dining table, with her a good distance away, separated by rank and importance.

Now, with the men and women reunited after dinner, he turned pages for Lady Farris as the countess played the pianoforte.

Tomorrow, she'd see him for the last time. She would dissolve back into her role of invisible companion, never to cross his path, let alone speak to him. Let alone kiss him.

He desired her. She desired him, yet her uncertainty kept her locked in place.

Damn it, this wasn't like her. Decisions, action, conviction in her purpose — these elements made up her life, especially after her parents' death. She saw what needed to be done, and by God, she did it.

Air. She needed air. Once she was alone, she could decide what to do about Noel.

Viscount Pickhill appeared beside her. "My lady, I would like your opinion on a question. There's a manufacturer of textiles in India —"

"I'll happily discuss the matter tomorrow, my lord. Let us enjoy the evening without talk of business."

"Of course, Lady Whitfield. Only —"

"Do excuse me."

She set her glass down and, before the gentleman could respond, she slipped from the chamber.

Lord Trask had boasted that his home had its own conservatory located toward the back of the house. A room filled with green growing things, and silence, seemed exactly what she needed. It would be a small taste of home, and its quiet.

She walked down the corridor, putting the parlor behind her, then came to a glass-fronted door. Pushing it open, she plunged into a shadowed room. There was enough light to see ferns hanging from the high ceiling, and plants, both exotic and more quotidian, abounded. The air here was thick and humid.

A stone bench sat tucked between two potted palms, and she sank down onto it, exhaling the breath she felt she had been holding for most of her life.

196

CHAPTER 14

As Lady Farris played Haydn's Piano Sonata No. 31 in A Flat Major, Noel saw Jess talk briefly with Pickhill before abruptly leaving the room.

With her gone from the chamber, it was as though someone had doused a light.

Her leaving was, in and of itself, not a source of panic. She could have easily gone to refresh herself in the retiring room. However, many minutes went by and she did not return. Alarm needled him. What if she'd fallen ill and needed help?

Lady Haighe entered the parlor, smoothing her hair. Surely she must have been in the retiring room, yet she didn't look panicked as if she'd come across Jess's insensate form slumped on the floor.

That still did not answer the burning question as to where Jess might be.

Once the piano piece was over, Noel bowed to Lady Farris. "My lady, an honor."

197

He then eased from the parlor. As soon as he was outside the room, he walked quickly down the corridor in search of her. He checked the upstairs drawing room first, but when that yielded no results, he paced from chamber to chamber. There was no sign of her. If she'd gone home, surely she would have informed Lord Trask of her departure. It stood to reason she was someplace in this house. But where?

It came to him then exactly where she might be. She'd said her upbringing was rural — perhaps she'd had enough of urban life these last few days, and sought out someplace that might bring her back to her early years.

There was the garden, but it was somewhat cool tonight, and she hadn't worn a shawl over her filmy gown. The conservatory made the most sense.

He went quickly to his destination, stepping into a room so warm and humid it was like drinking air.

"Jess?" He spoke lowly. "Jess."

"Here."

He strode toward her voice. She sat on a stone bench, wearing a look so troubled his heart clutched.

Noel immediately knelt in front of her. Seeing her like this — drained of the vitality that made her irresistible — was a stab to the gut.

"Talk to me," he demanded, taking her hands in his. A part of his mind realized that she wore no gloves, so their bare flesh touched. "Tell me if you feel faint or queasy or weak, or —"

"I'm well." She lifted her head and gave him the smallest of smiles. It seemed taut in the corners, and there was an echoing tightness in his chest. He hated the thought of anything causing her pain or worry.

"I can fetch you wine or sal volatile." He had to do something.

"None of those are necessary." Her smile turned rueful. "Much as I enjoy amusing company and thought-provoking discussion, I think I was born with an internal hourglass. When the sand runs out, I've had enough. I might cheerfully commit murder for a quiet corner, a cup of tea, and a copy of *As You Like It*."

He allowed himself an exhale. While he didn't like seeing her unhappy, at the very least, her troubles did not seem long lasting. "You've a low threshold for murdering people. I'd kill for a good Scotch whiskey."

"A duke outranks a baronetess," she said breezily, "so if either of us is to get caught for murder, I'd rather it be you. Less chance of hanging or transportation."

He grunted with a sudden realization, feeling like ten kinds of boor. Here he'd been concerned about her well-being, but he'd likely contributed to her distress, not eased it.

"Like a prime imbecile, I'm keeping you from your much-desired solitude." He started to rise, but she held tightly to his hands.

"Stay," she said with urgency. Then, more calmly, "Please."

The massive pleasure he felt from her urging him to stay was entirely unreasonable, definitely not ducal, but he didn't care. "As you wish."

"Do you know what I was doing here?" she asked after a pause. "I came here — to this place, away from the others, away from the Bazaar — because of how I feel about you. Because I want you."

The pleasure he had felt moments earlier was dwarfed with this new elation. She brought him to the heights of joy with an ease that ought to have panicked him — and yet he felt no fear.

A long, shuddering breath left him. "Four words," he murmured. "That's all it took from you and I'm as primed as a pistol. But, love, if you want me, why come out here?"

"I *shouldn't* want you," she said ruefully.

He stroked the tips of his fingers down her cheek, then along her throat, where her pulse sped. "I've never been much interested in *shoulds* and *oughts.*"

She gave a soft laugh. "Because you're a duke," she said. "You can do anything you want and there's no one to gainsay you."

"Untrue." He tilted her chin up so that their gazes met. "I met a striking young widow with a mind more cunning than any mechanical device. She told me to go slow, and I obeyed."

She glanced down at where his knees met the stone floor. "You don't have to kneel at my feet."

His voice was deep and gravelly, even to his own ears. "Perhaps I want to be on my knees before you."

Her mouth opened slightly, and the very tip of her tongue ran along her lower lip. A bead of perspiration traveled down the length of her neck to settle in the hollow of her collarbone.

They both considered what he'd just said, what he'd revealed. He was torn between arousal and rare apprehension, his cock already half-hard, his body aching for her.

"Tell me what you want," he rasped. "Tell me, and I'll do it."

She sucked in a breath. Her gaze moved over his face as if searching for something, an answer or the question itself. In the quiet of the conservatory, her ragged inhalations mingled with his own.

He'd never wanted anyone more. "Jess."

"Kiss me."

No sooner had she uttered her command than he readily obeyed, leaning close to cup his hands around her jaw. She angled her mouth up to meet his.

There was the briefest pause as they held themselves in suspension. It was a mutual savoring of the moment — the last second of rational thought — before their lips came together.

This time, they did not linger on preliminaries or gradual submersion. It was reckless and blazing as they opened their mouths to each other. He groaned when her tongue immediately met his. She could not wait to lap at him, just as he needed to devour her now, in great, greedy draws. Each kiss shot straight to his cock — he was now so hard it verged on painful, but it was the kind of pain he welcomed, making him feel alive and fully present.

He knew her taste now, and only when her flavor filled him again did he realize how much he craved it.

He positioned himself between her legs that had fallen open, and she arched against him, rubbing the length of her torso on his. Every lush curve of her seared into his flesh. Yet he had better means of learning the feel of her. He skimmed his hands down her neck, along her arms, molding his palms to the curve of her waist and then cupping her breasts. Her nipples were drawn into firm points and she moaned when he stroked them — through her bodice, then her bare flesh as he dipped his hands beneath the neckline of her gown. Softly, he pinched her nipples.

"Harder." She lapped at him hungrily. Then, "God, yes," when he did as she demanded.

"More," he growled. "Give me more commands." Ever since she'd verbally sparred with him the first day of the Bazaar, she had been the one in control. Having had a taste of bending to her mastery, he wanted to serve her forever, binding himself to her will so that he lived only to give her pleasure.

He was too inflamed to be shocked by this sudden need. It felt so perfect.

"Touch me," she gasped into his mouth.

"Where? Tell me where you want me to touch you."

"My . . ." She swallowed hard. "I want

your hand on my pussy."

He jolted with arousal. "You want me to make you come."

"Do it," she gasped. She dug her fingernails into his back, sharpening his need even more.

"Yes, Jess." Molten lust poured through him at his eager submission. He gathered up her skirts, the silk covering his forearms as he delved beneath them to find the stocking-clad flesh just above her knees. He went past her garters, and cursed roughly when he reached her bare thighs. "So fucking soft."

"Noel."

He loved the sound of his name on her lips as she gave the single syllable the weight of her desire.

With measured purpose, making himself go slowly so he could absorb each moment, he stroked up her thighs. His fingers reached the opening in her drawers.

His hand shook as he touched the silken, wet folds of her quim. She shuddered with a sound of ecstasy as he delved into her. He caressed her outer lips, then went deeper, gliding along her inner lips. He circled her opening before stroking up to her clitoris, and she rewarded him with her moan. Eagerly, reverently, he learned her intimate geography — what made her sigh, what made her cry out, what stole her breath.

He sank a finger into her passage, surrounding himself completely in her heat. She moaned his name again, but then seemed to lose how to form words when he joined his finger with another. As he thrust in and out, his thumb massaged her clitoris. Deep within her he found the swollen spot, and curved up to rub over it with each plunge.

"Yes. Yes, that's —" She was fire against him, pushing her hips into his palm.

"That's me," he rumbled. "That's me, fucking you with my hand." He pulled out, and she gave a sob of demand that he return. But he held up his hand, making certain she could see it. "See how slick my hand is? That's you."

Her eyes were heavy lidded, dazed, but she did look. The color in her cheeks deepened when she saw the evidence of her desire.

He stuck his fingers in his mouth. The taste of her was spiced and musky, and he lapped her up thirstily.

"When you want me to," he grated, "when you tell me, I'm going to lick your pussy. I'm going to devour you until you can't stop coming."

She dragged in a breath. "Now."

"Another time." He wasn't about to re-enter Trask's parlor with the taste of her all over him. That was something he would save for himself, and for her. "Now, I'm giving you *this.*" At his final word, he thrust his fingers back into her.

She keened, her head falling back. God-damn him, but she was the most incredible thing he had ever beheld.

He fucked her steadily with his hand. She let go of his back and gripped the bench for leverage to work herself on him. His vision swam with arousal as she unashamedly chased ecstasy. He needed her to come. He needed this to go on for eternity, only him, pleasuring her.

She bit down hard on her lip as her body went taut. Yet she couldn't quite suppress the sounds of her orgasm. He watched her face — she was in her own world now, one of release and sensation.

He wasn't finished. Just as her quaking subsided, he redoubled his efforts, stroking in and out with reverent intensity.

"Hard like that." Her words were almost guttural.

"Yes, Jess." His arm burned deliciously as he gave her everything.

She came again, silently. He could feel the

tremors through her body. They went on as she reached another climax. And then she went limp, barely able to support her weight on the bench.

"No more," she mumbled.

He obeyed at once, taking his fingers from within her. He cupped her mons and she purred in response.

She leaned forward and he did the same so that their foreheads touched. Her honey scent wrapped around him as their breaths slowed.

"Thank you," he murmured. He ran his hand down the length of her leg, then carefully lowered her skirts.

Her lips curved. "Shouldn't I be thanking you?"

"You gave me a gift. I've never —" He found himself unexpectedly bashful, which seemed ridiculous after he'd said such carnal things to her, after he'd *served* her — precisely why he felt tendrils of shyness. "I'm not used to serving like this, on my knees. Wanting a lover to tell me what to do. With everyone else, I'm the one in command. But having you hold the reins feels right."

She pressed a kiss to his lips. "I hope I was sufficiently dominating."

"I loved each second of it." At that moment, he wanted to drop every shield, leaving himself vulnerable. She could wound him irreparably, yet with the intimacies he'd given her, he knew in the deepest part of himself that he could trust her. "But we ought to get back to the others."

"What about you? You haven't . . . ." Her fingers skimmed over the aching length of his cock.

He hissed in a breath. "We've been gone too long. I'll tend to myself later."

"Damnation," she said. "I like picturing that. You, pleasuring yourself."

Her words put him on the verge of coming in his breeches like a lad. "Then think of that tonight, as you're lying in your own bed. Think of me with my hand around my cock, wishing it was your hand. Your mouth, your pussy."

"Demon," she admonished, her voice halfway between remonstrance and arousal. "I thought for certain that I couldn't possibly need another orgasm after the half dozen you just gave me. But you are determined, once again, to prove me wrong."

She presented too much temptation. He had to get her back amongst company, or else he was in serious danger of having her right here in Trask's conservatory, which, thinking on it, didn't seem like a bad idea.

She deserves better than a quick fuck on a stone bench. The plan had merit, but he craved her naked.

He fought a groan as he got to his feet. It hadn't felt painful being on his knees for so long, but his body now protested. At least the pain helped dull the edge of his arousal. He could walk back into the parlor without brandishing an enormous erection.

"My gracious lady." He offered her his hand.

She slid her palm against his as she rose to her feet, and just like that, the excitement he'd congratulated himself for dousing came flooding back.

"I like the way you say that," she murmured. "*My gracious lady.* As if you were a knight and I was a farmer's daughter."

"Don't you mean a princess?"

"I'm no princess," she said firmly. "Not if she's stuck in a tower, waiting for rescue. No," she went on, "I'm the lusty farmer's daughter who finds the weary knight in the barn and compels him to sate her desires. And he has to obey."

"Because he's sworn an oath to serve her in any way." Shuddering, he clamped his eyes closed. "I'm a hairsbreadth away from tupping you right here and to hell with anyone who might come in and see."

Her chest rose and fell. "I —"

"Lady Whitfield?" It was Lady Farris, and her footsteps neared.

Jess shoved Noel behind a large potted palm. It didn't fully conceal him, but hopefully the shadows would do the rest of the job.

"Here," Jess said brightly.

Lady Farris appeared. "Ah, good. You're on the verge of being missed." She eyed Jess, then looked at the potted palm. "You might want to wait here a few moments after we leave, Your Grace, before you return."

Fuck. Noel emerged from behind the palm. Still, few things couldn't be repaired with a dash of aristocratic sangfroid. "Lady Farris." He bowed.

Jess said, "We were talking. Nothing more."

Lady Farris held up a hand. "Don't fret. I can't pass along any scandal because I know nothing."

"Why would you keep silent?" In Noel's experience, information was a loaded weapon, ready to be fired. Everyone wanted to be armed.

"Because I've been where she is now," Lady Farris said, nodding at Jess. "Some men wagered on who would be the first to bed me after I came out of mourning. A friend came to my aid, fortunately, but" — her voice grew tight — "I never want another woman's body to be the target of speculation and gossip."

Jess took Lady Farris's hand. "Thank you."

"You've also my gratitude." Humbled by the countess, Noel bowed again. "If there's anything I can do for you —"

Lady Farris held up a finger in warning. "Do *not* boast of this to your friends."

"Never," he said firmly. God, the very idea was disgusting. And to speak of what he and Jess had done to anyone would profane it. He would keep it close and sacred — filthy, but sacred.

"And that's why I like you, Your Grace." The countess smiled before turning to Jess. "Shall we return?"

"I won't forget this," Jess said earnestly.

"I hope not," Lady Farris said, her smile widening, "for *his* sake."

Jess took her arm, and she and Lady Farris drifted toward the door. They hadn't gone a few steps before Jess murmured to the countess, "I'll join up with you in a moment."

She hurried back to Noel, then cupped the back of his head to pull him down for a searing kiss. He sank into her, lapping her up ravenously.

"I don't want this to end," he growled between kisses.

Pulling back slightly, her gaze roved over his face. She looked like a woman reaching toward a retreating light, grasping it before darkness fell.

He wanted to be that light, to burn brightly for her.

"Meet me at Covent Garden Market tomorrow," she whispered. "Dress as though you were an ordinary man, not a duke."

"It's impossible for me to be ordinary."

She gave a low, velvet chuckle that brought him back to moments earlier, when he'd been inside her, devotedly giving her pleasure. "Six in the morning."

"Madam, I never stir from my bed at such an unholy hour." He kissed her again. Her request was an odd one, but he didn't care. What she offered was more time alone with her, and that was a gift he wouldn't refuse. "You are the rare exception."

"An honor, Your Grace." She gave him a smile that was at once wicked and tender. No one smiled like her.

Then she was gone, racing back to Lady Farris, who lingered in the hallway outside the conservatory. Before she crossed the chamber's threshold, Jess looked back at him.

In her eyes, there was heat, mirroring his desire. But something else shadowed her gaze — knowledge that whatever hunger they shared, it would not, could not, last.

He wanted to prove her wrong. The thing they shared had no name and no sharp delineation, no easy definition, but it was precious to him and he did not wish to give it up. Yet he could not play the high-handed tyrant, and demand more of her than she was willing to give.

But, damn him, how he yearned for all of her.

CHAPTER 15

She had to tell him. She *would* tell him. The moment the Bazaar concluded later today, she would tell Noel everything about her deception. After last night, she had no other choice. He'd given her such ecstasy, and had laid his true self at her feet. He'd shown her, too, a part of herself that she hadn't known. To command and be served by a lover had given her exquisite pleasure — she'd no idea. She could not repay any of that with duplicity.

The idea had come to her in the conservatory, in the aftermath of what had happened. He had been fearless to reveal himself to her. And she had been unable to repay him with the same kind of honesty.

They had only a day left. She needed to know that when she and Noel parted, and he was left only with memories of her, what he remembered wasn't based on falsehoods and sham identities. She wanted to show him *her,* Jess, the farmer's daughter, the woman who took nothing for granted, and knew what it was to have only simple pleasures and not the heights of elegance and privilege.

She couldn't do that at the Bazaar, but there was more to London than Lord Trask's drawing room. There were places where a country girl might find a slightly familiar atmosphere, and that was what had made her think of Covent Garden. She knew her way around a market, and to be back amongst farmers and craftsmen would be a taste of home.

They would be surrounded by hundreds, but she and Noel would be alone together.

Before she could reconsider the idea, she'd blurted it to Noel. And he'd agreed.

Using the directions Lynch had given her, she now walked quickly toward Covent Garden Market. Fashionable London still slept, but the laboring people of the city were up, busily going about their lives, and pulling carts in their sturdy clothes. These were her people, far more than the Bazaar's wealthy elite. Today, she wore her own clothing, and while the garments of a paid companion were far more delicate than those worn by working folk, she was no baronet's widow, and attracted less attention.

Mayfair to Covent Garden was a fair distance, yet she didn't let her steps slow or falter, not when Noel awaited her.

She emerged at the west end of a large square. At one side stood a graceful, tall building with columns, but she barely spared it a glance. Instead, she scanned the busy plaza. How would she recognize Noel without his customarily expensive, elegant tailoring?

A man emerged from the crowd, and she saw then that her concern wasn't warranted. Even in a slouchy coat and threadbare trousers, with a slightly battered hat atop his head, she knew his long body and confident stride. He'd even forgone shaving, so that his jaw was shaded by dark stubble.

"Looking raffish," she said, approaching him. Once the distance between them closed, she leaned in to murmur, "And edible."

His eyes flashed. "Unkind to bring me to this public place and then verbally seduce me."

"I'll take pity on you because you've been so accommodating, coming here before your customary noon rising." She glanced at his clothing. "Where did you find such a beleaguered ensemble?"

He looked down at himself and grimaced. "Borrowed some old togs from my friend Holloway. His sartorial ability is inversely proportional to his intelligence."

"He must be a very smart man."

"Minx." He eyed her. "And you're back in the same dress you wore when I first met you on Bond Street."

She felt her cheeks warm — a combination of embarrassment about her less-than-stylish clothing and pleasure that he remembered what she'd worn that day.

"Today," she said, slipping into her broad Wiltshire dialect, "we're a pair of ordinary folk, out to shop the market."

He lifted his brow. "Where'd you pick up that accent?"

"Grew up rural." She narrowed her gaze. "You don't like it."

"On the contrary," he said, lowering his lids, "it makes me think about finding a convenient hayloft and doing all sorts of primal things to you."

"Now *you're* seducing me in public." But she didn't mind it. "Suppose there's nothing we can do about your accent? It's pure toff."

"The burden of being woefully overbred

217

— I had elocution lessons as soon as I started to speak. I know," he said brightly, "I shall pretend to be a gentleman who has fallen on hard times because I dared to court a Wiltshire woman that my family did not approve of."

He'd no idea how close to the truth he came. "Tragic tale. Shall we get to marketing?"

"Madam, lead the way." He held out his arm, and she tucked her hand into it.

The market itself was a sprawling, chaotic affair, far more bustling than any other she'd attended. Stalls were arranged against a wall, a few with canopies, while some were either tables or benches set up beneath the open sky. Baskets stood laden with goods, and carts also carried a bewildering array of produce.

Everything that grew from the earth was sold — asparagus, carrots, leafy lettuces and cabbages, baskets of mushrooms. Pie and sausage vendors also shouted to advertise the wares they carried in trays that hung from their necks, and wheels of fresh cheeses were stacked in pyramids. The air was rich with green scents and the loamy soil still clinging to crops.

It was wonderful and dizzying and reminded her powerfully of home, whilst it

218

also stood in marked contrast to the smaller local markets Jess had visited.

"Not so familiar with this place during the day," Noel said as they wove up and down between the rows of vendors. He nodded toward the tall, columned building at the other end of the piazza. "The Theatre Royal is more my haunt."

"The noise is less melodious." Voices of what had to be a hundred vendors clashed, verging on deafening.

"Depends on who's performing that night." He shook his head. "My God, I'd no idea what a veritable Babel this place could be."

"Markets usually are, though this one is of truly biblical proportions. Have you never shopped for your own food?"

He eyed her. "Dukes and ducal heirs are rarely tasked with marketing. Besides, I wouldn't know where to begin or how to manage it. I'd bobble the whole thing and wind up being arrested for disorderly conduct."

"Observe me, then, and learn." She winked at him before heading toward one stall selling an abundance of fruits. Addressing the red-faced woman behind the table, she said, "Morning, love."

"Morning, missus," the woman answered

in a thick London accent. Her eyes gleamed when she looked at Noel, despite his shabby clothing. "Fine day for it, eh, my lad?"

"As fine as the roses in your cheeks," he replied.

"Go on, now," she said, turning even more ruddy.

Jess smiled to herself. "Can't help yourself, can you?" she murmured under her breath.

"It's not my fault if women universally find me charming."

"Is that what you did with me? Flirt out of habit?"

His gaze heated. "Madam," he said lowly, "you ensnared me from the moment you gave those Bond Street bucks a verbal drubbing. But, then, you're well aware of how I love to bend to your will."

Now it was her opportunity to turn pink. "You're shameless."

"Under the right conditions." His smile was small and private, just for her pleasure. Jess gladly fell under its spell.

"What're you looking for, missus?"

The fruit vendor's voice broke through the haze surrounding Jess. Snapping to attention, she said, "These cherries seem nice enough." In truth, they were rosy red and looked as though they'd been harvested at their peak. "How much for half a peck?"

"Fourpence, love."

Noel dug into his pocket, but with a tiny movement, Jess stilled him. "Those strawberries look on the verge of spoiling. How's about you throw in a basket of 'em, and the half a peck of cherries, and I'll give you fourpence?"

The woman let out a long, gusty exhale. "You're trying to ruin me, you are." When Jess merely stared at her, she threw up her hands. "As you please. The cherries and the strawberries for the bargain price of fourpence."

Jess handled the rest of the transaction, pulling the coins from her hamper in exchange for the fruit.

"Mind you keep an eye on that bloke of yours," the vendor said, handing over a small basket of strawberries. She glanced at Noel, who studied the papery husks surrounding a heap of gooseberries. "A face like his will have half the morts chasing after him like cats swarming at Billingsgate."

"I've younger siblings," Jess confided, "so I know how to throw a punch."

"Right you are, love. Enjoy — the fruit and the bloke."

With the vendor's laughter ringing behind her, Jess tucked her purchases into her hamper before drawing Noel away. She offered him a strawberry, and when he took it, she plucked one for herself.

"A demon in the marketplace." He took a bite of strawberry and made a hum of pleasure.

"I'm not to be underestimated." She bit into the berry and the flavor was ripe with the season.

"I will never make that mistake."

They walked companionably together up and down the market rows, eating strawberries and dropping the hulls to the ground. As they strolled, Noel pointed out sights to her, such as a dog sleeping beneath one of the vendor's tables, and two children handing a peach back and forth between them as they took alternating bites.

It felt both comfortable and deliriously exciting to be with him like this. As if they were any couple doing a bit of shopping together for their evening meal, as if they *could* be any couple, with the possibility of a future together.

They had no future, but she clung to the pretense that, for a little longer, they did.

"Secondhand goods," a man cried from where he crouched beside a gray blanket. "Only the best. Anything you want, it's here."

"A moment," Noel murmured to Jess. He guided her to the man with his blanket covered in every variety of things. There were needle cases, shoes, scarves, poppets, and candlesticks. Turning his attention to the vendor, Noel asked, "How much for the pewter comb?"

"It's silver, it is. Swell bloke like you can have it for a penny."

Jess opened her mouth to protest the exorbitant price, but Noel gave a small shake of his head. He pulled a coin from his pocket and dropped it into the man's palm. "Here's a shilling."

"A moment, gov, and I'll have change for you." The man counted out the change before handing the coins to Noel. "Take the comb, and bless you for a gentleman."

Noel clasped the comb and made a shallow bow. "You've robbed me, sir, but I thank you for the privilege. Shall we continue?" he asked Jess.

"By all means." She held his arm again as they walked away from the secondhand goods.

"A favor." Noel handed her the comb. "Carry that for me?"

"Of course." She started to tuck it into her hamper.

"Do you mind holding it in your hand?"

It was an odd request, but she dipped her head in agreement. They continued walking the market, listening to the costermongers' and vendors' shouts and witnessing the bounty of British produce in June, all available to Londoners in one central — though chaotic — place.

Noel stiffened as a duo of well-dressed gentlemen headed toward him and Jess. Judging by their rumpled finery, they hadn't yet been to bed.

"Fuck," Noel muttered. "I didn't want to run into anyone I knew."

"Because you're embarrassed about your clothes?"

"Because," he said fiercely, "right now, I don't want to be a duke. I just want us to be the impecunious gentleman and his Wiltshire sweetheart."

Jess's heart squeezed — she wanted the very same thing. "Don't make eye contact." She pulled him toward a table laden with beetroots, and they both turned their backs toward the gentlemen.

Their cultured but insistent laughter sounded as they walked along the row. "Never tell me you can't hold your wine, Ablemayne," one of them brayed.

Noel picked up a head of lettuce and held it close to his face as he and Jess covertly watched the dandies. Only when the men moved on, oblivious to his presence, did they release the tension they held.

"Thank God they're as unobservant as that lettuce." He exhaled.

"Time's moving apace," she said, glumly observing the sun climbing higher in the sky. "We ought to go, since we're expected at Lord Trask's for luncheon and I am in need of a bath."

He consulted his timepiece, which was decidedly *not* the variety a man in frayed trousers might carry. "Damn. There's no help for it. Might I have the comb back?"

She gave it to him, and he slipped it into his pocket.

"You can't mean to use that," Jess said.

"Why not?" He looked surprised by her assertion.

"Surely you've got far finer ones. Ones actually made of silver."

"True, I do, but," he continued as they made their way out of the market, "none of them have been held in your hand. This way, every time I use it, I can imagine it's your fingers running through my hair."

Jess's steps faltered, and she blinked to stem a sudden rush of tears. "Noel."

She did not know how she'd go on after this, after him. It seemed that the future they couldn't share would be a slow, gray one. In that future, she would only remember what it was like to have such a man beside her.

"The change from the comb," she said, her throat tight. "I'd like a ha'penny, if he gave you one."

Noel pulled out the small coin and tucked it into her hand. "In need of funds?"

"You have something of me," she said, slipping the coin into her hamper. "And now I have a little piece of you to carry wherever I go. Neither of us will forget."

Soft wonder filled his face. He tugged her toward one of the canopied booths, positioning his body so that his broad back hid her from any passersby.

Then, cupping her jaw gently with both hands, he tilted her mouth up before bringing his lips to hers. The kiss was soft and silken, gentle with heat beneath it. She savored the taste of him, coffee and clove, and she'd never known anything as delicious or fleeting.

CHAPTER 16

Hours later, bathed and dressed in one of Lady Catherton's walking gowns, Jess headed toward Lord Trask's. It was the Bazaar's final gathering, which consisted of a luncheon before the company disbanded to return to their normal lives.

She would sink back into the obscurity of her position as a paid companion, overseas, far away from her family. As the hired help, no one would ask her for her opinion about financial matters. The most exciting part of her day would be sitting quietly in some parlor as Lady Catherton paid calls.

She would never see Noel again. Even if she wasn't going to the Continent, soon enough, he'd learn the truth about her, and would rightly never want to speak to her or see her. At the least, she had the ha'penny, now tucked into her reticule so she could have him with her whenever she desired.

Something else she could not ignore: this

was her last opportunity to save her family's business. Hopefully, her final gambit would work.

The butler greeted her with a bow as she crossed the threshold. He directed her toward the dining room, and as she moved toward it, her heart beat faster and faster.

In the hallway outside the dining room, she heard his voice, sonorous and husky. She paused to catch her breath as memories of this morning mingled with heated recollections of last night. *Tell me where you want me to touch you. You want me to make you come.* And he had. Over and over until she could barely remember why she couldn't have that with him always.

She was Jessica McGale, a farmer's daughter, and a paid companion. She fought for every coin. He was a duke, wealthy and powerful beyond reason.

"Who's out there, lurking in the corridor?" someone in the dining room demanded.

"Lurking implies nefarious intent." Affixing a placid smile, Jess entered the chamber. "I am not nefarious."

"But you are welcome," Lord Trask said as he stood next to the dining table. He had grown a good deal warmer to her over the past few days. Perhaps his negative beliefs about women in the realm of finance had altered. "Please, my lady, help yourself to whatever you like."

Despite the many people in the room, her gaze went straight to Noel. He stood with his hands clasped behind his back as he faced the door, wearing an expression of anticipation, as though he had been waiting for someone.

The smile he gave her was a flaming arrow right into her chest. She couldn't stop her answering smile, making his grow even more brilliant.

She joined the queue serving themselves a luncheon, which had been laid out on the sideboard. Two people ahead of her was Lady Farris, whose tranquil smile thankfully did not hint at what she'd come across last night. That was some relief. Some, but not much.

Noel took his place right behind her in the queue. He didn't reach for her, or whisper scandalous suggestions, or indeed do anything that someone might see. No one detected that Jess and the duke had known each other's touch and taste. But she knew. And he did, too.

"A good morning, Lady Whitfield?" he asked in a tone that was perfectly polite. As though he hadn't fucked her with his hand

and made her come like a goddess. As if he hadn't broken her heart this morning in Covent Garden Market.

"Passable, Your Grace." She reached for a fork to serve herself slices of roast beef.

"Allow me." His hand covered and stilled hers.

She almost told him not to bother because she absolutely could not eat a mouthful, not when he touched her and made her head spin. Instead, she merely nodded and yielded the fork to him. She watched his hand as he set a few slices of meat onto her plate, wishing she could look at something else because his hands truly were gorgeous and masculine.

"Thank you for attending to me," she murmured.

His eyes darkened, and it was as though they were back in the humid conservatory and he was telling her how much he, her servant, wanted to lick her quim.

Quickly as she could, she dished up more of her luncheon, then, with a last look at Noel, seated herself at the table beside Mr. Walditch. Lord Pickhill immediately occupied the empty chair beside her.

As if the guests had wordlessly conferred, no one took the seat at the head of the table. It seemed fitting that Noel should sit there, as though even in Lord Trask's home he was in command of everything.

Quiet fell as everyone ate, and she saw that her moment had come.

"I've a letter from the soap manufacturers, Baron Mentmore." She glanced around the table with a look of apology. "But I shan't disrupt everyone's luncheon with its contents. We can discuss it later — though it was rather fascinating."

"Don't keep us in suspense, Lady Whitfield," Mr. Walditch said before the baron could speak. "This saga has been rather intriguing."

"I don't want to hear about it," Lord Prowse grumbled.

"Then pay attention to your roast and cover your ears," Lady Farris said tartly, "because I'm also interested in what Lady Whitfield learned."

"There are more of us who want to hear than don't," Baron Mentmore encouraged. "Do go on. If that's all right, Lord Trask."

Jess barely breathed as she waited, fearing that the marquess would object to her bringing in an outside business.

Their host made a noncommittal wave of his hand, and she let out a long but silent exhalation.

She shot a look toward Noel — though he

continued to eat his meal, he had his head tilted in the posture she'd come to learn signified he was paying attention.

"As you heard," she said, "recently there was an accident that burned down several of their structures and cost them the use of much of their manufacturing equipment. This was all confirmed to me by Miss Cynthia McGale."

Lady Farris winced. "Terrible misfortune."

Several others around the table made murmurs of agreement.

"They are indeed in need of funds to rebuild and refurbish," Jess continued. "With enough investment capital, they could improve their operations — meet a greater demand if they were to sell their product here in London."

"Is it worth it to pour capital into a business that may or may not be able to resurrect itself?" Viscount Hunsdon asked.

"It might be an opportunity to take what was a small operation and transform it," Jess said. "Modernize it, whilst they continue to create a quality product."

"Fair point," Mr. Walditch said with a thoughtful nod. "It's not my usual avenue of investment, but your point about Brummell was well made. More baths mean more soap."

Hopefully, the lull in the conversation meant that everyone was contemplating the benefit of investing in McGale & McGale.

"A trip is in order," Noel said suddenly.

"Your Grace?" Mr. Walditch asked.

"Why not?" Noel looked around the table. "If the operation is in Wiltshire, it's a day's ride from one of my Hampshire estates. What's the village, Lady Whitfield?"

She blinked, slightly dazed at the sudden turn in her plan. "Honiton."

"I've heard of it," he said. "It's less than a day from Carriford. Anyone interested in learning more about this McGale & McGale can journey with me to Carriford. Allow me to treat you to some of my justifiably celebrated hospitality," he added with a crooked smile. "Spend the night there, then onward the next day to visit the soap makers. We gather our intelligence about them, then return to Carriford, and then" — he slapped his hand on his thigh like a man making a decisive plan — "back to London."

Panic was Jess's first reaction. This was *not* what she'd planned. They hadn't made arrangements at the farm for visitors, and certainly not ones who held the future of the business in their hands.

But . . . she could send a fast letter to Fred and Cynthia, telling them what needed to be done.

Yes. This could work. She'd manage it, and the trip could secure the funding they needed.

After a moment, she nodded.

"That's perfect," Baron Mentmore said. "I believe I'll join you, Your Grace. Good to get out of the smoke of London."

"Clear the lungs," Noel said sagely.

"I'll come, too," Mr. Walditch added.

"Myself, as well," Lady Farris said, and Lady Haighe nodded, also signifying her interest.

"It's settled, then." Noel tapped his fingers on the tabletop as if signaling that everything had been decided. "You'll accompany us, of course, Lady Whitfield."

She'd expected as much, so she was remarkably calm when she replied, "Thank you, but it's unnecessary for me to do so. I'm already convinced."

"You're going to the Continent soon," he said. "Stands to reason that before you embark on that journey, you'd want more information about the soap makers. You'll be better able to determine the amount you wish to invest, if that's your intention." His tone was even, and yet there was a hint of need in his gaze. As if he desperately desired to be in her company a little longer.

"Yes, do come with us," Lady Farris urged.

"Can't say no," Mr. Walditch said.

"I . . ." Panic clutched at her. She breathed deeply to loosen its hold, and took refuge in the calm, logical thought.

If she refused to visit the farm, she'd arouse suspicion. And if she told Noel about her deception, she might ruin her family's chance at gaining not one but *multiple* investors.

There was nothing logical about wanting to spend a little more time in Noel's company. She could have a few days with him, then she'd disappear from his life forever.

But first, she would write home immediately and tell her siblings of the visit.

"You make a convincing case," she said at last.

"Then you'll come?" Pleasure lit his eyes.

"A man cannot boast of his hospitality without putting it to the test."

His smile managed to be both self-deprecating and full of conceit. Somehow, only Noel could accomplish such a feat.

"I'll write to the McGales this afternoon," she said, "and inform them of our intent to visit."

"Very good," he said. "If anyone else decides that they'd like to drink up my cellar and devour my larder, meet at Rotherby House tomorrow at dawn. We'll caravan and do our level best not to lay waste to the countryside as we go."

The conversation moved on to other topics. Though she tried to pay attention, it was nearly impossible as her thoughts flew ahead out of the room and careened into the world. There was the letter she would have to pen the moment she returned to Lady Catherton's town house, and she'd need to secure Nell's services as maid for several more days, and all the other logistical elements she needed to take into consideration before embarking on this mad voyage home.

The meal concluded, and everyone rose from the table.

"How delightful to fly London's cage," Lady Farris said as she came with them.

"The duke *did* promise excellent hospitality."

"Is that what you call it?" The countess winked. "Ah, here comes His Grace. I do believe my presence is not required. I'll just speak with Mr. Walditch, shall I?" She drifted away.

Noel made his way toward her. It was

ridiculous to feel nervous around him when he'd literally been *inside her* last night, but there was something about him that made her sweat. As he stood before her, her body throbbed with want.

"My Lady Hawk," he said, his gaze hooded. "How you've enlivened us sad, dull creatures of the Bazaar."

"I guarantee no one considers you a sad, dull creature."

"But you *are* a hawk."

She pursed her lips. "Sharp beak and screeching?"

"A born hunter soaring overhead." Then, in a much lower voice, he said, "I was presumptuous. Again. Insisting that you come with us to see the soap makers." A rare look of uncertainty crossed his face. "It's only — I was not ready to say goodbye to you."

Goddamn him, making her melt like a beeswax candle. "Is that why you suggested visiting them? To spend more time with me?"

"It's a benefit," he said, "but not the motivation. You need not go if you truly don't want to. I'd never force your hand. I may be a duke," he added, "but I'm not a bully."

This was her opportunity. Her chance to

slip away without any further interaction between her and Noel. She ought to decline, and return to her gray half existence as a paid companion.

"I'll take the journey with you." The words spilled from her. She needed this, and him, just a little longer. She could play by the rules and still have a bit more time with him. And if she went, she could ensure that everything went smoothly at the farm. Much as she loved Cynthia and Fred, she'd feel far more certain if she herself watched over and quietly managed the visit.

He gave her another of his dazzling smiles. "Splendid." His gaze was warm and dark like a summer night. "That is most splendid. I'll see you at my home tomorrow. Dawn."

"My abigail will be cross with me to be awakened at such an early hour, but, yes, dawn."

"It's a delightful journey to Carriford." He nearly vibrated with eagerness and excitement, his ducal veneer gone. "The estate's one of my favorites. There's a meadow on the eastern part of the parkland I played in as a child, and it has the most glorious oak tree that's perfect for climbing. Wait until I show it to you."

His anticipation beguiled Jess — and it ruined her. If only she could give him

238

everything he deserved. Yet she couldn't. All
she deserved was his contempt.

CHAPTER 17

"Carriford's charming," Noel said to the passengers in his carriage. "The grounds are amongst the loveliest of all my estates. The old heap of stones was built in the late sixteenth century — but trust me when I say you'll be comfortable there. Successive Dukes of Rotherby were keen modernizers, so the walls aren't porous as sponges, and the rooms are warm. Small, but warm."

Since boyhood on, he'd looked forward to Carriford. But never in all of his thirty-four years did he feel the excitement he did now, heading there with Jess.

He probably sounded like the veriest ninny, rattling off facts about Carriford. But the hell of it was he didn't give a damn.

He'd show her everything. He wanted her to love it as he did. It shouldn't matter — she'd be gone to the Continent soon — but it did.

"We're nearly there." He nodded toward

the window. "That gristmill with the water-wheel means we're but a mile away."

Everyone, including Jess, Lady Haighe, and Mr. Walditch, craned their heads toward the landmark.

"It's lovely," Lady Haighe said irritably.

"That distresses you?" Jess asked.

"Lovely things make me aware of my mortality, and I already have reminders of that when I rise from bed every morning and my body aches for no reason at all."

Noel shared an amused glance with Jess. Fortunately, she sat opposite him, beside Lady Haighe. There was a good chance that if he'd had to ride to Carriford with Jess's thigh pressed against his, he'd arrive a slavering madman. Having Mr. Walditch next to him was far better.

The caravan toward his country estate consisted of his carriage and Lady Farris's own vehicle, which transported her, Baron Mentmore, Lord Pickhill, and Mr. Parley. Their servants trundled behind in a more sturdy coach.

It was all Noel could do to keep from jouncing his leg in impatience. The late afternoon light would gild Carriford's West Terrace, which he'd show Jess as soon as she had settled in her room. He'd made very specific instructions in his letter to the butler as to the placement of Jess's bed-chamber. Hopefully, she'd be pleased with his decision.

"Do you host many house parties at this estate?" Mr. Walditch asked.

"Not for some time." He wouldn't mention one weeklong bacchanalia a few years ago that had seen him playing nude billiards with an actress, and the garden fountain that had been filled with wine so that anyone might drink by scooping their hand into its contents. Even shy, scholarly Holloway had been his version of wild, fencing with McCameron in the long, vaulted gallery.

"I think I see some towers." Jess pointed to the sloped gables that barely poked above the ash trees. "Is that it?"

"We're passing through the gates just now." He waited in anticipation as the carriage rolled up the long, curving drive that led to Carriford's front entrance. Instead of looking out the window, however, his gaze held to Jess's face, eager to see her response to his estate.

A shame that the soap makers weren't located in Cambridgeshire, where his grandest home, and the seat of the duchy, was situated. Surely its fifteen bedchambers and thirty public rooms would impress her.

He discreetly rubbed his palms on his thighs in an attempt to dry them. He gave an inaudible, self-deprecating snort. When was the last time he'd wanted to amaze anyone? When did he ever feel the need to show off? Him — a duke.

Jess didn't seem to care that he was a duke. She saw beneath the gilded trimmings to the man. And she liked him just the same. Hell if that didn't fill him with humble gratitude — and the need to give her relentless pleasure.

"That's Carriford?" His eyebrows climbing up his forehead, Mr. Walditch stared out the window.

Noel glanced quickly from Jess to the window. Sure enough, the house emerged from the trees, rising grandly and with the dignity of an elder statesman who kept a prized place beside a king. The warm brick walls still held a glow from the day's light, and though the building itself wasn't massive like some of his other estates, it possessed a solemn grandeur that always struck him whenever he viewed it. A row of servants stood on the gravel drive, awaiting the arrival of the house's master and his guests.

He took all this in within half a second. Jess was his main concern.

She gazed out the window, her eyes wide,

her lips parted. Was that shock? Did she find the place to be too old-fashioned? If only he'd had time — he could have scheduled more improvements. Tear down a wall or two. Replace the old timbers with modern plaster in the style of Adams.

"It's . . ." She leaned closer to the window and stared out. "Oh, Noel. It's marvelous."

Gratification coursed through him, almost obscuring the fact that she'd called him by his Christian name in front of Lady Haighe and Mr. Walditch. He was faintly aware of the two other occupants of the carriage exchanging glances.

"My mother thinks it gloomy," he said, striving for nonchalance.

"It's not. At all." Jess brought her gaze back to his. "It's something out of a fairy tale."

"The knight and the farmer's daughter?"

Lady Haighe and Mr. Walditch conversed with each other, and seemed to not have heard Noel's carelessly made remark. Not that they'd understand its significance, but he should be more bloody circumspect.

"The very tale I was thinking of," Jess murmured, smiling.

God, the things he wanted to do with her . . .

The carriage came to a stop in front of

the house. A footman opened the door, and, summoning his ducal dignity, Noel stepped down. He helped Lady Haighe alight from the carriage, and then Jess.

As he greeted Gregory, the estate manager, and Vale, the butler, the second carriage arrived. The passengers emerged to gaze with admiration at the house and its staff.

Noel faced the assembled guests, careful not to let his gaze linger too long on Jess. "Gentlemen and ladies of the Bazaar, welcome to Carriford."

Jess had actually stuck her hands beneath her thighs, pinning them to the carriage squabs, to keep from pointing out the selfsame landmarks that she'd observed not so long ago as she'd traveled to London from Lady Catherton's home.

What if someone from her village had taken employment at Noel's estate? One careless whisper could ruin everything in a matter of seconds.

She did *not* have to manufacture interest as they'd neared his estate — if for no other reason than he seemed to grow more and more animated the nearer they came to it. He was always sophisticated, ready with his dry wit. But she saw it in his shining eyes, in his ready smile, and the way he sat on the edge of the seat, his gaze constantly returning to her face.

He wanted her to like his home. She wanted to like it, too, wanted to like anything he gave to her, and surely that way was dangerous.

"Welcome to Carriford," he said as she and the others assembled on the front drive.

Everyone, including Jess, made appreciative sounds. She couldn't speak much beyond that because he lived in a sodding ancient manor that was as old as it was lovely.

He performed introductions. "This is Gregory, my estate manager. If you've any questions about the running of the place, he's a font of knowledge."

A Black man with silvering hair bowed. "My lords and ladies."

Noel continued. "This is Vale, the butler." A man dressed in severe dark clothing bowed. "And this estimable woman is Mrs. Diehl, the housekeeper." A woman of surprising youthfulness curtsied, her freckles standing out against her fair skin.

"Should you require anything at all," Mrs. Diehl said, "from baths to beer, Mr. Vale and I will do our utmost to see your every need fulfilled."

Jess couldn't stop herself from glancing at Noel. She did have *one* need she very much wanted fulfilled, and only he could accomplish it — but she had to keep distant from him, for both their sakes.

In that quick moment, his gaze met hers. His eyes were hot, and heat traveled the distance between them.

Somehow, she managed to haul her attention away from him and distracted herself by admiring Carriford's facade. It had an air of enchantment, as though lords and ladies of an earlier time would emerge in just a moment to take the air.

"Rooms first?" Noel asked. "A tour of the house and grounds?"

"An old woman needs her rest," Lady Haighe grumbled.

"When I see one," he said with a smile, "I will suggest she do just that."

Lady Haighe sniffed, but it seemed she couldn't hold back her own reluctant smile.

Some of the others voiced an interest in going to their rooms so they might also rest from the journey.

"A tour sounds lovely," Jess said. She'd accompanied Lady Catherton to a friend's estate, and as soon as they had arrived, Jess had been put to work, communicating with the staff about the countess's preferences and dislikes. There had been no time for leisure.

Not today. Today, she was Noel's honored guest.

While some were shown to their chambers, Jess, Lady Farris, Mr. Walditch, and Lord Pickhill followed Noel as he guided them into the house. In the interim, the baggage was taken down from the carriages as the valets and ladies' maids arrived.

"The Great Hall," Noel announced, stepping into an immense chamber with tall ceilings. A huge fireplace dominated one wall, flanked by heavy wooden chairs. "Lords of the manor held quarterly audiences with their tenants to hear any complaints or requests."

"Doubtless with wolfhounds sleeping in front of the fire," Jess said.

His look was appreciative. "Deerhounds. But you're close. Very close."

"Perhaps you have been here before," Lady Farris said. "In another life. You might have been a lady, seated just so to protect the panniers."

Jess bit back the comment that if she had been alive back then, she surely would have been one of the laborers, her rough hands clutching her apron as she came to petition her lord for a new barn after a fire, and certainly not a lady protecting whatever the hell a pannier was.

Noel took them from the Great Hall into the corridor, where he showed them several parlors with wooden paneled walls covered in tapestries. The air smelled of beeswax polish and lemon, clean, but rich with history.

"This Venetian goblet has a tragic past," he said, pointing to a stunning glass cup in a cabinet. "The unfortunate Charles I drank from it on a brief stay at Carriford. And this," he continued, nodding toward a leather glove that looked tiny enough for a doll, "was left behind by one of Charles II's mistresses when she had used Carriford as an assignation spot with the monarch. Fortunately, there was just the *one* mistress and not the entire platoon of them. There aren't enough bedrooms at Carriford for that kind of debauchery."

"You sound sad about that," Jess teased.

"I come from a long line of reprobates and rogues," he said with a bow. "It would be such a shame for their descendant to disappoint them. Let us move on and let their ghosts cavort in peace."

The Long Gallery boasted curved ceilings and a floor made of wood so old it seemed to undulate in polished waves.

"Surely on rainy days you played ninepins in here," she said. "I would have."

"Our nurse forbade it," Noel said, then added with a wink, "but that didn't stop us. Oh, and I enjoyed sliding around in my drawers and stockinged feet whenever my parents and tutors were away, singing bawdy songs at the top of my lungs."

She pressed her lips together, trying without success to keep from grinning at the image of a young Noel, full of mischief, impossible to be denied anything.

The house itself was lovely, but when he brought them outside to the gardens and grounds, she knew with certainty that there was no place in England that held such enchantment. There were hedge mazes and arbors and, beyond the gardens, rolling expanses of grass that invited bare feet and reckless running at top speed.

As Lady Farris, Mr. Walditch, and Lord Pickhill talked with Mr. Fields, the aptly named head gardener, Jess admired the charming arrangement of wrought-iron furniture beneath the spreading branches of an ash tree, as though anticipating a small group of lords and ladies to take tea and cakes in the afternoon heat.

She felt Noel drawing closer, a palpable

sense of him that strummed through her body.

"You're pleased?" He ran one long finger over the curlicue of a flower set in the table.

"Anyone who lived here would be lucky indeed to call it home."

He exhaled. "I am. I'd call myself a lucky bastard, but my lineage is verified in state documents."

"Did you spend much time here?" While she had been helping her family bring in their crop, tending their bees, spending winter days cutting and wrapping soap, he had been at this place, waited on by servants and sliding through the Long Gallery and leading his charmed life.

They were so different in a multitude of ways. He was a duke, raised in privilege, with nothing forbidden to him. He could dream any dream with the belief that it could truly become reality — but his whole life already was a fantasy come true.

Could he ever understand the desperation that had driven her to carry on such a lengthy deception? And if he did understand that, could he forgive her for the fabrications she'd told him? She'd done her best to stick as close to the truth as she could, but there had been times when a lie had been unavoidable. Seeing this beautiful

251

home and his joy in it only affirmed what she believed: she and Noel had no future beyond the next few days.

"Not much," he said. "To my dismay. We spent more time in Cambridgeshire, at Roston Abbey, where the seat of the duchy is located. That estate is far grander in scale."

"Surely not as grand in magic." She trailed her own ungloved hand along the clever ironwork. Then held her breath as his hand came closer to hers, and closer still, until the very tips of their fingers touched.

He might as well have kissed her.

God above, if she ever brought him to her bed, she'd surely lose her wits from sheer pleasure.

"You think Carriford magical?" he asked, though his voice was low and rough.

She turned to him. "Years from now, I'll dream of this place."

His eyes were dark and immeasurably deep. The way he looked at her — as though he'd scaled a mountain and found her at the summit — was a look she'd remember until her last breath.

"I'm glad." His words rumbled. "There's a house full of people — but I don't give a damn about their opinions. It's what *you* think that matters."

"I'm no more qualified to appreciate a fine

home than anyone else," she said gently. "Lady Farris has likely seen more country estates than I have, and Mr. Walditch surely owns a magnificent home."

"But when I look at Lady Farris," he said, his voice intent, "I don't feel the world disappear around me so I am aware only of her. And I assuredly do not want to give Mr. Walditch the moon and the stars and all the things in the sky. I feel those things only for you."

Her throat tightened. "Noel."

"This place is special. And so are you." His gaze held hers and she understood what he'd meant a moment ago, because her awareness was only of him.

God help her — she wanted him to look at her that way forever. They didn't have forever, though. "What do you know of Honiton?"

If he minded her abrupt change of topic, he didn't say. "Nothing. Didn't even know the place existed until you brought the soap wrapper."

Good. He had no expectations of the place, or where she fit in within it. She'd paid extra to the rider delivering her letter, ensuring that he stopped only to change horses, so that her brother and sister had time to inform the village what to expect.

Hopefully, Fred and Cynthia had spoken to everyone, or at least made certain that word would circulate so that no one mistakenly called her "Jess" or "Miss McGale," or remarked on her fine dresses and the genteel company she kept.

"You must be curious to see the McGale & McGale operation," she said.

"As I said at the docks — Hell, was it only a few days ago? As I said, there's always something to learn. Discovering and learning are life's greatest pleasures. Well," he amended, his gaze heating, "*some* of life's greatest pleasures. There are others."

"To be sure," she said huskily. "Many others."

They could not seem to look away from each other. She faintly heard the voices of the other guests and the head gardener, and beneath all that, birdsong and the drone of insects. Though it was late afternoon, the day was still golden with warmth and languid, and it would be so easy to slip her hand into his and lead him down one of Carriford's garden paths, where, in the privacy of a green bower, she could show him how much pleasure he gave her.

It would be so easy, so right . . .

Someone coughed, a discreet servant cough.

Noel moved his hand at the same time Jess stepped away, putting needed distance between them.

"Apologies, Your Grace," Vale, the butler, said from several yards away. "I was reluctant to disturb you, but the gentlemen were most insistent."

"Gentlemen?" Noel raised an eyebrow. "One of the guests."

"Indeed, no, Your Grace. These gentlemen just arrived. They demanded that I pass on a message." Vale coughed into his hand. "They said, 'Tell the toff bastard that we're desperate for his company. Desperate, but not serious.' Those were the words I was instructed to say verbatim."

Horrified by the insulting message and the impertinence of the men who demanded Vale deliver it to Noel, Jess looked at him. She expected to see seething anger or even cold disdain on his face.

Instead, he wore the widest smile she'd ever seen from him.

"Convey to them the following message." He planted his hands on his hips. " 'Don't expect a place in the country when you sodding buffoons come calling without warning. I'll be there in ten minutes, so don't go burning down the house.' "

"Yes, Your Grace." Vale bowed before withdrawing.

When they were alone again, Jess said, "Those men sound awful. Rude. You can't mean to let them in your house."

"I can and I will. There's always room in my home for the Union of the Rakes."

"The what?"

Looking boyish and eager, a far cry from the urbane duke, he grinned. "The Union of the Rakes. A terrible name we coined for ourselves at Eton, and unfortunately the moniker stuck."

She followed as he strode toward the house.

"There were five of us that day in the library." He paused by Lady Farris, Lord Pickhill, and Mr. Walditch. "I have additional guests to see to. When you're finished in the gardens, just head into the house and Mrs. Diehl will see you settled in your rooms. Dinner is at seven."

He didn't wait to hear the others' response before taking a step in the direction of the house. She lingered behind.

He threw a glance over his shoulder and, with a mischievous lift of his brows, indicated he wanted her to accompany him. So she did.

They both crossed the threshold leading into a corridor. "Five of you? A library?"

"We were being punished for various infractions. The senior boy made us sit in the library all day and write an essay about who we thought we were. The task eventually fell to Holloway, who wrote one essay for the five of us." He stopped and shook his head, but his smile remained in place. "Thought for certain we'd wind up killing each other before the day was over. Turned out, we forged a friendship that's endured for twenty years."

"No small achievement."

"Five boys couldn't be more dissimilar. Myself, a ducal heir, Holloway, a commoner who was a brilliant scholar, McCameron, a Corinthian. Then there was Curtis, a criminal, and a . . ." He snorted. "I'm not sure what Rowe qualifies as. An eccentric, I suppose. Mayhap in our differences we found a kind of common ground."

"You like them so much you let them insult you." It was impossible not to see the affection in his face, not to hear it in his voice. He'd never spoken of anyone with such fondness as he did these men who comprised his select cadre of friends.

He lifted a warning finger, though there was no anger in the gesture. "Don't ever say that in front of them, or I shan't hear the end of it. They do so love to torment me."

257

"Men who torment a *duke*." She smiled widely. "I *must* meet them."

"Brace yourself." He waved her forward as he walked toward the front of the house.

She could hear masculine voices in the Great Hall, rumbled words intended only for a few ears, followed by laughter. She thought she heard someone threaten to hit the other with one of the medieval flails attached to the wall.

"I'll set the dogs on the lot of you," Noel said as he and Jess stepped into the chamber. Three men turned to face them.

"That's fortunate, as Curtis here is wearing beefsteak for drawers, and is particularly hard up for any attention below his waist." This comment came from a man with almost vulpine features, his cheekbones impossibly high, his eyes the pale blue of a glacier.

"Just because I don't let any Tom, Dick, or Harriet into my breeches — like you — doesn't mean I lack for amorous company, Rowe," growled a man with a square jaw and shoulders as wide as a doorway.

"Both of you, button it. There's a lady present." The man who uttered this had a Scottish accent and a bearing that could only be described as martial. His spine was straight and his gaze was keen and assess-

258

ing, as if he was taking the measure of a battlefield. He bowed. "Beg pardon, ma'am."

"Lady Whitfield," Noel said, "I must insult you by introducing you to my friends."

"You are this month," the one called Rowe said. "The check cleared."

She couldn't believe that Noel could permit such insolence, even if these men were his old schoolfellows. And yet he only laughed in response.

"Lady Whitfield, this is William Rowe."

"The political writer," she said, shocked at both Rowe's relative youth as well as his easy manner with Noel. He also did not seem unusually eccentric to her. "Your articles — they're incredible. That one about the certain decline of the ruling class was especially fascinating."

"Lady Whitfield is a genius," Rowe said to Noel, startling a laugh from her.

"This towering edifice is Theodore Curtis," Noel continued, gesturing toward the man whose muscles seemed to strain his jacket.

She gaped at Curtis. He had the body of a Samson, and, according to Noel, had been on the wrong side of the law in his youth. "The barrister? You defend the poor. I've read transcripts of your appearances in

259

court and the eloquence of them has occasionally moved me to tears."

"I agree with Rowe," Curtis said. "She's a genius."

"Finally," Noel said, "and least of all, this is Major Duncan McCameron, late of the 79th Regiment of Foot."

"The hero of the Battle of the Pyrenees." Jess couldn't stop herself from staring.

"You're well-read," Rowe said with a smirk.

Noel sent her a look full of admiration. "There's no one — Holloway included — who's got a thirst for knowledge like her."

"When you know things," Jess said, "you can take over the world."

"You best Wellington for ambition." Noel beamed. "That's a compliment, my lady."

"I took it as such. And you keep distinguished company."

"Ma'am." McCameron bowed again, all military precision. "It was duty, nothing more. I'd take issue with the liberal use of the word *hero*."

"But that's what the press dubbed you," Jess objected.

"They are out to sell papers, ma'am. Nothing more."

"McCameron is, as usual, nauseatingly modest." Noel walked to the Scotsman and thumped his fist against his chest. It was a measure of the major's strength that he swayed only slightly from the force of Noel's wallop. "Ply him with enough whiskey, he's sure to tell you a thrilling tale of him against an entire battalion of Bonaparte's best riflemen."

Jess turned a wondering gaze to Noel. "You told me they were your friends with a ridiculous name — you said nothing about being bosom companions with some of England's shining lights."

All four of the men laughed. "Shining lights?" Rowe repeated. "Good Lord, the things that pass for respectability these days."

"What the deuce are you reprobates doing here, showing up without a word of warning?" Noel asked, though there was no irritation in his voice.

Curtis shrugged his massive shoulders. "Rowe wanted to delve into some manuscript archive in Leicester, and, as we were passing by Carriford, we thought we'd duck in and give our regards."

"It's the height of the Season, and you assumed I'd be here." Noel's gaze was steady. "Or perhaps you hoped I wouldn't be here. You know there's an open-door arrangement for the Union regardless of whether or not I'm in residence. Free beds and a meal for any of you."

It was a generous policy that went above his usual bonhomie. Clearly, he cared very much for the men who made up the Union of the Rakes.

"You ass," McCameron said with affection. "Of course we hoped you'd be at Carriford. The beds and meals here aren't that exemplary."

Noel snorted. "And Holloway? Where's our scholar?"

Curtis rolled his eyes. "Too busy in London with his wife. Only a new book can make him as happy."

"I think books fall a distant second to Lady Grace," Rowe noted. "Would be that we'd all find someone who gave us the same contentment." His expression turned suddenly melancholy, and he moved to look out the windows that fronted the house.

Was Jess imagining it, or did Curtis send Rowe a look fraught with longing? She'd heard that some men preferred the company of other men. Was Curtis one of them?

She wondered if Rowe knew how Curtis felt.

Jess glanced at Noel. He watched Curtis with a faint frown, as if trying to puzzle out a riddle. Was it the fact that a man might desire another man? Perhaps his confusion came from another possibility — one of his dearest friends seemed to desire one of their close circle.

"I've a houseful of guests currently," he said after a moment. "If two of you don't mind sharing a bed, then I ought to be able to accommodate you."

"Sleeping on the floor should present no difficulty for me," McCameron said.

"You're not sleeping on any floor in my house," Noel replied.

"I can sleep outside, too."

"Goddamn it, McCameron, you're getting a bed at Carriford."

The Scot lifted his hands in a placating gesture. "As you like."

"Curtis and I can share," Rowe said distractedly — and seemed completely unaware that Theodore Curtis had gone perfectly still. "Isn't that so?"

"Doesn't matter to me," Curtis said quickly. Too quickly.

Another pause fell, and Jess could only speculate what any of the Union might have been thinking at that moment. Noel walked to the bellpull and tugged.

Jess hurried up to him. "I can share a room with Lady Farris or Lady Haighe," she murmured.

"Absolutely not. I picked out a particular room for you and —" He stopped, and his jaw clenched. It seemed he'd said too much.

"A specific room for me." She tilted her head to the side as she considered it. Perhaps he'd put her in a room close to his, because he'd hoped that at some point during the night, one would visit the other's chamber.

Enticing. And . . . a little irritating, that he might be presumptuous enough to put her near him for easy access.

"The Gillyflower Room." An actual blush spread across his cheeks. "It's very pretty — the wall hangings, and such. Has a view of the gardens, too." As if reading her thoughts, he added, "My bedchamber is clear on the other side of the house. But your room is the prettiest of all."

"I — Oh. Thank you."

Before she could think of anything more articulate, Mrs. Diehl appeared. "Your Grace?"

"Prepare the remaining bedchambers for my new guests," he instructed. "Major Mc-Cameron in one, and Mr. Rowe and Mr. Curtis in the other."

"Yes, Your Grace." The housekeeper curt-sied before hurrying away.

"Such consideration as a host," Jess murmured. "Just as promised."

"I always deliver. Besides," he said with a shrug, "the bare minimum is hardly deserving of praise. That's like congratulating a man for covering his belch."

"This has been very educational." At his lifted brow, she explained, "The things I'm learning about you. They're a continual surprise. A *good* surprise."

But it wasn't good. It was, in fact, awful. She was deceiving him, and the more she discovered about Noel — his kindness, his generosity of pocketbook and spirit, his inquisitive nature that he had to keep hidden behind a veneer of rakishness — the more she understood that all the preventative measures she'd taken against opening her heart to him were in vain.

If she wasn't careful, she could easily love him.

CHAPTER 18

"Remember when we were here and Curtis challenged you to an axe throwing contest in the Long Gallery?" McCameron asked, coming to stand beside Noel.

Like Noel, he'd changed into clothing more suitable for dinner, and Noel had to wonder if McCameron missed his dress uniform.

Noel chuckled. "Observe." He pulled back a tapestry to reveal gouges in the parlor's wooden paneling. "Part of the house's lore now."

"Never to be repeated?"

"A rake by reputation I may be —"

"And action," McCameron added.

Noel inclined his head in acknowledgment. "But I'm nearing my thirty-fifth year — all of the Union is — and, much as it pains me, it's likely best to leave behind weeklong bacchanals. Rakishness isn't the same as immaturity."

He and McCameron watched from the edge of the room as guests from the Bazaar mingled and chatted with his old friends. There was no worry that any members of the Union of the Rakes might embarrass him — they were all men of the world, and knew precisely when Noel's manners needed loosening and when they needed to be constrained.

"Does that mean you'll seek the usual accoutrements of a duke?" McCameron asked. "Wife, heirs, and the rest."

"Been talking with my mother? She's eager for the 'dowager' to come before her 'duchess.' "

"Her Grace and I have *not* been corresponding, but you're the only one of us who has the obligation to get shackled."

Such cynicism from McCameron wasn't unexpected, given his history. Still, it pained Noel to hear the edge in his friend's voice and see the buried sadness in his gaze.

"My father married at the advanced age of forty-one," he said. "With such an example, there seems little hurry for me to marry, regardless of what my mother believes. It will be years before I put out the word that I'm on a bride hunt. Besides," he continued, "the thought of courting some girl fresh from the schoolroom holds little appeal."

"What about pretty sandy-haired widows with amber eyes and incisive minds?"

Noel's gaze went right to Jess, who talked with Rowe and Mr. Walditch. She, of course, looked enchanting this evening in a dress the color of the sky just before dawn, pearls hanging from her ears but her neck deliciously bare.

"Judging by the length of your silence," McCameron said drily, "I can only assume that you've given the matter consideration."

"She's recently out of mourning. If she's anything like the widows I've known, she'll want as much liberty as possible before taking another husband. *If* she wants another husband. Can't see much to recommend husbands to anyone."

His own parents' union had been a pleasant but not especially passionate one. In truth, he couldn't remember them kissing in his presence, but then, they had both been scrupulously aware of decorum at all times, even at home in just the presence of their children.

McCameron said, "She might, however, want the security that comes from marriage. If she hasn't mentioned it to you, it could be because she's set her cap for someone else."

Noel glanced at his friend, who spoke

from painful experience. He didn't know what to say — never truly did — when it came to McCameron's heartbreak, and so he kept silent.

But the notion badgered him — picturing Jess married. And not to him.

"You're grinding your teeth," McCameron noted.

"And your hearing needs attending to." He studied the ornately carved ceiling. "Listen, McCameron, if I've been overbearing about anything —"

"All the time," his friend answered brightly.

"What I'm *trying* to say," Noel pressed on, his jaw tight, "is that if I have been a bit too domineering or high-handed about making decisions, or doing whatever I please without asking for anyone's opinion, I, uh, I'm sorry." Those last words were mumbled.

Brows raised, McCameron regarded him. "I think you're right. I *do* need my hearing attended to. Because I just heard you apologize."

"Do you accept my apology or not?" Noel irritably demanded.

"I do," his friend said. "And if this new, slightly more humble Rotherby is at all Lady Whitfield's doing, then I must congratulate her on achieving that which no amount of

Eton tutors, university dons, and members of the Union of the Rakes could."

"You're an ass," Noel muttered. "But thank you for your forbearance."

A bright, musical laugh sounded, and both Noel and McCameron looked to its source. Lady Farris stood flanked by almost all the remaining male guests, and as Noel and his friend watched, she swatted at Curtis's arm in playful remonstrance.

"You're scowling at her," Noel observed. "Can't understand why. A delightful woman, Lady Farris."

McCameron snorted. "Do you know she asked me if I knew the way to the roof because she wanted to go there tonight and watch the moon rise? She said, and I quote, 'What a lark that would be, standing on the roof and seeing the moon crest the horizon.'"

"It shouldn't matter a rat's arse to you if she wants to climb the chimneys."

"Couldn't she take up something less dangerous like, I don't know, making flowers out of paper? Can't break your neck making paper roses."

The surliness in normally even-keeled McCameron's voice gave Noel pause.

In truth, he worried about McCameron. The war had ended, his friend had returned, and yet since then, McCameron had drifted, aimless, from one thing to the next. He took occasional employment reviewing accounting ledgers for sundry noblemen and businesses, but nothing had ever truly captured his attention. But he said nothing about what might be behind his lack of purpose, or his plans and hopes for the future.

Something had to be done.

"Your Grace, my ladies and lords, and gentlemen," Vale intoned from the doorway, "dinner awaits." He bowed and withdrew.

As the host, and the highest-ranking member of the group, it was Noel's obligation to escort the highest-ranking female into the dining room. He went to Lady Haighe and held out his arm.

"Would you honor me?"

She eyed his arm. "That depends."

"On what?"

"On what food you intend to serve us. I don't want to be led into cold soup and boiled potatoes."

"Fear not, my lady," he said. "I am assured that there is an abundance of roast lamb and more than enough tarts made with fruits grown in my very own glasshouse."

When all the ladies partnered up with escorts, Noel headed the procession into the dining room.

During dinner, the conversation moved easily from one topic to another, there wasn't too much disagreement over political policy, and the food was, as he'd expected, excellent.

"This is my third serving of buttered roast artichokes," Jess said, helping herself to more of the vegetables. "I advise everyone to take what they want before I decimate the entire platter."

"My cook can always make more," Noel said. "He'll ask for an increase in pay if he knows how much we've enjoyed his dishes." He shrugged. "A worthwhile expense."

"Don't mistake me, it's an excellent preparation, but the artichokes themselves are at their peak."

"They're from Carriford's garden," he said.

"Give a raise to your gardener, too. The meat of the artichokes is . . ." She seemed to search for the right word. "Luscious. And in the silky butter sauce . . ." Her eyes closed and she licked her lips.

He couldn't look away. Wouldn't have been able to even if the other guests suddenly began throwing plates and glasses against the walls.

For the first time, he resented the presence of the Union. Hell, he resented everyone who wasn't her. This dinner would be far better if it was only the two of them, using their fingers instead of silverware, licking and nibbling and feasting on food and each other.

Conversation moved on, but he barely attended to a single word. He couldn't stop picturing what it would be like to take an intimate supper with Jess, plying her with delicacies made from his own estate's garden, watching her rapture from each dish, before taking her to bed and pleasuring her for hours. Then summoning another meal and making love to her until the sun rose.

Dinner ended, and the ladies retired to the drawing room to leave the men to their postprandial tobacco and spirits.

He rose to pour himself a stiff drink, and McCameron met him at the sideboard.

"Never seen you do that before," his friend noted.

Noel lifted his eyebrow. "I'm fairly certain you've seen me help myself to a whiskey."

"The whiskey in your hand isn't an uncommon sight," McCameron said, "but I've never seen you watch a woman leave a room before."

"Women make a far more appealing sight

than a room full of boorish dolts," he said offhandedly.

"I didn't say you watched the *women,* I said you watched *a woman.*" His friend crossed his arms over his chest. "Trying to bed her? Is that what she's doing here?"

The question did not seem to be given hostilely. McCameron seemed genuinely interested.

"I put her in the Gillyflower Room." Noel sipped at his drink.

McCameron gave a small grunt of understanding, because he'd been to Carriford enough to realize the distance between the Gillyflower Room and Noel's own chambers.

"And yet you watched her leave the room," his friend said. "Watched her like a prowling tiger eyeing a doe."

"Do tigers eat deer?"

"For the sake of argument, let's say that they do."

Evenly, Noel said, "I'd tear the fucking world apart for a chance to share her bed."

"Might not come to that. Given the way she stared at you all night."

Noel's entire body tightened, yet he managed to drawl, "And what way was that?"

McCameron's grin was sly. "As if the doe was exceptionally eager to be devoured."

CHAPTER 19

Jess pushed back the bed linens and sat up. She ought to be asleep, but there had been a honey-soaked pastry served with dinner's final course, the taste of which haunted her even hours after retiring to bed.

Easier to focus on the honey's flavor rather than Noel, asleep somewhere in this beautiful house.

He'd picked this room for her. The walls were covered in hand-painted wallpaper, and while the bed was made of dark chestnut wood, it had been carved into elegant gothic designs that made it seem like a vessel bound for the shores of a fairy kingdom.

Any lady would be happy to have such a room for her bedchamber. Jess was no lady, but she loved the space, and her heart softened to think of Noel selecting it specifically so she'd enjoy it.

He had watched her throughout the dinner and afterward, and there had been dark need in his voice as he'd wished her good night at the conclusion of the evening.

She wanted him. So badly she shook with it.

No — impossible. If, by the grace of some heavenly deity, he did decide to invest in McGale & McGale, she couldn't allow him to think that she'd slept with him as a means to secure his money. Learning the truth about who she was would only make him view their every interaction as a betrayal.

Yet . . . if she told him everything, told him *why* she did what she did . . . He was a man with heart. He wouldn't cast her aside because she'd fought to keep her family together. Would he?

And tomorrow, he and the others would visit the farm. Nervousness mixed with eagerness jumped through her — this was what she'd wanted for McGale & McGale. The culmination of her work at the Bazaar was less than twenty-four hours away. Hopefully, Cynthia and Fred would do their parts, and the end of the day would see their business with at least one new investor.

Her growling stomach interrupted her swirling thoughts. She pressed a hand to her belly, trying to quiet it. The food served tonight had been incredible, and she wanted more of it.

After grabbing a shawl, she peeked out of her room, and no one was in the hall. The last time the clock had chimed, it had been a quarter to one in the morning.

She took a candle and crept down the corridor.

Every country house had its idiosyncrasies, but thanks to her employment with Lady Catherton, Jess had enough of an idea about most houses' layouts so she could find the kitchen and larder easily.

In short order, she arrived. It was a large room with a high, smoke-stained ceiling. The fire had been banked, and, to her relief, no one was about. But her true aim wasn't here.

She found the larder quickly and shut the door behind her. Light from her candle revealed marble shelves lined with covered jars, while haunches of meat hung from hooks.

Jess put her candle on a table in the middle of the room, then approached the shelves as she rose up onto the tips of her toes to reach the honey pot.

Footsteps sounded in the corridor. She froze, then cursed the fact that she had forgotten to douse her out-of-reach candle. Surely whoever was outside in the hallway could see light coming from under the door. If it was the butler or housekeeper, they'd likely investigate to make certain none of the staff was eating what belonged to the master.

But servants were quite forgiving of anything the master or his guests might do. She was Lady Whitfield, after all. Not Jess McGale.

The footsteps approached and then stopped outside of the larder. She arranged her shawl, straightened her shoulders, and tipped up her chin.

The door opened, and Jess's plans to behave regally fell away.

It was Noel. Dressed only in his shirtsleeves, breeches, and boots.

His open shirt exposed his chest and the shadow of dark hair that dusted his pectorals. As he entered the larder and closed the door behind him, his muscles shifted beneath the fine lawn of his shirt.

"What are you doing here?" she asked, hating herself for the asinine question.

He raised a brow. "The master of the house is permitted to go wherever he likes, whenever he likes." Then he ruined the aristocratic hauteur of his reply by saying, "And Cook told me that he'd put a meat pie aside for me in case I needed something

278

to nibble on in the middle of the night."

"Do you often come down to the larder after midnight?"

He set his candle down beside hers. "As habits go, it's my least dissolute. You're here for a snack, I imagine."

"I am discovered. We share the benign inclination to ransack larders when everyone is asleep."

She didn't do it often at Lady Catherton's home, and when she did, she made certain to grab only a few rusks or sugarplums. But she remembered all too well the lean years on the farm, when she'd gone to bed hungry and there had been nothing to eat in the middle of the night, and hardly anything for the morrow's breakfast.

She could never tell Noel, of course.

Being alone with him in this tiny chamber made her heart pound. To keep herself from blurting truths about herself, she asked, "Anything here you want?"

"I've a taste for something sweet." His gaze smoldered.

She inhaled sharply, but managed to say, "I have been told that I'm too astringent."

"Only to men with an immature palate." His eyes locked with hers, he prowled around the table until he was right beside her. "Do you want me, Jess? Even a fraction of the way I want you?"

"I do," she whispered. "God help me, I do." There were very good reasons why she had to keep away from him, but she couldn't think of a single one — not when his body radiated warmth and his gaze was even hotter, and without his coat, his thighs and arse were revealed in his tight buckskin breeches. Lord was he beautiful.

His arms enfolded her, bringing her body snug to his. His hands cupped her hips.

He growled and she made a kind of mewl as the thinness of her gown provided no barrier to sensation. Already, he was aroused, his cock thick and rigid against her belly. She rubbed against it, drawing from him a long, moaned *"Fuck."*

She brought her arms up and threaded her hands into his hair. She curled her fingers, tightening her grip on him. Not too much. Just enough to sting.

"God, yes," he rumbled, his eyes closing. "Kiss me."

She lifted up to meet him as his lips crashed down onto hers. The kiss was fevered and urgent, openmouthed with need. His tongue lapped at hers, and each stroke reverberated through her, centering in her breasts and quim. He kissed her as if he'd been formed for this singular purpose,

280

and he finally had a chance to do exactly the thing for which he'd been made. Her shawl slipped down to the ground.

He brought one of his broad hands up to cup her breast. But even the whisper-thin cambric was too much of a barrier, and he tugged at the ribbon of the neckline until it gaped open. She bit back a cry as his bare hand, hot as a brand, stroked her. When her nipple tightened into a point, he pinched it lightly. Enough to make her gasp.

"I want to talk to you," he growled. "Or perhaps you prefer me silent."

"Talk," she said at once.

"Been thinking about this." He rumbled each word, his voice deep and low. "Since we arrived at Carriford. Your skin against mine. My cock hard as iron as I pleasured you. I want to pleasure you. May I? Will you let me?"

"I will." And she knew with certainty what he wanted — he'd said so in the conservatory — and she wanted it, too.

It felt perfect to hold dominion over him, this man who was so powerful. To receive the gift of his submission and honor it with her own power.

All along, every interaction, every word and glance, where she had met him parry for parry, led to this moment between them.

And it was glorious.

Somehow, he'd known. Seen within her that need to be in command, something that no one — not even she herself — had understood. She had done her best in her life to be in control, but she had been born too poor, and a female. The world gave her no power, and she had not realized until now, until *him,* how much she hungered for it.

"Taste me."

He groaned. "Yes, Jess. I will lick your pussy."

She nearly came right then. But she managed to keep her release at bay for a moment. "My bedchamber . . ."

"Too far." He clasped her waist and lifted her up, setting her at the table's end. "Too far for a starving man."

His hands trembled as he raised the hem of her nightgown.

She clasped the edge of the table as he eased back. He was a beautiful man, and the candlelight turned him into a vision of Eros himself. She could see the long, heavy length of his shaft pressed tightly against the front of his breeches, and she sucked in a breath when he stroked his hand over it.

"Am I wrong, Jess? Am I wrong to touch myself when I think of you? To pump my hand on my cock and imagine it's your mouth or your quim, taking me in, surrounding me?"

"You *are* wrong," she said imperiously. It felt perfect to speak to him in this way, as though she'd been waiting for eons to find a man strong enough for her to command. "On your knees and perform your penance."

Noel slowly sank to his knees between her legs, his gaze blazing and ripe with intent. He slid his broad hands up her bare legs, pushing up the hem of her nightgown. She could barely catch her breath as sensation built higher and higher still in time with his hands. Her rasping gulps for air combined with his own rough inhalations.

She didn't sleep wearing drawers, and soon he'd hiked her nightgown up to bunch at her waist, revealing her to him. Cool air touched her hot, sensitive flesh. A vestigial fillip of embarrassment made her reach to cover herself — the conservatory had been enveloped in shadows and she hadn't bared herself in this way.

He clasped her wrist. "Please, no. Let me see your beautiful cunt. Let me see *you.*"

Shakily, she tugged her hand free and returned it to the edge of the table, which she gripped tightly.

"Thank you for your trust," he murmured.

She was able to nod, but forming words at that point was beyond her capability. Her hold on the table tightened further as he leaned close to kiss his way up one thigh.

She thought for certain he'd taste her then. Instead, he kissed his way up her other thigh, stroking her legs with his hands until she shook with arousal. "Taste me," she gasped. *"Now."*

"What if I'm disobedient?" His eyes gleamed. "What if I want to take my time and look my fill of you? I haven't been able to think of anything other than what it would be like to be on my knees with your gorgeous pussy mere inches from my face."

Her eyes drifted shut. *"Noel."* He kept undoing her, piece by piece. She was enthralled by him.

She felt his breath against her quim, and held her own breath. Then —

"Oh, damn." She moaned as his tongue slipped between her folds in one long, slick stroke. Her moan rose again as he swirled his tongue around her clitoris, then dipped back down again to slide through her inner lips. When he lapped at her entrance, she thought for certain she'd lose her mind, but then he stroked a finger up into her and she knew that any chance she had of retaining her sanity was gone.

He devoured her as he thrust his finger into Jess's passage. He worshipped her profanely until she had no will left, no other choice but to come.

"That's it," he rumbled.

Her orgasm hit like a wild summer storm, pummeling her with pleasure so intense she couldn't sit upright. Heedless of what things she might knock over onto the floor, she fell back as another climax slammed into her.

"Honey," he growled. "You taste of honey."

"It's the soap," she murmured.

She felt his hair tickling her thighs as he shook his head. "Not perfumed soap. It's *you*. Like sweet, fragrant honey warmed by the sun to coat my tongue. I want to swallow all of you."

Heaven help me. Yet the only kind of divine assistance she wanted would ensure that she experienced only this for the rest of her life.

"More," she gasped. "Kill me with pleasure."

There was a wicked smile in his voice as he said, "I will keep you alive for a very long time — especially if that means I get to eat your quim for eternity."

She would be dead of ecstasy. Of that, she

was certain. But the hell if she didn't care. "Fewer words and more of your mouth on me."

"Yes, Jess." His words vibrated with erotic rapture.

"And don't touch yourself," she added. "Not until I say you can."

He grunted his response, but she could tell her command pleased him. And then she was lost once more as he licked and drank from her.

Her anchor to consciousness slipped as she was lifted up on an endless succession of climaxes. As he lapped at her, his thumb circled and stroked her clitoris, while he added a second finger to his first inside her channel.

She lost count of her orgasms. She lost her hold on everything but the feel of him devotedly serving her.

And yet . . . "I need more," she rasped.

He rose up over her, and his jaw was tight with desire. "Tell me what you need."

"You." She slid her hands down his shirt and plucked at the fabric.

He whipped off his shirt in one fast, heedless motion.

How was he so beautiful? It hardly seemed fair — his body was taut and his abdomen ridged and his arms were magnificent and it was as though some cosmic architect had decided to put all of her work into the fashioning of this one man.

She raked her fingers across the coarse silk of the dark hair on his chest.

He snarled. "If anyone is going to kill anyone, *you* are going to kill *me.*"

"It's your punishment for making me wait for more." She sank into the pleasure that rose up from dominating him.

He kissed her deeply, and she tasted herself on him. "What more do you want?"

"Your . . ." She couldn't quite get the word out, finding tiny fragments of inhibition lodged within her desire.

"My cock. You want me to fuck you with my cock." He rocked his hips against hers. The sensation of his buckskin-covered erection sliding over her wet quim made her moan.

"Yes — fuck me," she gasped.

"How shall I do it, Jess? I could give you my cock slow and gentle, or hard and rough." He continued to torment her with his shaft slipping over her.

"Slow and gentle first. Then hard and rough. As rough as you dare." She dug her nails into his shoulders. "But do it *now.*"

His cheeks were flushed, his eyes gleaming. He held her gaze as he worked a hand between their bodies to undo the fastening of his breeches. She knew he'd freed himself when he sucked in a breath, and she looked down to see him holding his erection in a grip so tight it surely hurt.

"One thing," she murmured.

He went still. "Anything."

"I cannot risk pregnancy."

He nodded once. "I'll be careful."

The last fragment of her tension fell away, and she exhaled, preparing herself for what was to come.

He straightened to standing, and guided his cock to slide through her folds, making her moan.

"You're so wet."

"You made me so."

He shook his head. "*We* made you wet. You and I together. Because you need this, don't you? You need my cock in you, just as I need your cunt around me."

His words would shatter her. "Don't play with me any longer. This is the last time I'll tell you: fuck me. If you don't fuck me now, I'm going to —"

He thrust into her in one long, thick pump. She bowed up from the table, uncaring about the rigid surface at her back. All she felt was him inside her, filling her completely.

"Does this satisfy you, Jess?" he growled. "And this?" With each question, he drove into her. His strokes were slow, but the force behind them shook her. "Like so."

Her whole body was alight with sensation. "Just like that."

"I'll give you everything. Everything you want." He fucked her, his pace unhurried and steady.

His tempo was almost too leisurely, yet pleasure built higher within her. In gradual waves, ecstasy rose up. She loved the way he fit, how her body had to stretch to accommodate him, and his determination to give her as much sensation as she could handle — to give her *more* than she could handle.

"That's it, Jess," he crooned. "Let me fuck you like this."

She jolted when his fingers found her clitoris. "Oh, God."

He timed his strokes with his caresses on her bud, and in a rush, another orgasm took her. A long, keening sound tumbled from her lips as she drowned in pleasure, as if she was crying out for help, but didn't truly want anyone to save her.

He had stilled as she'd come, but just as the waves of ecstasy began to recede, his pace increased. "You've had slow and gentle. Now I'll give it to you hard and rough."

The table beneath her shuddered with the force of his thrusts, and yet she didn't care. She didn't care if it collapsed beneath her, or if the bricks of Carriford crumbled to the earth. She didn't care about anything except his exquisite brutal strokes. Something fell off the table, a plate or other piece of china, and shattered on the floor. He didn't ease his thrusts, and they were both lost to the frenzy.

She careened out into ecstasy. It was made all the better by his harsh, rasping breaths, and the quiet grunts that told her he was consumed in this moment and the wonder of their bodies together.

"Please, Jess," he growled. "Come for me. Show me I'm giving you what you want. I need you to come."

She did. Jess would have believed it impossible that she could have so many orgasms in one night, but he was in all things a marvel, and she came again in a final climax that scoured her clean of everything. Every thought, every sense of who she believed herself to be, of what she believed sex could be. All of it. Her orgasm eradicated everything except sensation.

Her body seemed to liquify as she collapsed against the table. And she realized that, in all this time as he'd tasted her and pleasured her, not once had he any kind of release. Surely he suffered from enduring as long as he had.

"Your turn," she gasped. "I want you to come."

Sweat that filmed his forehead and torso gleamed in the candlelight. "Yes, Jess."

And then he pounded into her. Three hard, wild thrusts, before he pulled from her. He groaned as his seed shot from him, coating her belly. "Fucking. Holy. Hell."

They both stilled, panting. He rested on one elbow, bracing himself above her, and she felt his breath on her face. She still could not shape anything resembling thought, and so she drifted on amber-hued swells of fading pleasure. Her limbs seemed incapable of movement. This was where she belonged. Her eyes closed as peace settled over her.

After many moments, he shifted and rose up. She didn't open her eyes, but murmured her thanks when he wiped a piece of fabric over her stomach, cleaning her. With the same tender care, he tugged her nightgown down so she was covered.

"Did I please you?" he whispered at her ear.

"*Please* is too mild a word. I think . . . I

think I've ascended to another level of exis-tence."

He chuckled softly. "That makes me happy. But something does not make me happy."

She opened her eyes to see him standing, bare chested but his breeches fastened, with his hands on his hips. Frowning, she lifted herself up to sit on the table. "What is it?"

"You came down here for something to eat, and I went ahead and fucked you before I fed you."

"Firstly," she said, "*you* didn't fuck. *We* fucked."

He inclined his head. "And secondly?"

She smiled. "We're still in the larder."

"Such wisdom." He took a plate down from the wall.

"When it comes to knowing where the food is, I'm most assuredly wise." Her lips twitched when he laughed. But when she moved to assist him in collecting a few items to eat, he held up his hand. "At least let me clean up the mess we created."

She eyed the pieces of the fallen platter and potatoes that had scattered across the floor.

"Very well," he said with reluctance.

As she collected the shattered china and bits of potato, he put food on the plate. The domestic scene felt quiet and comfortable — despite, or perhaps because of, the fact that they'd just had the most intense sex of her life not minutes before.

Once she'd tidied up and set the pieces of the platter on a shelf, she turned to find Noel waiting with a food-laden plate. There were pieces of meat, and a hunk of cheese, some bread, an orange, and, blissfully, a whole fruit tart.

In companionable silence, they ate from the same plate.

"Do you . . ." She swallowed. "Have you done that often?"

"A man shouldn't boast of the number of his sexual encounters." His lips quirked, a touch of self-deprecation in his smile. "I did, however, have a relatively early start to the practice."

"I was the lucky recipient of all that practice. But what I meant was, do you often act submissively with your lovers?"

"Ah." He glanced away, and she wondered if she'd gone too far, pushed him in a way that made him uncomfortable. Yet before she could apologize, he looked back at her and said in a low voice, "Never. Not before you."

She lost her breath. That he'd given her such trust humbled and overwhelmed her.

Only with her had he been so vulnerable. He — who held the nation's power in his very hands, whose words shaped destinies large and small — gave her the gift of his submission. Because he trusted her.

She didn't deserve his trust. Not by a league.

"Thank you," she said softly. She cupped his jaw with her hand. His morning shave had been long ago, and his stubble lightly abraded her palm. He was so potently masculine. She loved the contrast between them, but they were also alike, because she had strength, too. They complemented each other in ways she never would have anticipated.

How unexpected he had been, and how incredible that she became herself so fully when they were together. This was what she'd desired without knowing it, who she wanted to be, and who she needed at her side. Fearlessly, he showed her the way to the powerful woman within her, celebrating that woman and permitting her to do the same.

An invisible bond anchored them to each other, something she'd never felt before, not with anyone, not even Oliver. The rightness of it stole her breath.

Oh, God. No.

CHAPTER 20

"You've got no goddamned business looking so cheerful at this hour," McCameron grumbled from the sideboard as Noel sauntered into the dining room for breakfast.

Noel heaped crisp streaky bacon on his plate. He was ravenous. "It's my sodding house, so I may look as cheerful as I please."

"Sleep well?" McCameron spat.

"I did, thank you very much." In fact, he'd had the best sleep of his life.

His slumber had been deep, likely born from the utter exhaustion that came from bringing a woman to orgasm many times while denying himself release, and when that release had been permitted, he'd nearly torn the centuries-old house apart with the force of it. He'd never had a climax so devastating. He'd loved it, but it left him a shaking husk, so after kissing Jess one last time and escorting her back to her room, he'd collapsed in his bed.

When he had dreamt, his dreams had all been of Jess. Not frustrating images of what he wanted and could not have, but memories of them together, heaving and panting and lost in pleasure.

He'd been aloft on clouds of contentment, though awakening this morning without her beside him had been somewhat lowering. He wanted her in his bed. He wanted to wake with her in his arms and ask about her dreams, if they had been restful or unsettling or silly.

He wanted that — every morning.

The thought made him pause. "Damn."

"Now what?" McCameron demanded. "You came in here whistling like a ruddy ship's bosun and now you're keeping me from the ham."

"Choke on it." Noel handed his friend the serving fork. "Cantankerous bastard."

"You'd be chewing iron, too, if your room had been right next to Lady Farris's." McCameron and Noel made their way to the table, where several other guests, including Mr. Walditch, Lady Haighe, and Baron Mentmore, already sat, quietly eating their breakfasts.

"Let me guess, she read poetry aloud into the small hours." Noel took a bite of toast.

"Practicing and failing at juggling marble busts."

"Nothing like that," his friend said sourly. "But I could hear her. Moving around. Doing . . ." He waved his hand.

"For a tactician, you're being remarkably vague."

"She went in and out of her room all night. God only knows what she was doing. Nothing orderly or appropriate." McCameron poked his fork moodily into his eggs. "There's a proper way of doing things, a rightness and order. Not her."

"You're out of uniform, Major," Noel said gently. "Regulations and discipline don't apply in peacetime."

"They should."

Noel regarded his friend. Something needed to be done for McCameron — he was too tense, too rudderless.

Curtis and Rowe came into the dining room, and Noel called, "Good morning, gents."

"Morning," Rowe mumbled, but Curtis said nothing. Both of them wore tight, distracted expressions, and they seemed determined to keep a distance of several feet between them. They wordlessly filled up plates, and Curtis took a seat a good four chairs down from where Rowe sat.

Dear God, what had happened to everyone last night?

Well, he knew what had happened to him. He'd had the most incredible sexual experience of his life. Hell, it had been the most incredible experience, regardless of whether or not it had been sexual. He'd allowed himself to be completely exposed — and she had kept him safe.

He had never dreamt of the pleasure that could come from being sexually dominated. But it wouldn't have felt right with anyone other than Jess. He'd felt her strength, and rather than fight against it or feel the need to be the one in charge, he'd ceded to that strength.

It was like falling backward into the air, knowing that she would catch him.

As if his mind had summoned her, Jess entered the dining room. She looked exquisite in a pale green gown trimmed with coral ribbon, as if she was the living embodiment of a summer day. The moment he saw her, his mouth flooded with her taste of sun-warmed honey.

Like the other men, he rose when she came into the room. Hell, he would have floated up to the ceiling with the pleasure seeing her gave him.

"Good morning," she murmured.

298

A few mumbled "Good mornings" answered her, but Noel said in a clear voice, "Good morning, Lady Whitfield."

Her gaze held his, and she smiled a full, genuine smile. That smile sank into his chest like a thrown knife, but instead of wounding, the blade invigorated him.

Last night had exhausted him completely, and yet he never felt more energized. It was as though yielding to her and giving her everything had in turn nourished him in a way he'd never experienced before. It had been more than sex and physical pleasure. For the first time in his long history of making love, it had been a communion.

She was right for him — in every way.

"Hell."

"What?" McCameron demanded.

Noel hadn't realized he'd spoken aloud. "Nothing. Remembered I'm due for a visit to the tailor."

His words hid a stunning revelation. Jess never asked him for anything; she didn't have demands or agendas. If anything, she seemed uninterested in the fact that he was a duke. He wasn't a means to an end for her, someone with whom she had to curry favor, or use. He simply *was,* and for her, that was enough.

Sweat beaded along the back of his neck

at the thought of confessing his feelings. He was only truly open with the Union. Yet last night, he'd been so raw and vulnerable with her and she hadn't abused his vulnerability. She'd held it carefully, protectively.

If there was anyone with whom he could trust his inner heart, it was her.

"Where's Lady Farris and the others?" Jess poured herself a cup of tea, then sat down next to Lady Haighe.

"Apologies," Lady Farris said as she sailed into the room. The men stood upon her entrance, but she motioned for everyone to take their seats. Her windswept hair was partially up, but several silvered locks had slipped their pins to flow over her shoulders. "There's a tree that's absolutely wonderful for climbing."

"A tree?" McCameron asked incredulously. "You climbed . . . ?"

"It was the best way to watch the sunrise." She said this as if it made perfect sense, and to question her logic was the height of folly.

McCameron muttered and took a sip of coffee.

"I told the McGales to expect our party in Honiton by noon," Jess said. "We should start out now, so we aren't late."

"Good point." Noel threw back the last of his coffee and motioned for a footman.

When the servant approached, Noel gave him instructions to have the carriages made ready to leave within a quarter of an hour.

Once the footman had gone, Noel addressed the room. "We'll be off shortly."

"Never seen soap made before, so this ought to be a novel experience." Lady Farris rested her chin on her fist as she looked at McCameron. "Are you joining us, Major?"

"A pity, but no," McCameron said stonily.

"I shall weep disconsolately for the duration of my journey." She gave him a bland smile before turning to Jess. "Are you as eager as I am to learn about the manufacture of soap, Lady Whitfield?"

"My early years were spent in the country," Jess replied, "so I know a small amount about how soap's made." She popped a hulled strawberry into her mouth, and her moan went straight to Noel's cock. "My God, these strawberries should be fed to anyone on their deathbed. It will be a sweet journey to Eternity." After sipping at her tea, she continued. "From what I remember, making soap's an arduous task. And certain parts of the process can be" — she wrinkled her nose — "pungent."

Then she laughed. He leaned into the musical, husky sound, wishing he might hear it every day for the rest of his life.

He'd had an informal relationship with his past lovers, as they did with him. No expectations, no grasping for anything the other wasn't willing to give. If a woman he'd bedded wanted to move on to another paramour, he had made no objection. Not once had he ever believed he could want more from a lover beyond a few nights of pleasure.

It was different with Jess. He couldn't slake his thirst for her — and he didn't want to. But he could not forget that soon she would go to the Continent for an unknown amount of time. She would go on with her life. Take other lovers.

And he would be here in England, wanting her.

Jess watched as familiar landmarks rolled past the windows of Noel's beautifully sprung carriage. It had taken the entirety of the morning and into the early afternoon to reach Honiton. She resisted the impulse to point out the river that wended its way beside the road — that selfsame river flowed past her family's farm.

With each mile closer, her excitement and trepidation grew. She'd never played cricket, but she imagined this was what a batsman felt on the pitch at the close of a match, confident in their ability whilst also understanding that their bat could either secure the win or lose it all.

Never had the stakes been so high — yet with the possibility of failure also came the prospect of victory.

She felt Noel's gaze on her, hot and intense, as he sat opposite her in the carriage. Everything had changed between them, and yet it could not. She still had to ensure that her family's business survived. Focus was essential, but throughout the morning, she'd accidentally poke a bruise left behind from their delicious, torrid lovemaking and be transported back to the larder. Back to his kisses, his exquisite tongue, and his glorious thrusts.

God how she adored him. And she couldn't have him.

Now is not *the time to start pining,* she mentally snapped. *Pay. Attention.*

"We're almost there," she said, nodding out the window.

"How can you tell?" Noel asked.

Yes, right. She'd never been here before. "The cottages are closer to each other, and I think I hear the tolling of a church bell."

Noel, Lady Farris, and Mr. Walditch all nodded. Jess nearly told them that the village truly showed itself to its best advantage at Christmas, when fir garlands were hung on gates and Mrs. Osterby tied red ribbons on everyone's front door.

Soon, the carriage reached the village green. It was bound on all four sides by shops and a taproom, with a stone cairn erected to the memorial of the men lost in the war in the center of the square itself.

"Someone is supposed to meet us in the village," Jess said, "and then they will guide us to the establishment itself."

Noel rapped on the roof of the carriage, and it came to a stop outside Lucy Devin's mercer shop. Jess heard the carriage behind them also stop, and within short order, everyone stood on the high street.

Jess glanced up and down the road. Where the deuce was Cynthia? "They are supposed to be here," she offered by way of explanation. "We can wait."

She recognized every passerby, from Emma Ferring, the vicar's wife, to John Lennox, who often wandered about in his bare feet, even in the depths of winter. Nearly everyone stared at her — and why shouldn't they, since she'd arrived in an expensive, glossy carriage and stood with people far more elegant than had ever graced the homely little village.

Thankfully, however, it seemed that Fred and Cynthia had briefed everyone that for today she was Lady Whitfield, an outsider. So the pedestrians' gazes never lingered on her for too long. Besides, if anyone did stare, she had the convenient excuse that they were simply staring at a wealthy stranger.

It was Noel, however, who attracted the most attention. Regardless of the fact that they were in a tiny village deep in Wiltshire — or perhaps because of it — he drew everyone's notice. No wonder. He radiated wealth and power, and in his expertly tailored clothing, with his absurdly handsome face, he'd draw anyone's regard.

"No need to wait." Noel tipped his head toward the mercer shop. "I'll ask in here for the direction of the McGale business. It won't take but a moment. Join me, Lady Whitfield? The shop looks charming."

"I cannot resist anything charming." Despite Jess's outward calm, her stomach briefly clenched. The fewer interactions she had with the villagers, the better her chance of avoiding a potentially dangerous situation.

He opened the door for her, and the bell chimed in that same double ring Jess had heard for most of her life. *Ring-ring!* She'd always loved that bell because it meant they were getting cloth to make new dresses — a rare treat.

Fortunately, there were no customers in the shop. But Lucy Devin stood behind the counter, and gazed at Jess with recognition. Thank God Noel had turned to examine a bolt of wine-colored fabric, because he didn't see Lucy open her mouth to greet Jess, nor Jess giving her head a small shake at Lucy.

The shopkeeper frowned. Thankfully, however, she said, "Fine afternoon, sir. Got lots of fine merchandise for you today."

"Afternoon," Noel said, turning back with a polite nod. "We're looking for the Mc-Gale farm."

Lucy looked at Jess, and Noel followed Lucy's glance, so Jess made herself peer into the glass-topped counter and pretend to admire a bowl full of sparkling beads.

" 'Tis but a short ride from here," Lucy said. "Follow the high street north out of the village. It follows the river, which flows past the McGale farm. You'll see the gate plainly on the right side, just a mile after the church."

"My thanks," Noel said.

"Of course, sir. Madam."

Jess exhaled.

The bell chimed its double ring, and a man entered the shop in the clean but coarse garments of a farmer. Jess recognized him immediately as "Oaty" Williams, a man of her parents' generation. Oaty paused just on the threshold.

"Aye, Lucy, there's some carriages outside that look right costly," he said, then tilted his head. "Jess? What're you about in them fancy togs?"

She wanted the floor to open up and consume not just Oaty and Lucy's mercer shop, but the village green and an additional half mile, as well. Sadly, that option did not seem imminent.

She felt Noel's confused look on her.

"Tess?" She frowned as if in confusion. "My name's not Tess."

Oaty took a step toward her. "But —"

The door swung open, and praise everything, Cynthia dashed inside. She panted, her hand pressed to her side.

"Your Grace," Cynthia gasped. "My lady. So glad. You made. The journey."

"My lady?" Oaty scratched his head. "It's —"

"I'm Lady Whitfield," Jess said, iron in her voice. "Not this Tess person you're speaking of."

"She doesn't resemble Tess in the slightest," Cynthia said. "For one thing, she's far prettier than Tess. Wouldn't you say, Lucy?"

"I . . . uh . . . yes. Yes, Tess is completely different from this woman. Um, Lady Whitfield."

"Wouldn't you like to show Mr. Williams some new fabric, Lucy?" Cynthia said. "Perhaps *take him into the back room?*"

Lucy blinked. She strode forward and grasped Oaty's arm, then tugged him behind her. "This way, Oaty. We've some lovely calico that would look stunning on Ellie."

Oaty let himself be pulled along, yet he objected, "But it's —"

Lucy dragged him through the door that led to the storeroom, and shut it firmly behind them, quieting Oaty's protestations.

Cynthia fixed a smile on her face that was so manic as to be almost vicious. "In any event, I'm Cynthia McGale. My brother, Fred, awaits us at the farm."

"Peculiar bloke," Noel murmured, glancing back and forth between the closed storeroom door and Jess. "Mistaking you for someone else."

"Poor Oaty hasn't been quite right since we had to fish him out of the well," Cynthia said. "Confuses his goat with his horse and tries to ride his goat into town. It's sad, honestly." She shook her head mournfully.

"We don't want to keep anyone at your farm waiting," Jess said, her words pointed. "I imagine there's quite a lot to see, and we ought to move things along if we plan to return to His Grace's estate before nightfall."

"I came over in my gig," Cynthia said cheerily, "so I can lead your carriages to the farm."

"By all means, let's put a bit of distance between us and . . . Oaty," Noel said. "Before he mistakes me for the butcher and tries to order a haunch of beef."

Noel placed his hand on the small of Jess's back as he guided her out. Under different circumstances, she would have accepted his touch gladly. It might have even enflamed her, small and mundane as it was. Yet these circumstances, however, made Jess stiffen. Hopefully, Cynthia wouldn't notice.

Cynthia noticed. Of course. She shot Jess a questioning look. Jess gave her a silent threat of bodily harm if her younger sister was to press the matter. Cynthia responded with a sly little smirk.

Apparently, there was no age barrier to a younger sibling's irritating behavior.

Everyone clambered back into the vehicles to prepare for the short journey to the farm. Cynthia brought her gig around, pulled by the family's gray mare, and then they were off.

Riding in an expensive ducal carriage toward her family's farm was far removed from her usual experience of being in the gig or driving the farm's wagon or even being on foot. It was unsettling to see Noel's profile silhouetted against the fields that she'd known her whole life, as if she sat down to the battered wooden family kitchen table and was served a meal of delicacies on golden plates.

They finally reached the farm, and everyone gathered in the yard outside the main house, where the family lived. Cynthia appeared, with Fred at her side.

Her brother glanced from the carriages to the refined company — lingering in awe on Noel — before his look skipped to Jess and her borrowed regalia. Yet, like Cynthia, her brother said nothing that gave her away.

"Your Grace, my lords and ladies," Cynthia said with a friendly smile, "what an honor to have you here at McGale & McGale. As some of you know, I'm Cynthia McGale and this is my brother, Fred."

Fred bowed. "Refreshments before we begin our tour?" He bent down and scooped up the farm's orange tabby, then gave the cat a scratch between its ears. The mouser purred its approval. "We've excellent mead made from our very own honey."

After setting the cat back down, Fred motioned to a trio of the farm's laborers who, Jess knew, helped in the soap production process. Today, Katie, Sam, and Dot had exchanged their sturdy garments for their Sunday best, and they brought trays with mugs of mead forward to the visitors. Inwardly, she cheered whomever had thought of this excellent strategy of plying the guests with the delicious, mood-lightening drink.

Noel stepped forward to take two mugs. He passed one to Jess, then took a sip. "Extraordinary."

"An old family recipe," Fred said proudly. "Proprietary, too. Though," he added with a wink, "with the right inducement, I'm sure someone will be willing to give up their secrets."

Jess coughed loudly, and glared from behind the fist she'd brought up to her mouth.

"Everyone finished their mead?" Cynthia asked. When the company nodded, she said, "If you'll follow Katie, she'll begin the tour of our operation. Lady Whitfield, a word? I have a question about today's planned agenda."

"Of course." Jess smiled and waved the group forward, including Noel. "Go on ahead. I'll catch up."

"This way, everyone," Katie said, holding up her hands as she walked backward. "There's much to see and I'm sure you'll have questions, so let's begin."

Once the visitors had moved on — Noel casting a glance at her over his shoulder before joining them — Jess turned to her siblings. Her mind spun out into a hundred different scenarios: their half-dozen workers had failed to show up today, or they'd neglected purchasing enough tallow, or the bees hadn't produced enough honey. Whatever the situation, Jess would handle it.

But before she could speak, Cynthia demanded, "A *duke*, Jess?" Her eyes gleamed excitedly. "You never said anything about a duke fancying you."

"Handsome as Hades, too," Fred added, waggling his eyebrows.

Jess scowled at her brother. "Shut it. And whether or not Noel, I mean, the duke fancies me doesn't matter. We're here to keep McGale & McGale going." She glanced toward the open-walled structure where they made lye. Katie gestured to the barrels as she likely explained the way in which wood ash was boiled with river water to create the lye for their soap.

Noel stood with the rest of the group, listening to Katie. Having him on her family's humble farm ought to feel strange or odd, his elegant figure a stark contrast to the workaday buildings and equipment. And yet it was as though she had been waiting forever for him to come here, and at last, he was in his rightful place.

"Did you . . . ahem." Fred looked at her meaningfully. "With him? For the business?"

Her gaze flew back to her brother. "God, no!" The thought was appalling, churning her stomach. "I'd never."

"That's not what we believed at all." But Cynthia spoke too quickly.

Jess closed her eyes and counted slowly to five. When she felt sufficiently calm, she opened her eyes and said, "I'm getting back to the others to, you know, *legitimately* save our family business." She walked away, her pace sedate and even in case anyone from the Bazaar looked in her direction. When she rejoined the others, she made certain her expression was calm and interested.

As Katie continued to explain how liquid lye was created, Noel leaned close to whisper, "Making mischief behind the scenes?"

"I don't hide my mischief — I do it in

plain sight." She explained in a low voice, "Just a few logistical questions about the post-tour luncheon." She continued to smile at him, hoping he believed her, willing everything to work out. Because it had to. There simply was no other choice.

CHAPTER 21

Throughout the tour, Noel couldn't stop himself from glancing at Jess. The information the McGale siblings presented them was fascinating — Noel used soap daily, but had virtually no idea what the process of making it entailed — yet he found himself looking for her whenever they moved from one step of the procedure to the next.

She watched it all with a careful expression, taking note of everything, listening carefully. She also sent discreet glances toward the Bazaar guests, as if assessing their reaction to the business.

It was only natural — in a way, Jess had been the one to bring McGale & McGale to everyone's attention. Surely she'd be invested in whether or not they agreed with her assessment.

Mostly, though, Noel gazed at Jess because he simply liked to see her. He watched the play of thoughts across her face, and savored the sunlight caught in her hair, and noted a thousand details that he tucked away to revisit and cherish later.

There was a poem he dimly recalled from school. Typical male, the poet had gone on and on, employing every verbal trick in the book so he might get under the lady's skirts. Two lines, though, kept sticking in Noel's head: *But at my back I always hear / Time's wingéd chariot hurrying near.*

Jess was not his forever. Hell, he didn't know if she was his *now.*

"You're aware of what happened four months back," Cynthia McGale said in her broad Wiltshire accent. There was something familiar about the way she spoke, the rhythm of her words, but he could not quite identify what that was.

Cynthia nodded to a heap of charred timber, the grass around it scorched.

"The fire," Noel said.

Fred McGale said grimly, "That building was where lye and rendered fat were combined in the saponification process. Dangerous work."

"That's what caused the fire?" Lady Farris asked.

"There's the rub," Cynthia said. " 'Twas a lightning strike that started the blaze. We all heard it and ran out, me and Fred and —"

She stopped abruptly. "And my other sister."

"But you couldn't save the structure or anything in it," Jess said, her words firm. "Correct, Miss McGale?"

"We lost the building and equipment, my lady," Cynthia said, "and that's why we need you. Because we know that if we got everything back up and running, made a few improvements and had our production volume increased, we'd be a roaring success."

"Which would also be dependent on our investors spreading the word," Fred McGale added. "If people knew about us, they'd want our soap."

"How do you know that for certain?" Lady Haighe asked.

"Because everyone who tries McGale & McGale soap becomes a repeat customer," Cynthia said. "We know this for a fact — and have the record of sales to prove it."

The visitors murmured amongst themselves, and Noel had to admit that what the McGale family offered sounded promising.

"We'd like to see the accounting ledgers," Jess said. "To see how profitable the business was before the fire."

"Our sister — the one who isn't here — kept them," Fred said. "They show McGale

& McGale's profitability when we did have all of our structures and equipment. We would be happy to provide that for you, Your Grace."

"Here they are." Cynthia motioned toward one of the workers, who brought forward two volumes. She handed the books to Noel. "Feel free to look at them during our luncheon, but I'll need both back before you leave today."

"My thanks." He flipped one open to find very thorough auditing of business costs and profits. "Where is your other sister?"

"She's . . ." Fred cleared his throat. "Working. She has been employed off the farm for several months."

"Neither one of us has seen her in some time," Cynthia added.

"Shame," Noel said, returning his attention to the ledger. She'd done a fine job of recording the expenses and revenue. The handwriting looked oddly familiar. He tried to place where he'd seen it, picturing in his mind a woman's hand recording something in a notebook with that same penmanship.

Ah, well. It didn't signify. What *was* of importance was the careful and detailed accounting in the ledger, revealing the sustained profit of the McGale operation.

When everyone had finished examining

the books, they were returned to Cynthia McGale's care.

"Luncheon next, I believe," Jess said.

"Right this way, my lords and ladies," Fred McGale said.

He led the group to a long table that had been set up beneath the branches of an oak. Wildflowers in ceramic jugs were placed at intervals down the middle of the table, and a collection of unmatched plates marked each person's place. Since they were not in a formal setting and he wasn't required to seat himself according to rank, Noel offered Jess a place beside him. She smiled and took the proffered chair.

The McGale siblings and two of the farm's workers brought out platters of simple, homey food, including roast chicken, cucumbers dressed with vinegar, and apples baked in honey-sweetened pastry.

As the sun inched lower in the sky, it cast golden light through the oak leaves, and between having Jess beside him, the mellowness of the mead, and the languid June air in this bucolic place, Noel couldn't recall a more enjoyable day.

Beneath this sense of calm and peace, anticipation sparked through him. He had another night with Jess beneath his roof.

Another night before their time together ran out — but it didn't have to come to an end. Tonight, he'd show her with all the ways he could how much she meant to him.

"My lords and ladies," Cynthia McGale said, holding up her hands, "Your Grace. Thank you all for your visit today. Have you any further questions?"

After a moment, Lady Farris said, "I have none. The moment I return to London, I'll have my man of business prepare the necessary documents."

Mr. Walditch, Mr. Parley, and Baron Mentmore added their own plans to invest. By the time they'd voiced their intentions, the McGales looked as though they were on the verge of joining hands and dancing in a victorious circle.

Even Jess grinned, clearly pleased that she'd guided everyone to a worthwhile venture. He felt it from her, the sense of relief so profound it eased through Noel's own bones.

"Potential is ripe here," Noel said. "I'm in."

"I think this calls for a celebration," Fred said. "More mead, and I baked a honey cake in hopes of this very outcome."

The glasses were all refilled, and moments later, Cynthia came out bearing a large platter with an impressive golden-brown cake. Strawberries and blackberries adorned the top of the cake and encircled its sides. She cut slices for everyone, adding a dollop of whipped cream with the berries.

As everyone ate and drank, contentment gripped Noel. He resisted the urge to stroke his hand down Jess's thigh beneath the table, but he felt her beside him just the same.

Conversation went on, slightly drowsy from the long day and the excellent meal.

Jess stood. "Please don't get up," she said when Noel and the other men began to rise. "I just need a good stretch of my legs before we return to Carriford."

"A walk sounds the very thing, Lady Whitfield," Noel said as he got to his feet. "Machines that get too little use turn rusty."

Together, they strolled away from the table. They took a path past several fields full of growing crops. The air was filled with green scent and the fragrance of rich soil — though he was ignorant of what precisely they grew — and bees droned beneath the late afternoon sky.

A glance behind him confirmed that everyone at the table continued to chat amongst themselves and with the McGales.

Noel reached down and took Jess's hand.

They'd removed their gloves for eating, so their palms pressed snug against each other. Her fingers were like the opening stanzas of a poem he knew by heart.

He stroked his thumb back and forth over hers, her skin soft but not in the same way as most ladies. There was a slight hardiness in the feel of her, as if she did more than pour tea, write letters, and practice at the pianoforte.

"You must feel at home here," he murmured.

She glanced at him. "Why do you say that?"

"You mentioned a rural upbringing. Unless you made that up to hide the fact that you and your jewelthieving family traveled from glamorous city to glamorous city, breaking hearts and stealing precious gems."

"We only turned to stealing so that we might pay for our dear old gran's medical treatments." She guided them off the path and down a sloping hill, where tall grasses brushed against their clothing. When he stiffened at the sound of something rustling in the brush, she said, "Don't worry — there are several mousers at this farm that keep everything rodent-free."

Grateful, he exhaled. "I'm certain Mc-Cameron would give me a roasting if he knew my loathing of mice and rats. An inescapable part of being a soldier, he said. That, and weevils." He shook his head. "No, thank you, kindly."

She made a quiet scoffing noise. "Farm life's not for you, then. Because there's no avoiding a host of wriggling things and creatures with pincers and many, many legs."

They reached the bottom of the hill, and stood on the banks of a cheerful river, water streaming over rocks and gently chuckling. The last strains of daylight played upon the river's surface.

"So, your life wasn't just rural, it was downright agrarian."

"I grew up on a farm," she said after a moment. "There were no glamorous cities or carefully plotted robberies. Just cows and goats and a fair share of manure." She shot him a look. "You wouldn't have liked it."

"Here, now," he said in mock affront, "I once had to wear a woolen waistcoat instead of one made of silk. Never say I'm not adaptable." With his free hand, he stroked a finger along her cheek and then down her neck. Her warm, silken flesh thickened his thoughts far more than any mead they had imbibed.

"Carriford suits you well enough," she

said, leaning into his touch. "Is a farm entirely too rustic?"

He looked behind him at the fields that stood at the top of the slope. "Don't know if I'd make for much of a farmer. But with the right inducement, I'd be willing to try." He stroked across her lower lip, and smiled when she playfully nipped at him. "If it means hayloft trysts with you, then I am certainly amenable."

He regarded her. "On Bond Street, and at the Bazaar, you were in your element. Lady Hawk. I've never seen a woman, no, never seen a *person* so confident and knowledge-able about the world of finance. Surely, I thought, this is where she belongs. This is who she is."

She said nothing, but her gaze was clear and direct.

"Yet here you are, at this farm, and there's something about you, something . . . looser."

"A woman with loose morals?" She lifted a brow.

"The very best kind. But my meaning is that you've got a softness out here, a cen-tered calm I didn't feel in London." He shook his head. "Pay me no regard. I think the smoke-free air has addled my brain so I can only spout nonsense. Which makes me ideally suited for politics."

"You would begin a policy of government-mandated carousing." She squeezed his hand, and an echoing squeeze centered in his chest. "Perhaps I'm Lady Hawk and also the girl from the farm. Perhaps people don't have to be fully one thing or the other. For example, there's you."

"One hundred percent ducal stock, which makes me phenomenally overbred. Unless," he added thoughtfully, "my mother had a wild affair with the groundskeeper — but I doubt it, given that I have my father's eyes, nose, and severe reaction to shellfish."

"That's not what I mean."

"I swell up and itch all over —"

"Noel." She pressed her lips together as if fighting a smile. "Lord Trask warned me about you."

"About my sensitivity to shellfish?" He raised a brow.

She stroked a finger along the base of his thumb. "He said you were a dazzling comet — with the underlying message that you were all flash and fire, with little substance."

"The rotter," Noel said without rancor. "Thank God I'm too indolent to challenge him to a duel."

"But there's deep nuance to you." She stepped closer to him, the distance between their bodies mere inches. "The way you are with your friends, the way you care for them . . . you have a good heart. A wonderful heart."

In a whisper, she said, "And it's softer than you think it is. Perhaps more than you want it to be — but you can't help yourself. You're made the way you're made, and it's beautiful."

His eyes grew hot, and his throat tightened. "Damn," he muttered. "I want to say something, *anything,* that's droll or urbane and" — he swallowed — "and safe."

"You don't need to," she murmured.

"Not with you." He tipped his head forward so that their foreheads touched, as they had last night in the larder. "Because I'm safe with you. I trust you."

Her eyes squeezed shut. "Oh, Noel."

He kissed her. A velvety, slow kiss full of desire and gratitude. Because she'd reached into the very core of him. With her, he was simply himself, just as she was herself, and as his tongue stroked against hers and he tasted her flavors of honey and spice, he sank into the place they created together. A place that was theirs alone.

"Want to lay you down in the grass and have you beneath me," he growled between kisses. "Hot and soft and fierce. I need to be inside you."

"I want you there."

"Tonight."

She pulled back slightly, and a look of pain crossed her face — too quickly for him to be certain that he'd seen it at all. Her eyes opened and he saw focused resolve there. "Midnight. In your bedchamber."

"You'd prefer my room to yours."

"I want to see you in your native habitat."

Ah, she'd kill him with her insight. "It's a bit of a trek."

"One I'll make willingly."

God, how he loved the way she took what she wanted. "Delightful woman. Go all the way down the main corridor, then left, then turn right at the Chinese vase, and I'm the third door on the left. It's somewhat confusing."

"I've an excellent sense of direction. Never more so than when I'm motivated."

They kissed again, mouths open, hearts open. It anchored him and he vowed to himself that this night he would give her everything.

CHAPTER 22

In the end, Jess could not stop herself. It was a mistake, a terrible mistake, but she had to make it. At midnight, she stepped into a pair of slippers, draped a shawl over her shoulders, and left the Gillyflower Room in search of Noel's bedchamber.

Cool air swept around her as she walked, navigating the corridors of the old, rambling house. Darkness surrounded her — she hadn't taken a candle to prevent detection.

Her family and the business were safe. Jess's gamble had worked, and the thought alone was nearly enough to make her run through the countryside, clad only in her nightgown, shouting her relief.

Yet there was a cost. There always was.

In all the ways in which this scenario had taken shape in her imagination, losing her heart to a duke had never entered her mind.

Yet she had, and tonight would be her last night with him before she disappeared from his life forever.

Moonlight spilled into the hallway from tall, diamond-paned windows. Her body moved of its own accord, following a silent call. To him.

Jess paused outside his room. Just beneath the door, light flickered. Her heart leapt into her throat as she raised her hand to tap on the wood.

The door opened before she could make contact with it, revealing Noel. Firelight cast a glow around him, and in his untucked shirt, his waistcoat undone and his coat gone, he was in beautiful disarray. It looked as though he'd dragged his hands through his hair many times as he'd waited for her. Dark stubble emphasized his lips and the angles of his jaw, and his eyes were dark as mystery as he gazed at her.

Her breath caught. He was so beautiful. Even his damned bare feet were beautiful.

He held out a hand to her. She stared at it before sliding her palm into his.

Gently, firmly, he tugged her inside. He shut the door behind her. Locked it.

As she leaned against the door, he stepped close to her. His chest brushed against hers, and he cupped his hands around her hips. Their rough breaths mingled in the narrow space between them.

"Wasn't certain you were coming," he said, his voice low and sonorous.

She closed her eyes as the heat of him penetrated every last corner of her being. "I'm here now. For tonight. And then —"

"No need to speak of *then*. Let's have *now*. Jess." He growled her name as he brought up one of his hands to cradle her jaw. A man with such large hands should not have been able to touch her with this reverence, yet he did. He tilted her face up.

She lifted onto her toes and, wrapping her hands around the back of his neck, brought her mouth to his. Their lips opened to each other. They kissed long and deep, each stroke of their tongues urging need higher. It was a kiss that felt both familiar and astonishingly new, as though she'd crossed a doorway she had walked through a thousand times, to find not an expected comfortable room, but a chamber of wonders.

Her breasts grew tight and sensitive, her nipples firming into points that brushed against the unyielding expanse of his chest. His hips pressed into hers, and she was branded by the length of his arousal as it curved along her belly. Instinctively, she rocked against him. Small flares of pleasure lit inside her.

"Been hungering for you all day," he

growled. "Wanted to carry you off into the fields and fuck you beneath the sun."

She made a low, needful sound, because she wanted that, too. "Tell me what you want now."

"You. In all the ways I can have you." He reached up and threaded his fingers with hers. "Tell me what to do. Command me."

Without relinquishing their hold on each other, she pushed against his hands, putting a small distance between them.

"You want my commands?" At his nod, she said haughtily, "Show me your cock. Take it out."

His nostrils flared and his jaw went taut — with arousal.

He took his hands from hers, and they trembled slightly as he worked the fastenings of his breeches to free his straining erection. It was thick and full and reached upward in a luscious curve. Already a tiny bead of moisture glossed the slit.

"Here's my cock, Jess," he growled. "Hard and aching. What shall I do with it? Order me to fuck you."

"Not yet. Touch it. Let me see your hand stroking yourself." The command was outrageous and deeply arousing to speak, but saying the words was nothing compared to watching him wrap his fingers around his shaft and pump. "Look at me while you do it."

His gaze flew to hers, infinitely dark. Watching his face contort with pleasure brought slick heat between her legs and made her breasts heavy.

"What pace?" he rumbled. "I could fist my cock slowly, imagining I'm deliberately plunging deep into you. Or I could go hard and quick, pretending I'm fucking you in a frenzy."

God, how could she keep standing when he spoke to her like this? "Slowly. I want to watch you bring yourself close to coming. But you aren't to come, do you understand? Do not let yourself climax."

She looked down to see how his length grew longer, and seemed to fill his hand even more.

"You will kill me," he said hoarsely.

"You won't die. But," she added with a sly smile, "you'll come close."

"I need something from you first." He released the hold on his cock and brought his palm up to her lips. "Lick."

Her knees nearly buckled as she ran her tongue over his hand. There was a hint of salt and musk on his skin, the flavor so delicious she moaned. With his gaze holding hers, he fisted his cock. His strokes went smoother now that she'd provided lubrication, and the cords of his neck stood out as he stroked himself.

"Fuck," he snarled. "I need to come."

"Not. Yet. If you feel yourself on the verge, you must stop."

His hand stilled, and his chest rose and fell with harsh, ragged breaths. He'd never looked more aroused, and she certainly had never *felt* more aroused. If she was to touch herself, not only would she find herself soaking wet, but she'd climax with a single stroke.

A moment went by, and then another. His breath slowed.

"Touch yourself again," she demanded. "Slowly. You must go slowly."

An animal sound rose up from him. "Yes, Jess."

He pumped into his hand, and she loved every moment of it, seeing this powerful man bend to *her* will, working himself into a haze of agonizing pleasure because it was what *she* decreed.

"I'm close," he panted after several more strokes.

"Stop."

Even as he groaned, his hand froze. He truly was hers to command. And he gave her that power over him.

"Good. Very good."

"Jess." He bowed his head, then looked up through his lashes. "Please, I ask you to . . ." He swallowed hard. "Suck my cock."

Torrential heat poured through her. She hadn't known that mere words could bring her to the very precipice of her own release, and yet his did.

"Go." She pointed to a wingback chair beside the fire. Only then did she take in the details of his bedchamber — its dark wooden paneled walls, the heavy but ornately carved escritoire and clothespress, and the massive four-post bed that dominated the room. It suited the lord of the manor. It suited him. "Strip, then sit there, and I will show you what wicked servants get when they make demands of their mistresses."

Noel pulled off his shirt so quickly he thought he heard it tear. His breeches followed, and then he was nude.

She was still clothed. The difference in their state of dress — him, completely exposed, while she had not revealed any part of herself — whipped his excitement into a fury.

He strode to the chair and lowered himself down. His cock was like a second heartbeat, so hard and aching as it angled upward toward his navel. He'd never delayed his release like this, and the pain and pleasure of it was beyond measure.

She walked to him, her head back, and in her finely woven nightgown, with her hair loose about her shoulders, she looked like an elfin queen ready to command her armies.

"Hold the armrests," she instructed him.

He obeyed, clutching them so tightly his knuckles went white. And then he held his breath as she slowly lowered herself to her knees and licked her lips.

Noel was forced to squeeze his eyes shut, because the picture she presented — preparing herself to take his cock in her mouth — brought him close to climax. Then he realized something, and he opened his eyes again.

"A moment." He pulled a cushion from behind him, and slid it under her knees.

She bestowed him with a grateful smile. "Thoughtful."

"I live only to serve you."

She inclined her head in gratitude, then instructed, "Hands back on the armrests."

He obeyed, panting as if he ran full speed across the rolling fields, and hissed as she wrapped her fingers around his cock.

"Mm," she murmured. "Beautiful." She lowered her head and licked the crown.

"Fuck." His voice came from somewhere deep and dark. And then he didn't know any more words as she took him in her mouth. She bobbed up and down, her tongue swirling around his shaft.

She lifted her head enough to speak. "Who gave you permission to be silent? Talk to me. Tell me what you feel. If you don't, I'll stop sucking you."

"*Please* don't stop." He loved begging her. "I'll do anything you wish."

"Then talk."

"I love your mouth. I love the look of it. The — *fuck yes* — feel of it." As he spoke, his words barely more than growls, she took him back into her mouth. "All that wet heat. The velvet of your tongue on my cock. Sucking me. *Good God.*" She swirled around the head of his cock, timing the strokes of her hand on his shaft with her licks. "Just want to — *Christ.*"

"Want to what?" she murmured between strokes.

"I want to hold your head and pump into your mouth."

Her gaze heavy lidded, she pried one of his hands from the armrest and placed it on the back of her head. His heartbeat raced at the feel of her hair against his palm, and what it meant.

"I give you permission," she said regally. "Fuck my mouth."

He swore again, and once more when she positioned the crown of his cock between her lips. Then any attempt at keeping himself in check burned away, and he thrust his hips up, plunging into her mouth. They both held her steady as he did what she commanded. She dug her fingers into his thigh, urging him to use her as he wanted — though they both knew it was she who held all the power.

Pleasure built, gathering low and spreading through him in a web of fire. His release loomed and he tried to pull back, tried to take himself from her mouth.

"Jess," he rasped. "Going to come."

Yet she remained where she was, and tightened his hand on her head.

God above, was she truly going to let him —

His climax ripped from him. Wave after wave of ecstasy slammed his body after the release he'd been denied finally broke free. His back arched and he groaned, his entire body going rigid with the force of his orgasm. And she took it. She swallowed him, never pulling back until he gave up the last of his seed.

"My God, Jess . . ."

She'd completely ensnared him. He was hers, for all time.

He could not find words. They seemed so small and confining, when what he felt was beyond language.

Carefully, he eased her back enough so he could stand. His legs were unsteady, yet they held strong enough for him to gather her up in his arms and carry her to the bed. Tenderly, he laid her down, taking note of how her thighs shifted against each other, and the stiff tips of her breasts beneath the cambric she still wore.

He stroked his hands up her ankles, her calves, and then he snared the hem of her nightgown. "May I?"

She nodded, and in an instant, the garment was gone. He tossed it to the floor as she kicked off her slippers. At last she was naked, in his bed.

"You're so goddamned beautiful," he muttered. "So soft and curved. My hands were made to touch you. May I touch you?"

"Yes. Noel, yes."

His hands discovered all of her, from the roundness of her belly to the indentation of her waist, to the silk of her breasts and taut nipples. And she was responsive, so responsive, writhing and moaning as he touched her. She was lovely in her pleasure — incredibly, he began to harden again, even after his devastating orgasm.

"I want to fuck you again," he growled as he brought his lips to her stomach. "But first I want you to come on my tongue. Do you want that, too?"

"I want that." Her words were gasps. "Want you."

He grazed his fingers over her mound, and her thighs parted as he found her slit. "My beautiful Jess. You're incredibly wet."

She glossed his fingers with her desire. He stroked her, fingering the delicate folds, and when he circled her clitoris with his thumb and slipped two fingers into her passage, she bowed up with a cry.

"I can't wait anymore." He lowered his head and licked her. He groaned as her flavor filled him, honey and spice. She was lovely everywhere, and he loved this part of her, so he showed her with rough reverence how grateful he was to be given the honor of pleasuring her. He used all of his skill, strategic licks and sucks and even gentle nibbles. All the while, he thrust his fingers in and out. The exquisite place within her was swollen, and he curved his fingers to stroke over it. When he sucked her clitoris between his lips, she clutched his head to her — a reversal that he adored.

She cried out and went rigid, grinding herself against him as she came. He happily drowned in her. The moment her body relaxed, he flicked his tongue over her bud again, his fingers working her relentlessly. He adored the sound of her climaxing again.

By the time he'd brought her to another orgasm, his cock was as hard as if he hadn't had release in months, not minutes.

"Noel," she commanded hoarsely.

"You want my cock in you?"

"Now."

He climbed fully onto the bed and lay back, tugging on her hands. "Ride me, my lady."

Her whole body was flushed and pink and wonderfully supple as she clambered atop him. She straddled his hips, and he guided his cock to her entrance. With her gaze holding his, she sank down onto him, impaling herself. She moaned. "Oh, God."

He gripped her hips as she held tightly to his shoulders, then she did as he'd asked. She rode him. Hard. Her hips slammed against his, and he surged up to meet her. It was rough and relentless. He watched his cock disappear into her, then dragged his gaze up to her face. She had her head thrown back, her eyes closed, her mouth open as she mewled with each stroke.

Her fingers gripped him, her body tensing as she gasped another climax.

As the last waves seemed to leave her, he moved quickly, arranging their bodies so that she was on her hands and knees as he knelt behind her. "Yes?"

"Yes," she rasped.

He drove into her in a single thrust. She pushed back into each pump of his hips, and he was lost. Being inside her was the greatest pleasure he'd ever known, and he wanted it to last forever. It would not be long, though, before he had to spill.

He brought one of his hands around her hips. His fingers found her clitoris, circling it, rubbing against her sensitive flesh as he fucked her steadily.

"Oh, God," she gasped. "I —" She let out a long, full-throated moan of release.

A moment later, he pulled out. He grunted as his entire being was suffused with pleasure, and his seed shot from him.

She collapsed onto the bed. He grabbed a cloth from the washstand and cleaned her, before setting the fabric aside. He lowered down beside her, and then, sated, exhausted, exhilarated, he gathered her up in his arms. She snuggled against him, her breath soft and warm against his chest.

"How?" he murmured. "How does it keep getting better and better?"

"No idea," she said drowsily. "But it does."

Time slipped away and he couldn't stop it. He had power over so many things in life, but not that. Having her in his arms now, he could not imagine the nights ahead where his arms held only his memories of her. He needed her as he needed sunshine. Existing in permanent grayness was possible — but she would bring brightness and joy.

"You should see this place in the winter," he murmured. "Sometimes it snows — not abundantly, but enough to cover everything with sparkling diamonds."

"How marvelous."

"It is, rather." He rubbed his lips over the crown of her head. "My friends, the Union — this is a place for us. When we were younger, wilder —"

"*This* is a tamer version of you?" She shot him a wry look.

"Quiet, madam, or I will hold you down and fuck you with my mouth until you scream yourself hoarse."

"I fail to see how that's supposed to deter me."

He nipped at her shoulder. "As I was saying before a saucy minx interrupted me, I bring my close friends here, but no one else."

"Yet you opened your doors to the Bazaar."

"I opened my doors to *you*," he amended. "They happened to come along. That happens often — crowds gather around me. Always more and more people."

Leaning on her elbow, she propped her head on her hand. "You're a popular man. Everyone wants to bask in your radiance."

He lay on his back to stare at the canopy. "Everyone wants something from me. They've told me whatever I wanted to hear, stuffed me with falsehoods and pretty fabrications, all to advance themselves. It's been that way since . . ." He mulled it over. "Since always."

"Sounds lonely."

"Sometimes." He turned his head to look at her. "I've got Rowe and Curtis and McCameron and Holloway — you haven't met him yet. They're genuine. In twenty years, they've never once fed me beautiful lies." He snorted. "Can't dine forever on untruths. You feel full, but you wind up starving to death."

"It's an empty diet," she said softly.

"That's why I don't stomach it anymore. I

used to, but the older I became, the less acceptance I had for it. The deceivers and the lying sycophants have no place in my life. I don't have to endure that kind of dishonesty." He captured her hand with his own and brought it to his lips. "There's nothing to endure with you. Every moment with you is the best I've known. I know you, Jess. I trust you. With everything."

Now is the time. She had to feel how his heart sped up as he spoke the words he had never said before. "I have feelings for you, Jess. Strong feelings. I don't want you to go to the Continent." He held her steady with his gaze. "Stay here, with me."

Her soft, loose-limbed body stiffened. The moment he felt the change in her, icy fear stole through him. That fear grew and became monstrous as she disentangled herself from his embrace.

She rose from the bed. Lifting himself up on his elbows, he watched her as she hunted down her nightgown and drew it on. Her face was a tight mask and she blinked hard, as if chasing away tears.

"Jess?"

"I —" She grabbed her shawl and threw it over her shoulders. When she finally met his gaze, her eyes were tormented, and her lower lip trembled.

Remorse. That was what he saw in her face. A scouring sorrow that took the beautiful pleasure they'd made and turned it into something ashen and cold.

She dashed her knuckles across her eyes. "I can't, Noel. I can't —"

Then she was gone, fleeing so quickly she barely had time to close the door behind her. Alone, naked, stripped bare of everything that had once protected him, Noel lay back in his vast, empty bed and stared at the canopy overhead.

What have I done?

CHAPTER 23

"I can't speak for you," Lady Haighe said as she and Jess waited in the foyer while their luggage was loaded onto the carriage. "But I will be exceedingly happy to return to London today. Mind, His Grace's house is lovely, and portrait-perfect Wiltshire farms are delightful — but there's not enough to gossip about in the country."

Jess attempted a smile. Weariness made her bones heavy as iron — she'd been unable to sleep — and she felt ready to break apart at the slightest touch. "I'm certain you've missed nothing of importance while we've been away."

"Let us hope so." Lady Haighe sniffed. "It is *so* dull out of the city."

Jess couldn't agree. In the two nights that she had been away from London, her life had careened between exalted heights and profound lows. She pressed a hand to her throbbing head. Lack of sleep always gave her a headache, and now was no exception.

"Still waiting?"

Nerves alight, Jess turned at the sound of Noel's voice. He descended the front stairs, and in his elegant traveling clothing, with his freshly shaven face and artfully tousled hair, he was every inch the polished, perfect duke. One would never know from looking at him that only eight hours ago he'd been begging her for sexual release, or that he'd pleasured her with his mouth until she'd thought she would perish from ecstasy.

This morning, she learned that she could be both anguished and aroused at the same time.

She tried not to flinch from his searching gaze as he reached the foyer. What could she tell him? She wished from the very depths of her soul that she could say, *I have feelings for you, too. I want to stay with you.* Because she did. She wished so much it was a steady agony beneath her skin.

He deserved to hear those words spoken to him. But he couldn't — not from her. Not when she didn't deserve his adoration or his company.

"Mr. Vale said it would be only a few more minutes until we were ready to leave." Somehow, she managed to speak levelly. "He offered for everyone to finish their breakfasts at leisure. Lady Haighe seemed especially eager to get our journey under-way, so I opted to keep her company as she waited out here." Also, for Jess, the prospect of eating was entirely impossible.

Noel offered Lady Haighe an easy smile. But Jess saw the tiny lines bracketing his mouth, and, upon closer inspection, there were shadows beneath his eyes. She'd done that — cost him his peace because of her deception.

He said, "Eager to return to London's bustle, Lady Haighe?"

"There's a decided lack of scandal in the country." The older woman harrumphed.

Jess's gaze automatically found Noel's, remembering their words to each other. She'd never forget the sight of him stroking himself at her command.

"Although," Lady Haighe added slyly, "things were emphatically more interesting for the younger set. Isn't that so, Lady Whit-field?"

Jess cleared her throat. "I wouldn't know."

"If she doesn't know," Lady Haighe said pointedly to Noel, "then you didn't do your job properly."

"I'm an excellent host," he answered.

"Beg pardon, Your Grace," Gregory said as he approached. "Before you return to

London, I hoped we could review a few more estate matters in the study."

"I'll be there momentarily." Noel bowed. "Excuse me, my ladies."

Once they were alone, Lady Haighe studied Jess. "Are you all right, my gel?"

"Why shouldn't I be?"

"Because," Lady Haighe said, stroking a hand down Jess's cheek, "you look on the verge of noisy tears. Which seems out of character. Did he hurt you?" Her expression hardened. "If he did, I don't care if he's a ruddy duke. I'll plant my knee in his bollocks."

"That's very kind of you." Jess rubbed her knuckles against her eyes, forcing back the very tears that Lady Haighe had noticed. "There's no blame for Noel — I mean, His Grace. It's all my doing." She could say no more, but the urge to confess everything pushed at her. "He's a good man. A wonderful man."

"And you care for him."

"I do." This was wonderful and exhilarating and so painful that she couldn't seem to catch her breath.

"Have you told him?" Lady Haighe asked. Jess shook her head. "I can't."

"Why not?" the older woman demanded. "His affection for you is clear. And you couldn't be more plain if you wore a sign on your chest and rang a bell in the midday square. So, it's established. You both adore each other. Nothing else is relevant."

"Things are exceptionally complicated." Which was a very mild way of saying that if Noel knew the truth about her, who she was and what her purpose for being at the Bazaar was, everything would collapse in an unsalvageable heap. If she told him every-thing, if he understood that she had lied to him throughout their time together, her family's business could be ruined. Yet if she said nothing, what she and Noel had to-gether would be predicated on a lie. Eventu-ally he would find out, bringing her right back to where she started. He'd be furious. Brokenhearted. Rightly so.

If she *was* honest with him, and if by some miracle he still invested in McGale & McGale, she didn't know if his feelings for her would be strong enough to continue. Could he care enough for her to see past her deception, and past his anger that was sure to come?

She was strapped into an iron maiden, waiting for the spiked door to shut.

"Child." Lady Haighe took Jess's chin between her thumb and forefinger in a grip that was astonishingly strong. "We've one

350

certainty in life. Death comes for all of us. It doesn't care who we are or what good or evil we've brought to the world. We all turn to dust."

"That's rather grim."

"It *is*. Which is why I'm telling you that when you have a chance at something as rare as love, you *take that chance.*" Lady Haighe smiled sadly. "I found love, but because I was a scared girl, and because his skin was the wrong color for my family, I took the safe chance and married someone else, but the one who'd captured my heart . . ." The widow sighed. "He walked away. Found himself a lovely wife and they've gone on to have a beautiful family."

Lady Haighe released her hold on Jess to wipe at the sheen gathered in her eyes. "He found love and happiness again. And I've led a good life, but it's been one without him. So listen to me, and listen well. You and His Grace have forged a rare bond. Don't smash it apart because you were too afraid."

Jess swallowed as gratitude swelled, though she still didn't know what she ought to do. "Thank you."

The widow raised an imperious brow. "And if you ever tell anyone I was tender-hearted toward you, I will deny it vehemently. I've a reputation to uphold."

"Naturally."

Lady Haighe glanced out the window beside the front door. She clicked her tongue. "Are they still loading the bloody carriages? How dull country life is." The widow opened the door and strode out. "Are we leaving or do we plan on growing roots in the Hampshire soil?"

Jess turned a slow circle as she stood alone in the foyer. She took in all the details of this room in Carriford, from its wooden paneled walls to the parquet floor, to the portraits of ancestors and several dogs — deerhounds. It was a wonderful house. Some fortunate woman would marry Noel and come here with their children and they'd have golden days and velvet nights.

That woman wasn't her.

She knew this because she understood that no matter what, she had to tell Noel everything. He deserved it. He might pull his investment from McGale & McGale, and demand that the others withdraw in solidarity, but that was a chance she had to take.

Once he learned the truth, he'd want nothing more to do with her. She would be banished from the kingdom of his heart, and spend the rest of her life in exile, with only the memory of the last few days to keep her company.

Conversation in the carriage for the return journey was minimal. It seemed everyone was worn thin, between the Bazaar and the trip out to Wiltshire.

Jess stared out the window as the carriage drove away to preserve Carriford's image in her memory.

Her gaze moved to Noel. Tension ripened between them, heavy almost to bursting. But they couldn't speak candidly in front of Lady Haighe and Lord Pickhill, leaving the air thick with everything unsaid.

She'd bolted last night, and he'd been so open, so vulnerable. She'd repaid his courage with cowardice. But that would come to an end once they reached London.

Jess rehearsed what she would say to him, yet all the words she grasped seemed too clumsy to express how much he'd come to mean to her. It would be wrong and manipulative to tell him of her deception, then follow up with a declaration of her feelings. Emotions weren't to be used like weapons or traps, hurting or ensnaring someone.

Noel had donned his ducal mask, appearing as unruffled as if he'd been sitting in his favorite chair at Brooks's.

Lord Pickhill broke the silence. "Almost forgot that the Season's still going strong. We've a few more weeks of assemblies and balls and God only knows what before we can rest for the duration of the summer." He chuckled. "There's to be a ball tonight at the Earl and Countess of Ashford's home. There aren't many from the Bazaar who were invited, but you must be, Your Grace."

"I'm obliged to attend," Noel said. "Been trying to coordinate my schedule with Ashford and the ball's the only opportunity we'll have to speak to one another about a bill he'd like to sponsor."

"Surely *you* will attend, as well, Lady Whitfield," Lord Pickhill pressed. "There will be an abundance of men of marriageable age who will be delighted by a pretty widow such as yourself." When she didn't answer, he added, "You *do* intend to marry again, do you not?"

She felt Noel's focus on her, but she kept her attention on Lord Pickhill.

"I am not marrying."

Silence fell as tight as a knife against the throat.

Finally, Lord Pickhill coughed. "The roads are good this time of year, at least. Don't you think so, Lady Haighe?"

"No one cares about the state of the

roads, Pickhill," Lady Haighe answered. "But," she continued, when he deflated, "I'll be happy to talk about horse racing. The Meloy family's supposed to breed and train the best horseflesh in England."

Lord Pickhill seized the topic and said with forced brightness, "I saw one of their stallions race not long ago. Magnificent creature."

The conversation continued, yet Jess paid it no heed. She was aware only of the tension emanating from Noel, and how her own body felt strung taut to the point of snapping.

It was a very long ride back to London. The miles ticked by, and anxiety climbed. Thank God she wore gloves to keep her fingernails from digging trenches in her palms. As it was, her hands ached from being clenched for hours.

Signposts on the city's outskirts announced their imminent arrival. And then they were in London proper.

Noel had given his carriage drivers directions to each of his guests' homes because they were not going straight to Rotherby House. Instead, the carriages containing the guests, their servants, and their baggage stopped at each person's residence. The route must have been planned at Carriford, because it became evident that Jess would be the last guest delivered to their doorstep.

They said goodbye to Lord Pickhill, and then Lady Haighe, and then, abruptly, Jess was alone in the carriage with Noel. But the vehicle didn't move.

She blinked at him, words drying up as her heart pounded so hard surely he had to hear it.

"I need to tell my coachman your direction," Noel said flatly. "However, I don't know where you live."

"Number eighteen, Hill Street." It was, in fact, four doors down from Lady Catherton's actual address, but she didn't want him to know where she resided and potentially speak to anyone who knew she was not, in fact, a baronet's widow.

Noel relayed the information to the footman, who in turn passed the address on to the coachman, as well as the driver of the second coach that carried Jess's maid. And then they were off again. It would be a short ride, less than five minutes.

Now. Tell him now.

But every time she opened her mouth, no words came out. It was as if she'd exhausted all her supply of language. All the speeches she'd planned on the ride from Carriford were gone. Noel returned to his tense silence, so nothing was said.

The carriage came to a stop. She glanced out the window to see that they'd arrived at their fictitious destination. From her vantage, she could see the town house where she actually resided. She heard the sounds of her trunk being taken down from the second carriage, and her abigail speaking with the driver.

Jess had to do it. Had to tell him the truth, and suffer the consequences.

A familiar carriage came to a stop farther up the street. A footman jumped down and opened the vehicle's door. He reached forward to help out the carriage's occupant.

It was Lady Catherton.

Here. Now.

She'd arrived at her house without any notice.

"Jess — ?"

Dragging her gaze back to Noel, she blurted, "I can't see you again. I'm sorry, Noel. I'm so terribly sorry."

His expression blanked, as though she'd shot him in the center of his chest and he could not comprehend how the bullet had lodged between his ribs. "I —"

"Please," she begged. "I can't say more. I have to go."

She leapt from the carriage and shut the

door behind her before he could say anything. "Drive on," she hissed at the coachman.

"Don't," Noel said. He appeared in the carriage window. "Jess, no. Not like this."

"It has to be," she said desperately. "I'm leaving. That can't be changed. You'll forget me, and . . . and I want you to."

The confusion in Noel's gaze iced into angry hurt. His jaw firmed. "I see."

She wouldn't allow herself the luxury of tears. Instead, she said to the coachman, "Drive, for God's sake."

"Your Grace?" the servant asked.

"You heard her," Noel intoned. Not a hint of emotion or affect in his voice. "No reason to linger."

He sat back, disappearing into the carriage, then the vehicle rolled forward.

Throat aching, Jess saw that Lady Catherton hobbled slowly up the front step of her town house, her pace slowed by the silver-tipped cane in her hand.

Jess turned to Nell standing beside the trunk. "Your services are no longer needed. I will pay you the balance of your salary as soon as you help me carry my baggage inside. We must move quickly." She grabbed one handle of the trunk. "We'll use the back entrance."

The maid frowned, but took the other handle. Together, they carried the trunk down the street. As they passed Lady Catherton's house, the lady herself navigating the front stoop, Jess made sure to duck her head and hope that the brim of her bonnet hid her face.

"Miss McGale!" Lady Catherton called into the open door. "Miss McGale, where are you?"

"Hurry," Jess urged Nell. They turned into the mews.

Sweat slicked down Jess's back as she and her abigail awkwardly muscled the luggage down the low steps leading to the servants' entrance.

A footman opened the door. He looked puzzled as he glanced between the trunk and Jess.

"Take this up," she said to him. "Immediately."

"Yes, miss." He hefted the trunk into his arms and moved into the house.

"And this is for you." Jess set a stack of coins in Nell's hand. "Plus a bit extra for your assistance."

The abigail tucked the coins into her reticule. "Will you provide a character?"

Jess grimaced. "I can't even provide a character for myself. My apologies." She hurried inside.

She raced through the kitchen and then up the stairs. As she ran, she heard Lady Catherton calling again, her voice echoing in the foyer. "Miss McGale! Oh, is that my trunk?"

Oh, no.

Jess sped down the corridor. She came to an abrupt halt in the foyer, slapping a smile onto her aching, tight face, and blinking away the sweat that trickled into her eyes.

Lady Catherton looked at her as she stood beside the trunk that Jess had used for her trip to the country.

"My lady." She dipped into a curtsy, barely managing to keep from tipping over. "What a pleasure to see you so soon."

Lady Catherton's normally porcelain forehead pleated in perplexity. "You're usually so prompt, Miss McGale. Goodness, you look like you've been racing up and down the garden."

"Because . . ." Jess coughed. "Because I have. I read somewhere that a little physical exertion has been proven to maintain one's health. Must keep myself in good form to better serve you." She patted her chest. "There. Healthy as a plowhorse." She cleared her throat. "This is an unexpected arrival."

"I sent word two days ago. I wrote I was feeling better and my physician deemed me fit to travel and then depart for the Continent. Didn't you get my letter?"

Jess's gaze shot to the side table and the platter atop it. A missive bearing her name, written in Lady Catherton's hand, rested on the platter. Jess snatched it from the table and crumpled it in her hand, trying to hide the evidence that she hadn't been home to receive it.

"Oh, yes, the letter! Of course! I meant I didn't expect you at this *hour.* You must've made good time, with accommodating roads."

Lady Catherton peered at her. "What are you doing in my clothing?"

"Most of my garments were damaged in transit," Jess improvised, "so I'd been relying on the same gown for the past fortnight. To make matters worse, your trunks were accidentally put into storage before I could unpack them. Your letter explaining your injury came before I'd fetched the trunks." She went on, "I'd intended to get the trunks out, but there had been so many matters that required my attention, I hadn't had the opportunity. It's been so hectic, you know."

"If my trunks were in storage, why are you in *my* dress?"

361

"I inadvertently packed one of your gowns in with my own clothing, and it was one of the few garments in my bag that wasn't damaged. So while I have been repairing my own clothing, I'd no choice but to wear your gown. I apologize that it's a little rumpled, but I've been wearing it for several days in a row — with clean linen beneath, of course."

She didn't explain that she'd just been in a ducal carriage for several hours, instead gesturing toward the trunk that sat on the foyer floor. "Here's one of your trunks now, finally retrieved from storage. Have it brought to Lady Catherton's room," she said to the waiting footman. "Her maid will air out her garments."

"Yes, miss." The servant bowed and carried the trunk upstairs.

Lady Catherton tilted her head. "Things appear to be in chaos, Miss McGale. That is unlike you. Are you all right?"

"Apologies, my lady. Your time here in London will be smooth and without incident." *God, I hope that's true.*

"Where is my correspondence?" Lady Catherton asked.

"I have it collected in your dressing room."

Her mistress gave a nod. "Do join me in my bedchamber in ten minutes. In the interim, be so kind as to take off my clothing and wear one of your own garments."

With that, Lady Catherton slowly ascended the stairs with the help of another footman.

Jess waited until her mistress had reached the next story before she turned and raced down the hallway to the servants' stairs. She took the steps two at a time. The moment she reached her room, she flung her bonnet to the floor and struggled out of her spencer and gown — no easy feat without a maid to assist her. As she dragged on one of her own plain dresses, Noel's face kept appearing in her mind, his confusion and then pain. Agony threatened to drag her down, but she had no time for it now. There was only survival.

She splashed water on her face and rubbed it nearly raw with a towel. After attempting to smooth her now-disheveled hair into a somewhat demure bun, she glanced at herself in the tiny mirror above her washstand.

A wild-eyed woman stared back at her. One who didn't know what the next minute would bring.

The little clock on her mantel showed that Jess had but a moment before she was due in Lady Catherton's room.

Jess bent down and, with a wince, tore the hem of her dress to give credence to her story about her clothing being damaged. She was careful, however, to ensure that the tear could be easily repaired. There wasn't money to buy anything new, since the extra money Lady Catherton had sent her had gone into paying Nell.

She headed from her cramped little bedchamber to her employer's expansive suite of rooms. Her feet kept speeding up and she forced them into a sedate pace. After collecting herself outside the door to her mistress's bedroom, she knocked.

"Enter," Lady Catherton said.

Jess did so.

Lady Catherton had installed herself in a chair by the fire as her maid scurried around the room. She glanced toward her dressing table. "My correspondence, if you please. Go through it and tell me what you find."

"Yes, my lady." After a week of openly stating her mind, speaking so humbly stuck in Jess's throat. She swallowed around her aching pride and picked up the large stack of letters.

For several minutes, she read aloud the names of the correspondents. To each name, Lady Catherton would reply either "Skip" or "Read."

Finally, Jess read, " 'The Earl and Countess of Ashford.' " Why did that name sound familiar?

"Read."

Jess broke the wafer and unfolded the single sheet of paper. " 'Your presence is requested on the evening of the twelfth of June for a ball —' " She frowned. "That's tonight."

Lady Catherton said to her maid, "Make certain that you air out my yellow silk, and press it. I'll also want —"

"Apologies, my lady, do you mean to attend?"

Lady Catherton frowned as if confused by Jess's bewilderment. "I do. And I know you'll wear your finest dress, though if it has been damaged, it might require some repair." She turned to her maid. "I'll want the pearl-and-diamond earbobs, and —"

"I'm coming with you?"

Her mistress held up her walking stick, looking at her injury with frustration. "This blasted ankle ensures that I cannot move quickly or indeed much at all. I'll need you beside me to fetch refreshments and bring guests to me."

"I see." Jess had accompanied Lady Catherton to smaller assemblies in the country, but nothing on the scale of an actual ball given by an actual earl and countess.

She stiffened as realization struck her. *Please, no.*

The Earl and Countess of Ashford were the hosts of the same ball Noel would attend.

Jess pressed a hand to her throat, and made several strangled sounds.

"Something ailing you?" Lady Catherton asked.

"As it happens," Jess said in a raspy voice, "I have a touch of the grippe. It would be best if I stayed home tonight."

"Unfortunately, I cannot spare you. The earl and countess rarely entertain, and I fully intend to be there. Afterward, you can go straight to bed with some broth."

Panic clutched at Jess, truly squeezing her throat tight. "I can arrange for someone else to accompany you."

"Miss McGale." Lady Catherton fixed her with a level stare. "I consider myself a relatively tolerant person, but I must point out that I pay you to be my companion, and so I have to insist that you accompany me tonight. Now I will rest, and when I wake, I will take supper. After that, I will dress for the Ashfords' ball. We will depart here at nine o'clock."

There was no choice in the matter. Jess

had to accompany her employer to the earl and countess's home — where Noel would also be.

Under other circumstances, she would have looked forward to finally attending a London ball. Even better would be seeing Noel dressed in his evening finery. Surely he would be a magnificent sight.

At the thought of trying to keep him from Lady Catherton, and the possibility that he might learn the truth about her identity, all she felt was dark, smothering dread.

CHAPTER 24

Noel launched himself from his desk chair. He'd tried to review the mountain of documents and letters that had amassed in such a short amount of time. There were plans for a mill he intended to refurbish on his Lincolnshire estate, and several letters relating to the bill he intended to discuss with Ashford that night.

While his gaze moved over the words, he took none of them in. Everything might as well be written in Aramaic.

He scooped a sheaf of papers into his arms and stalked to the fireplace. The hell with it. He'd burn the lot.

"Excuse me, Your Grace," his butler said from the doorway. "Mr. Holloway is here. Are you at home to visitors?"

Had it been anyone other than a member of the Union of the Rakes, Noel would have sent them away without a second thought. But he *was* one of the Union, and that gave him automatic entry into Noel's home. Besides, Noel needed distraction, and cerebral Holloway's wisdom was welcome.

"Send him in."

"Yes, Your Grace."

Noel stomped back to his desk and dumped the papers onto its surface. He then went to a table and poured out two whiskeys. Holloway had always been an aficionado of fine spirits, and while his financial fortune — and personal happiness — had improved since marrying an earl's daughter, he still didn't indulge often in expensive liquor.

Holloway strode into the study.

"What good fortune that I happened to enter just as you poured yourself two drinks," Holloway said, taking the offered glass. "Two-handed drinking is never a good strategy, Rotherby."

"I'm reevaluating that statement as we speak." Noel sipped at his whiskey. It burned, but not enough.

Holloway studied him. Noel stared right back as he did his best not to squirm beneath his friend's examination, but it was ruddy hard when the perceptive Holloway had Noel within his sights.

"It's a woman," Holloway said at last.

"It's not," Noel answered.

Holloway snorted. "The very fact that you immediately deny it proves without a doubt that it's a woman. But then," he mused after taking a sip, "it never has been a woman before, so I've nothing to base my hypothesis on except instinct. Still, I'm almost entirely certain that the downward cast of your mouth and your rigid shoulders indicate that you're brooding because of a woman."

"My shoulders aren't rigid." Noel loosened them. But . . . "Goddamn it, you're right." He turned away from his friend and walked to the row of bookshelves lining one wall. He read the titles but absorbed none of it.

"Up until very recently," Holloway said, coming to stand beside him, "I was the last person to give anyone advice about women, especially you."

Noel shrugged. The fact that he'd often had someone to share his bed reflected nothing about who he was as a person.

"She was a damned surprise," he muttered.

"A good surprise? Or an unwelcome one?"

"Started out good. Very good. Now it's a goddamned misery."

"Ah." Holloway rocked back on his heels, his gaze roaming upward. "Most cultures have group celebrations for matrimonial unions, and some societies even ritualize less formal pairings. But not many have traditions when those unions fragment. Which is a shame — broken hearts must be suffered alone."

Noel gripped his glass tightly. "Soon after I'd become the duke, I had renovations done on this place."

"I remember. Scaffolding everywhere, and the sawdust made Rowe sneeze."

A faint smile touched Noel's lips. "One of the workmen left a saw in a corner. The blade was jagged, capable of cutting through nearly anything." His jaw was tight. "I feel exactly like that saw blade."

"The lady in question, she knows your feelings?"

Noel threw back the last of his drink and returned to the decanter. Apparently, it was a two-whiskey afternoon. "She knows. And fled as if I'd told her about my love for cannibalism."

Holloway walked to him and held out his glass for a refill. "Civilizations all over the world have different thoughts about love. And the very fact that there are so many theories and myths about it shows that it's fucking complicated."

"Who the deuce said anything about

love?" Noel snapped. At Holloway's even, unblinking look, Noel slammed his glass down onto the table. Whiskey sloshed over the rim and onto his hand.

Scowling, Noel stuck the side of his hand into his mouth. He muttered, "I don't love her."

"But you're serrated as a handsaw, sucking whiskey off your hand, and in general acting like a moody ass. Yes," Holloway said carefully, "I can see that you clearly don't have feelings for the woman."

"Perhaps I do. What of it? It's not reciprocated."

"How certain are you of that?"

Noel crossed his arms over his chest. "She told me it was over. Didn't say why, though."

"What do you want for yourself, at least where this woman is concerned?"

"An abundance of questions, Holloway," Noel grumbled. "Now I'm your newest subject of study."

"What you are," Holloway said gently, "is my friend. The selfsame friend who trained me in all the ways of rakehood, rather than let me flounder and fail."

Noel swallowed around a hard mass in his throat. "If I hadn't, you would have caused mass panic whenever you appeared in public. It was for the nation's safety."

Behind the glass of his spectacles, Holloway's eyes were kind. "I ask again — what do you want for yourself and your lady?"

"I want to have her in my life," Noel answered at once. "Today and every day thereafter."

"Marriage?"

"I . . ." Hell. He'd never said anything to her about marriage. Only that he wanted to continue their liaison.

It didn't need to be an affair. It could be permanent.

His heart thudded heavily. But — "She's leaving the country."

"She might not, if you offered something more lasting."

Noel stilled. Then he flung himself into motion.

"I have to go." He took three steps toward the door, then came to a halt. "You're welcome to my cellar, Holloway, or my library or anything you damn well please."

His friend tilted his head to one side as he contemplated the bookshelves. "Most of your books are merely decorative, so I'll gratefully decline."

"Get stuffed," Noel said amenably before charging down the hallway.

He summoned his carriage, and within

minutes, he drove toward Hill Street. The entire way there, he clenched and un-clenched his hands. Once he reached her doorstep, once he saw her again, he'd get down on one knee . . .

Oh, but he wanted to kneel for her. He'd gladly be on his knees for her forever.

A lifetime with Jess, giving her endless pleasure, gratifying her every wish. It sounded just like heaven.

If she accepted him, he'd count himself one fortunate bastard, and spend every minute of every day of every year ensuring that she knew what a gift she'd given him.

If she refused him . . . he'd have to find some way of moving on with his life without his heart.

He didn't wait for the carriage to come to a stop before bounding out the door. Ner-vousness tensed his muscles — when was the last time he'd been nervous about *any-thing* — but he leapt up the front steps. He rapped sharply on the door.

No one answered.

He knocked again, and yet again, no one came to the door. He strained to hear a servant's tread or any movement at all within, but there was nothing. Not a sound, just utter stillness.

"There's no one there."

Noel turned at the sound of a woman's voice. A girl in a maid's tidy apron, a basket on her arm, stood on the pavement. When Noel stared at her, she made a quick curtsy.

"Come again?" he pressed.

"Begging your pardon, my lord," she said. "But nobody lives there."

He frowned. "She left for the Continent today?"

The maid shook her head. "There's been no one in that house for a month."

"But this is —" He checked the address. "Number eighteen."

"It is, my lord. The last tenant owned a heap of woolen mills, and he brought his wife and daughter for the Season. They hied off back to Leeds when the daughter ran away with a pianoforte tuner." At Noel's continued silence, she shifted uncomfortably. "I'm due home. Good day to you, my lord."

She hurried down the street before ducking into the mews.

Dazed, Noel walked slowly back to his carriage. None of this made sense. Jess had been here — he'd dropped her off only hours earlier. Did he see her go inside? She'd been distracted and on edge, so perhaps she had accidentally given him the wrong address.

Yet all of his conjecture meant nothing. Jess was gone.

"You're quiet as a churchyard, Miss Mc-Gale," Lady Catherton said as they rode to the Ashfords'.

"My apologies," Jess murmured. "Is there something you'd like to discuss, my lady?"

"Not particularly," her employer said. "But some conversation will help pass the time until we arrive."

Though her throat squeezed with anxiety, Jess forced herself to say, "I don't know much about the earl and countess except what I've read in the papers. In *her* newspaper, specifically. She owns and publishes the *Hawk's Eye.* She was born a commoner and is now a countess. Isn't that remarkable?"

"Remarkable — and scandalous."

It almost made one believe that happiness could be within any woman's reach. Almost. Jess knew better than to imagine the world could bend and change its shape for her.

She continued to talk with Lady Catherton, pure nonsense flowing from her — the latest fashions she'd observed during her time in London, gossip she'd read in scandal sheets like the *Hawk's Eye* — all the way to the Ashfords' grand Mayfair home. She operated a puppet, projecting her voice into the inanimate thing as it performed.

The carriage joined the queue of other elegant vehicles lined up outside the earl and countess's home. Finally, Lady Catherton's carriage came to a stop and a footman opened the door.

As the servant helped her mistress out, Jess had the wild impulse to grip onto the carriage's cushioned seat and refuse to let go. She'd have to be pulled out like someone taking an angry cat from a basket.

"Help me up the stairs, Miss McGale."

Swallowing her terror, Jess climbed down and took her place beside her employer. Lady Catherton put her hand on Jess's shoulder and held tightly.

Right. No bolting, then.

They merged with the guests ascending into the Ashfords' home. Once inside, they went up the staircase, moving slowly on account of the crush and Lady Catherton's ankle. Each step closer to the ballroom took a year off of Jess's life.

At last, they reached the doorway to the ballroom. Jess tried to hustle past the butler, but Lady Catherton hauled her back with remarkable strength.

"He must announce us first," her employer reminded her.

There was no help for it. Jess gave Lady Catherton's name to the butler, and he bellowed to the room, "The Dowager Countess of Catherton."

Jess herself did not rate an introduction.

A few heads turned in Lady Catherton's direction, but their gazes passed right over Jess, as if she didn't exist.

Thank God for being insignificant. There was no sign of Noel. No accusations or revelations of the fact that she wasn't a baronet's widow.

She scanned the guests. The earl's ballroom was exceptionally grand and glamorous, filled as it was with Society's darlings. Several chandeliers hung from the vaulted ceiling. Beneath the lights, the floor swirled with ladies' gowns of every hue, precious stones winking around their necks and from their ears. Gentlemen in dark evening clothes provided an elegantly sober counterpoint to the gowns. Music filled the air, courtesy of an octet installed in one corner, and servants circulated with trays of refreshments.

It was a triumphant night for the earl and countess.

For Jess, however, it was a crucible.

"I wish to take a turn around the room," Lady Catherton said.

"With a gentleman, perhaps?" Jess asked hopefully.

"Not tonight, when I am recently returned from the country. I'm certain my conversation would be too dull for a gentleman."

Jess swallowed hard and then offered her employer a supporting arm. Together, they skirted the dance floor. Lady Catherton was greeted by many, and some even remarked on her imminent departure to the Continent.

Walking stiffly, Jess was certain she would run into Noel. Her entire body tensed in nervous expectation.

If only she could hurry Lady Catherton's pace, they might be able to leave sooner.

"Goodness," her employer said as they reached the halfway point around the room. "Who knew that a week of inactivity could make one so prone to weakness?"

"Let us finish our turn and then say our goodbyes." Jess was pleased she didn't sound too eager. "You've made an appearance, but you must now see to your health."

After a moment, Lady Catherton said, "I think that I'll finish my turn and then head for home. I must see to my health, you know."

Jess allowed herself an exhale as they headed toward the entrance to the ballroom.

"His Grace, the Duke of Rotherby!"

She froze. There he stood, in his black evening clothes, a vision of beautiful masculinity.

Plans spun quickly in her mind. She could slow Lady Catherton, and wait until Noel stepped into the crowd. Then Jess could rush her employer out the door.

"A moment, Miss McGale," Lady Catherton said. "Before we go, I need some time to catch my breath."

"Of course."

Jess guided Lady Catherton toward a chair against the wall, before helping her employer down into the seat. "There," Jess said with forced brightness. "Isn't that better?"

She quickly scanned the room, but there was no sign of Noel.

Lady Catherton grunted. She unfolded the fan at her wrist and waved it in front of her face. "It's rather hot. Do fetch me a lemon ice."

Arguing was useless. "I'll be right back."

Jess hurried off toward the refreshment tables, where servants doled out punch, cakes, and ices. She quickly took a lemon ice from a footman and turned back, intent on reaching Lady Catherton as fast as possible.

She drew up short before colliding with a

gentleman. She looked up the long expanse of his silk-covered torso, then higher, to the snowy neck cloth, and then to the jawline — which was unmistakable.

"Noel," she blurted. "I mean, Your Grace." She dipped into a curtsy.

"Jess." He regarded her, clearly perplexed. "You're here."

She cleared her throat, then held up the little silver cup in her hand. "I'd heard the countess favored lemon ices, and it's been an age since I've had one, so here I am." She made herself eat a spoonful of ice to give truth to her lie, before setting the cup onto a passing servant's tray.

Noel frowned slightly, then his frown deepened when his gaze moved down, taking in her simple gray silk dress that had clearly been let out a few times. Hardly the gown a baronet's widow would wear.

She tried to think of an excuse for her unfashionable and drab clothing, but he said instead, "We must talk."

CHAPTER 25

"I —" She glanced quickly over her shoulder toward Lady Catherton. Fortunately, her employer was distracted by chatting with a lady with plumes in her hair.

The butler boomed, "The Dowager Countess of Farris, Baron Mentmore, and Viscount Pickhill."

Her stomach sank. Three guests from the Bazaar, here, now. And Noel.

She felt as though she'd been thrown into the middle of a lake and could only slap at the water to stay afloat.

"Jess."

She dragged her gaze back to Noel. "Noel, I mean, Your Grace —"

"Miss McGale." Lady Catherton's voice sounded right behind her. Jess pivoted to see her employer standing a few feet away. "I think it's time we . . . I beg your pardon, Your Grace." To Jess's horror, her employer smiled at Noel and executed a flawless curtsy. "Ah, I see you've met my companion."

Noel looked back and forth between Jess and Lady Catherton. "Lady Whitfield is your *companion*."

"I —" Jess managed before her employer spoke.

"Lady Whitfield? I'm not certain who you're talking about."

"The person standing right beside you." Noel gestured to Jess.

"I do hate to contradict Your Grace," Lady Catherton said deferentially, "but this person is Miss Jessica McGale, my hired companion."

"Miss McGale?" Noel said, his gaze fixed to Jess.

There were only a few times in Jess's life when she'd truly prayed. When her parents both fell ill, and she'd sent pleas to Heaven for them to get well. She'd prayed, too, that the fire would not destroy the family farm.

Her prayers had gone unanswered. Now she prayed that something, somehow, would stop this cataclysm.

Yet again, her fervent appeal to the heavens went unanswered.

Because she saw it then — she saw the moment that Noel understood.

The heartbreak in his dark eyes nearly

made her crumple. She actually staggered as it seemed the floor would give way beneath her. But the floor remained in place, Jess continued to stand, and she watched in abject misery as the wounded man vanished. In his place was a cold, indifferent duke who gazed at her as if she was merely a speck of dust that had landed on his pristine black jacket.

Just as the music ended, Lady Catherton said, "Miss McGale is most assuredly not someone named Lady Whitfield."

"Come again?" Lord Pickhill appeared, with Lady Farris and Baron Mentmore beside him. "We've spent the week with her, haven't we?"

"She was Lady Whitfield then," Baron Mentmore said. "But now she's Miss McGale?"

"McGale & McGale soap." Lady Farris stared at Jess, and the wounded look in her eyes was a fresh stab of guilt. "You conspired to infiltrate the Bazaar and then plant the idea of investing in the soap operation."

"It was a ploy." Baron Mentmore's face darkened with outrage. "The whole time, a mercenary ploy."

Lady Catherton looked astonished. "Miss McGale — is this true? You've pretended to be a *lady*?"

384

"She wore that very gown," Lord Pickhill said, waving toward Lady Catherton's dress. "*Your* gown."

In an instant, Jess saw her family's fortunes break apart. Lady Farris and the others would withdraw their investment capital, the repairs going unmade, the operation crumbling, and her siblings scattering to the wind. She'd ruined the business, ruined them.

All the nearby guests stared at the spectacle of Jess being confronted with the devastating outcome of her lies.

She tried to speak, but words did not materialize. Her eyes had gone hot and dry, and she could only stand there, rooted to the spot by a burning spike that went straight through her.

Lost. It was all lost. Because of her.

"My plan worked," Noel said.

Silence. Then Lady Farris said, "Your Grace?"

His voice a wry drawl, Noel said, "A lark, really. It's all been so tedious lately, everyone and everything the same as always. I used to pull pranks all the time in my school days, so I thought it would be amusing now, finding someone of ordinary birth to pose as one of us. Adding her to the Bazaar would make it even more droll. Miss Mc-

Gale agreed to my proposed scheme — it was even better that she had a business in need of investors. A soap-making business, you know, and quite excellent."

Gaze moving over the crowd, fully in command of everyone's attention, he continued. "At my direction, she presented herself as 'Lady Whitfield,' then, through the subtlest of means, presented McGale & McGale to the others. She followed all of *my* instructions. And," he added with a smirk, "everyone fell for it."

Jess stared at him. Was he truly saying all this? Protecting her?

"You cannot be serious, Your Grace," Lord Pickhill said.

"Believe what I say or don't, Pickhill. It hardly matters to me." Noel lifted one eyebrow, the picture of hauteur.

Lord Pickhill tugged at his lapels and chuckled. "It was well done of you. Very comical."

"Amusing," Baron Mentmore said, and added his own laughter.

Lady Farris said nothing, but Jess struggled to meet her incisive gaze. Did the countess accept Noel's explanation?

Everyone else did. There was laughter and nods all around and murmurs that His Grace had pulled off a remarkable prank.

Noel's chuckle was dry as autumn leaves. "With that, I bid you all good night."

The crowd parted as he strode out of the ballroom. Jess stared at his retreating back. She felt so many things, shock and gratitude and sorrow all combining into one tempest within her.

"Miss McGale, please explain," Lady Catherton said tightly. "Are you in His Grace's employ or mine?"

Jess did not heed her employer — likely, *former* employer — as she raced after Noel, clinging to a thread of hope. She could explain, and he might understand.

She caught up with him on the landing. Still wearing his smirk, he said, "Well done, Miss McGale. Everyone was fooled. I bid you good night — and goodbye."

His eyes were wintry, and as she looked into them, she saw that there was no hope. He was lost to her.

She had expected this, but that didn't make the pain any less. She struggled to remain standing, her hand clutching the stair railing for support. "Goodbye, Your Grace."

And then he was gone, his footsteps resounding in the corridor, speedy and clipped as he quickly walked away from her.

She stared at the space he'd occupied for

a long, terrible moment. Behind her, she heard the chatter, the excitement over the duke's jest, with cheerful music from the orchestra beneath it all. Surely the papers would declare the earl's gathering a rousing success, and people would talk about it, boasting if they had been there to witness it all, or else bemoaning the fact that they had not been in attendance.

All of this came to her as if she stared through a spyglass at some distant shore, far, far from her.

She walked heavily down the stairs, into a world absent of Noel.

CHAPTER 26

Jess stepped out of the servants' entrance, carrying her battered satchel. She had to leave behind the extensive lady's wardrobe, but those garments had never been hers in the first place. She was back to being Jess McGale again, with Jess McGale's minimal belongings.

It would be a long walk to the coaching yard, carrying this bag. She hefted it onto her shoulder to redistribute the weight.

Sorrow weighed heaviest. She'd carry Noel's sadness and sense of betrayal all the years ahead. What came next, she'd no idea. Though Noel had saved her from utter public humiliation, there'd be no rescuing McGale & McGale. Their investors would surely withdraw their capital.

It would all be gone soon. Everything. She'd lost him — for what?

She blinked hard, pushing back tears. In the past, she'd been able to salvage some semblance of hope, some slender lifeline to cling to. Misfortune had befallen her many times, and many times, she'd pressed onward, determined to persevere. If not for her own sake, for the sake of her family.

Not this time. There was nothing to clutch tightly, no faint prospect that she might somehow recover things. It was a new world and she'd no idea how to survive in it.

First, she needed to return home. With any luck, there'd be a mail coach heading toward Wiltshire tonight.

She took a step and her foot connected with a stone. It careened across the yard and knocked against the stable wall.

"Bloody bad luck, getting sacked," Lynch said as he emerged from the stables. His coat was gone and his waistcoat undone, and he held a book.

"I didn't mean to disturb you."

He waved off her comment. "No one but me and the horses, and we don't mind a bit of to-do now and again." Lynch's mouth curved into a sardonic half smile. "Whenever us working folk try to step out of the box they've made for us, we get beaten back."

"Foolish of me to attempt it." She couldn't keep the edge of bitterness from her voice.

Lynch stepped closer. "We've got to try,

otherwise everything stays the same. The gentry get what they want, and we're left in the muck. Bunch of blackguards, the lot of 'em."

"Not all of them are bad," she said automatically. "Some try to do good with the power they're given." She dashed a knuckle across her eyes in a vain attempt to stem her tears.

"You'll find a way back onto your feet. Can't keep a good woman from rising up. Like the sun. Every morning she's up in the east."

"Thank you," Jess said. "For telling me it's all right to dream. It's just . . ." She swallowed. "It's terrible when those dreams break apart."

"They'll mend." He shrugged. "Or they won't. Life likes to kick us in the bollocks."

"It does," she said ruefully. She'd fought hard, but perhaps those efforts had been laughable. God knew, she'd been deluding herself to ever believe she could have Noel.

"I'll take that." He plucked the satchel from her hand and walked toward the stables. "I'm giving you a ride to the coaching yard."

"Kind of you — but the mistress won't like it."

He said over his shoulder, "Nothing kind

about it. I just like telling them abovestairs to kiss my arse."

A laugh broke from her, like a bird startled from the scrub. "I'd say you were a good man, Lynch, but I'm not sure you are."

"Then we're a pair, ain't we?" He set her bag inside the carriage. "Now get aboard while I hitch the horses, and we'll get you the hell out of London."

She climbed into the vehicle and waited. As she did, she fought to bring comforting images of home to mind, seeking solace in its familiarity of the house itself and the fields and all the places she loved best.

But all she could imagine was the vast open spaces of her broken heart.

"Your Grace," Beale said with barely suppressed horror as Noel stepped into the bedchamber. "What has become of your coat?"

At his valet's exclamation, Noel glanced down at himself. His coat had begun the evening in a much more unsullied state, and now, after a night wandering the streets of London before finding himself at a dockside tavern, it was rumpled and stained. At least the blood on the sleeve wasn't his. It had spurted from the mouth of a man who'd thought it a fine diversion to pick a fight with a toff.

The tooth Noel had knocked from his assailant's mouth now lay upon the floor of the tavern, to be swept up — or not — by an unfortunate taproom wench.

"And your eye is atrocious," Beale added.

Noel's hand drifted up to the swelling spot beneath his left eye. The man who'd accosted him had managed to get in a single punch, but that lone blow had been enough. Noel would surely sport a bruise for a goodly while.

"Have you been to bed?" Noel rasped as he lowered himself into the chair by the fire. This was hardly the first time he'd kept his servants awake waiting for him, but tonight he carried the stink of the docks and cheap gin rather than the smell of expensive wine and a woman's perfume.

Beale crossed the room and tugged on the bellpull. "I amused myself by playing craps and beating the footmen out of sixpence." A few moments went by, and Mrs. Hitcham, the housekeeper, appeared. "His Grace requires a bath immediately. And some beefsteak for his eye."

"Yes, Mr. Beale." The housekeeper curtsied before speeding away.

Noel leaned his head back and closed his eyes, weary beyond imagining but certain he'd never find rest again. He tried to put his pain in a neat container, labeling it *Betrayal* and setting it on the shelf. He wasn't the first person to face treachery at the hands of a beloved. Others survived such grievous wounds. Surely he could do the same.

Try as he might, agony kept pushing its way out of its box. It wouldn't be contained, wouldn't be labeled. It simply *was,* and that *was* had become all-encompassing, taking over everything. Stealing his breath and grabbing him by the throat.

Jess. His lovely, brilliant Jess. Another liar who had used him.

He'd stupidly believed she was different from everyone else around him. With the exception of the Union, she'd been the one person he could trust, with whom he could fully be himself. He'd told her things he'd never revealed to anyone — she hadn't needed or wanted the urbane, influential Duke of Rotherby. She'd wanted Noel, the man. He'd been both physically and metaphorically naked with her, completely unguarded.

And what had that gotten him? Treachery.

He dimly heard the door open and servants walk through to his bathing chamber, then the sound of water being poured into his copper tub. The servants retreated, and Noel was once again alone with Beale.

"Up, Your Grace," his valet commanded. "We need to peel that abomination of a coat from you. There's every likelihood that it will require burning, not washing."

"Do with it what you like." Noel heaved himself to standing, shucking his coat as he did so. He had never liked being dressed or undressed by a servant, so he proceeded to strip himself, handing his garments to Beale.

He padded into the bathing chamber. Dawn light crept through the curtain in the narrow window, and a low-burning lamp illuminated the steam rising up from his waiting bathwater.

"For God's sake, Your Grace, don't dally." Beale pointed to the bath. "In you go."

Noel grumbled, but he'd grown used to his valet's high-handed ways. He stepped into the tub and sank down into the water with a groan. He ached everywhere — but the hot water couldn't touch the hurt that burrowed deep in his chest.

"Bathe first," Beale directed, "beefsteak after. Here." He put a cake of soap into Noel's hand.

Jess was everywhere. She surrounded him, engulfed him in her scent of honey and sunshine, and his heart leapt up with joy.

Was she here?

"What the fuck is this?" he growled at the soap in his hand.

His valet paused as he straightened a stack of towels. "It's from that farm you visited in Wiltshire. McGann? McGill?"

"McGale." Noel lobbed the soap across the room. It hit the wall and slid to the floor. Yet the scent held to his hand, and he scrubbed at it. He lifted his hands to his face and inhaled. The smell of her clung to his skin. "Get me another goddamned soap."

He never spoke to Beale so curtly, certainly not about something as inconsequential as soap, but anger and pain rose up as the scent held fast to him.

"Yes, Your Grace." The valet opened a cabinet and pulled out another cake of soap. He held it out to Noel. "Will this do?"

Noel took the soap and breathed in its fragrance. It was his usual soap, purchased from a Bond Street shop, and perfumed with bergamot. "It'll suffice."

He worked up a lather and washed, his movements jerky and tight. Surely to Beale he seemed like the veriest madman, throwing tantrums over *soap,* but Noel was past the point of caring what anyone thought. He'd cared about Jess and her thoughts and

396

feelings, and here he was, a wounded animal retreating to its lair to howl.

As he bathed, he made a silent vow. He'd gone through life carefully shielding himself from sycophants and flatterers, protecting himself from those that saw him as a resource to be exploited. He'd thought Jess different. Like a fool, he'd lowered his shields and failed to protect himself from both of them. And he paid the price.

Never again. He'd keep the world at arm's distance, keeping everyone back. He had loved once, but he would not do so a second time.

He knew better now.

"Fred! It's Jess! Come down at once," Cynthia called up the stairs. She rushed forward as Jess took a weary step inside the house. "My dearest. What are you doing here? What has happened? Sit. You look fit to collapse."

Her sister guided her to a chair at the kitchen's long table. Jess lowered herself down into it, wincing at her stiffened joints. She'd jounced and bounced in the mail coach for hours, which wasn't sprung nearly as well as Noel's carriage. She had also been wedged between three other passengers on one side, her knees knocking against the passengers sitting opposite her.

The coach had driven past the entrance to Carriford. Jess's head ached so badly she'd pressed a hand to where it throbbed. That pain continued here, in the kitchen she'd known her whole life.

"Have you eaten?" Cynthia asked.

Jess shook her head. "Not hungry."

Her sister made a clicking sound with her tongue. "You'll eat." She bustled around the familiar kitchen, putting the kettle on the hob, pulling down a loaf of bread, and slicing cheese.

Heavy male footfalls sounded on the steps. Fred came into the kitchen wearing an expression of concern.

"What's happened?" Fred knelt beside Jess's chair and rested a hand on her head. "Oh, Jess, I'm sorry, but you look awful."

Jess coughed up a weary laugh. "I feel awful, so you aren't far off the mark."

"Dearest, tell us." Cynthia squeezed her hand.

Jess took a breath, and then related the whole story. Certain details were left out or alluded to. What happened between her and Noel in the bedroom — and conservatory, and larder — was secret. Yet she did tell her family that she'd been intimate with Noel, and that she'd taken his trust and ruined it with her machinations.

"The hell of it is," she said, "I don't know if anyone is interested in McGale & McGale now. We've likely lost our investors — knowing what they know, they might shun us. The repairs won't happen and that will be the end of the soap making. We'll lose . . ." She could hardly form the words. "We'll lose each other. I'm so sorry. I failed us all."

"Oh, love, no." Cynthia pressed a kiss to Jess's forehead. "You did nothing of the sort. It was a mad gamble, and a price has been paid, but you tried, and that's enough."

"But it isn't," Jess said. She looked at her siblings, and the low-ceilinged kitchen, where, for nearly all of her life, she had taken her meals and laughed with her family and cried when loss had come for them all.

Who was there for Noel? Hopefully, his old school friends would offer him solace. They might even curse her, but it wasn't anything she didn't deserve. She couldn't ignore the terrible hurt she'd caused him, and she didn't want to ignore it, because she could never forgive herself for damaging a man that deserved so much better than he'd been given.

"It isn't enough," she choked out. "I've let

everyone down, and I've let myself down, too."

"Jess," Fred said, taking her face between his palms and locking his gaze with hers. "You did your best. We don't forgive you because there's nothing to forgive."

She stared into her brother's eyes. In them, she saw tiny mirrors of herself, but they weren't as small as how she felt on the inside.

CHAPTER 27

Days managed to crawl by. Jess existed from minute to minute, marking time with each aching throb of her heart. Yet she did not shrivel up and blow away. She moved forward. Slowly, to be sure, but forward.

She'd avoided reading the newspapers. The *Money Market* column held no interest, and there would be accounts of the Duke of Rotherby's amusing coup. Even reading Noel's name would blind her with fresh pain.

The knock at the door came midmorning of the third day after her return home. Fred was out, tending to the many chores that a farm always required, but Cynthia joined Jess as she opened the door.

"Good morning, McGales." George Griffith, the postal carrier, waved a letter. "All the way from London."

Jess's stomach clenched. It could be Noel — damning her, no doubt.

George handed Jess the mail before heading off to continue his deliveries.

She didn't recognize the penmanship, but that could mean a secretary had actually written the letter — if Noel felt that he couldn't be bothered to write it himself.

The paper shook in her hands. A minute went by, and then another. Was she strong enough today to read Noel's condemnation?

"Going to open it?" Cynthia asked.

"It might be from Noel." Her voice sounded lifeless.

Cynthia cupped her hand over Jess's shoulder. "Might make it easier if I read it first, so you know if it's bad or good."

"I should do this on my own."

Her sister gently turned Jess around to face her. "There's the crux of it, big sister."

"How do you mean?"

Cynthia's lips pressed into a line, as if she debated speaking. Finally, she said, "It's always been you, on your own. You've taken all of it on your shoulders — the farm, McGale & McGale — and leave me and Fred pottering about. It's like . . . it's like you don't trust us."

The words hit Jess like a slap. "I trust you."

"Not so certain of that." Cynthia's gaze dropped to the floor. "When Ma and Da died, you took her words to heart. You ran everything — the harvest of the honey, the buying of materials, paying our workers. Fred and me became just more workers, not your partners."

Jess opened her mouth to contradict her sister, but what Cynthia said was true. She'd run around like a whirlwind, overseeing the entire operation, never letting her siblings shoulder the responsibility of keeping Mc-Gale & McGale afloat.

"The fire made it worse," Cynthia went on quietly. "Even though Fred and me took outside work but stayed home, you left to become Lady Catherton's companion. It was like you thought you needed to do more, go further. Then when you were going to move to the Continent, it was up to you alone to save the business. But, Jess, we've been here." She lifted her eyes to Jess, and in them, there was love and acceptance and frustration. "Me and Fred, we're here. But you've got to trust us, love. Let us help you."

Jess blinked back tears, but they fell anyway. "I'm the big sister. With Ma and Da gone, I thought it was all my responsibility. I thought . . . that I was protecting you."

Her sister's smile was fond. "We're not babes in arms, Jessie. Might even surprise you to know I'm not a virgin. I think Fred isn't, either, but he and I don't like to talk about such things with each other."

Jess gave a watery laugh. "You're both my world."

"And you are ours." Cynthia pressed a kiss to Jess's damp cheek. "Now, are you going to read that London letter, or shall I?"

"I'll read it." There was a chance that Noel had written about their intimate encounters, and Jess needed to preserve his privacy.

She opened the letter and scanned the contents. Her breath left her in a rush, and she managed to rasp, "Oh, my God."

"What is it?" Cynthia demanded.

"A shop on Bond Street wants to meet with me — with *us,*" Jess corrected. Stunned, she continued, "They want to discuss selling McGale & McGale soap. We're to bring as much stock as we have." Jess stared at her sister. "They said it was because the duke had recommended our product to a ballroom full of England's elite. Already, they've turned away dozens of customers looking to buy our soap."

Cynthia let out a little shriek before throwing her arms around Jess. "My God, Jess. This is unbelievable — the very best news."

Jess hugged her sister, who was as tall, if not taller, than Jess herself. How obstinate she'd been to believe that Cynthia and Fred were still her little brother and sister.

She fought to make sense of what the letter from Daley's Emporium had said. Here was the possibility that McGale & McGale might be able to salvage itself — because of Noel.

But . . . "Cyn, if we can't get the blunt to make the repairs and modernize, we can't meet demand. They'll place an order we cannot fill."

"A step at a time, love. Let us celebrate this good fortune for a moment and then we can think logistics."

"Wise girl," Jess murmured.

Cynthia broke the embrace first. "I've got to find Fred. He needs to hear the good news." After giving Jess another kiss on the cheek, Cynthia ran down the path toward the barn and outbuildings, calling for her brother.

Alone, Jess allowed herself to sink to the ground, right on the threshold of her home. She read the letter again. Elation filled her, mixed with caution, which was the peculiar alchemy of adulthood. She wanted to believe that everything would be all right, but there was no certainty.

The urge to talk to Noel hit her strongly. He could offer his thoughts and opinions, say something witty to lighten her worry. He understood her ambition — he understood *her.*

Jess started to rise so she might grab pen and paper, then she stopped herself. Her hands curled into fists in her lap.

Even if she did write him, he'd never open her letter. Likely, he'd throw it into the fire and walk away before it became ashes — a fitting symbol. They had been mere embers, then blazed together before turning cold and dead.

As she knelt in the doorway of her family's home, she looked skyward. Success beckoned, but the price . . . the price was immeasurable.

Noel tipped his head back, draining his glass. There was no satisfying burn that came from strong liquor. Come to think of it, he hadn't felt that heat in days, not since he'd first started down this determined path of carousing. It was as useless as drinking tepid tea. He threw the glass to the floor, causing the people at his table to jump and look like startled rabbits.

"Give me something stronger," he demanded to the room at large.

A man in a publican's apron appeared, smiling too wide so he seemed like a ghoul.

"What would you like, Your Grace?"

"Scottish whiskey," Noel said. "American bourbon. Water from the sodding Thames. I. Don't. Care."

"Yes, Your Grace."

"And more wine for my dear, dear friends," Noel added, waving at the assortment of bucks and demimondaines draped around the table, who cheered in response. "Who are you, again?"

"Your bosom companions, Your Grace," a florid-faced lordling declared. "Recall — we met at the opera earlier and you swept us up in your excellent hospitality."

The last few hours, hell, the last few days, were a haze that Noel neither wanted nor cared to remember. His head was full of shrill laughter and his mouth tasted like a puddle in the middle of Charing Cross Road.

"Still here?" he slurred to the publican. "Unless you've a twin brother who is currently fetching my goddamned drink."

"I have a sister, Your Grace, but no twin brother."

Vision swimming, eyes gritty, Noel stared at the man. The publican bowed before racing off to fulfill Noel's command.

Noel slumped in his chair, weary to the very fibers of his being. The days where he woke without a venomous headache and a dry mouth were less frequent than the days he could barely stir from bed. Even Beale's pointed coughs as he gathered up Noel's carelessly discarded clothing couldn't make Noel give a damn about getting up and facing the world.

But face the world he did. At balls and assemblies and opera boxes and supper clubs and everywhere in the whole of the city where people gathered to enjoy themselves and make merry. Noel would make merry until it fucking killed him. Trouble was, with a broken heart, merriment seeped out of him, pooling like congealing blood on the field of battle.

He went to bed alone every night and woke up just as alone. But he'd keep trying, by God. He'd celebrate, carouse, and cavort like a madman and pretend that he was the same rake he'd been a few weeks earlier.

Yet he couldn't summon any pleasure when McCameron entered the chophouse. Posture as upright as ever, McCameron made his way through the riotous throng, nimbly ducking as a chicken bone flew through the air.

"Duncan," Noel cried. It seemed as good a time as ever to call his friend by his Christian name. Flinging his arm wide, Noel said,

"Join us. We're a disorderly bunch in need of a strong, reliable, and sober presence."

"Sobriety is in short supply," McCameron said, eyeing the cups, mugs, tankards, and glasses strewn about the table.

Noel shoved the various vessels to the ground, the clatter barely heard above shouts and laughter. "We are now the most ab . . . ab . . . abstemious of gatherings."

At that moment, the publican returned with a bottle. "From my own still, Your Grace."

"Piss off," Noel said affably.

"Yes, Your Grace." He bowed once more and melted away.

"Sit, sit," Noel directed to McCameron.

"There are no unoccupied chairs."

"He can have my seat, Your Grace," some ash-pale buck announced magnanimously.

"I must decline your hospitality," McCameron said. He eyed Noel. "Can you stand?"

"Perhaps," Noel replied. "Wouldn't lay odds on it, though. Bad investment." He winced at the word *investment*. He'd always associate it with Jess. He'd associate breathing with Jess, likewise feeling any emotion other than being utterly cup-shot.

"You and me are talking, but we're not doing it here." McCameron wrapped an arm around Noel's shoulders and hauled him up from his chair. "Up you get. Time for a wee cozy chat."

"Good thing you're such a braw laddie," Noel said, affecting a Scottish accent. Even to his own ears it was terrible, so he didn't use it again when he added, "I've the strong suspicion that if I attempt to stand without your support, my legs will liquify beneath me."

For all McCameron's strength, Noel had several inches on him, which made balance a rare commodity as they staggered outside. His friend half carried, half dragged Noel down the street, until they reached a narrow alley. McCameron deposited Noel onto a large empty crate, but made certain to prop him against the brick wall as it was dead certain that sitting Noel upright was impossible.

"This is charming." Noel's head lolled. A rat scurried by, yet what did it matter? He could be devoured by packs of vermin and wouldn't care. "Got all the comforts of home."

"We've stopped by," McCameron said, folding his arms across his chest. "Rowe, Curtis, Holloway, and me. Your ruddy butler said you weren't at home to callers. When the fuck have any of the Union been *callers*?"

"Perhaps I thought I should expand my social circle. You should commend my efforts to pursue a path of personal growth." The bricks behind Noel's head were slick with an unknown substance, yet he let it soak into his hair.

"That lot at the chophouse are your new friends?" McCameron snorted. "Fine group if you like having your bunghole licked."

"Sod off." Noel sagged forward, bracing his arms on his thighs, his head hanging down.

"Holloway and Curtis told me what happened. With the woman." McCameron's words were surprisingly gentle, given that he was more familiar with barking orders at his men. "What you said at Ashford's ball — none of it was true. It wasn't a prank."

Noel glared at his friend. "Like hell it wasn't."

"You forget, I met her. I saw how you looked at her. How she looked at you."

"Like a swindler looks at their mark," Noel spat.

"Lady Whitfield —"

"Is no lady," Noel snarled.

"That's what upsets you?" McCameron planted his hands on his hips. "The fact that she's a commoner?"

"I don't give a rat's arse if she's a commoner. She used me." His throat burned and he tried to swallow around it. "Jess deliberately set out to seduce me so she could bring in investors to that sodding soap operation."

"*Did* she seduce you?"

"Yes," Noel answered at once. Then, "Maybe. No. I don't goddamned know."

"I didn't see everything," McCameron mused. "If she targeted you specifically, that's unforgivable."

The fog of alcohol did nothing to cloud his remembrance of the Bazaar. How drawn he'd been to Jess, how she had asked him to go slowly. Whenever she'd talked of McGale & McGale, she had spoken to other members of the Bazaar, and he'd added himself to the discussion.

"I made some inquiries," McCameron continued, "into Jessica McGale and the McGale family."

"You've too much time on your hands," Noel grumbled. "Nosing around my affairs like a hound."

"We're not all of us titled toffs used to pissing our lives away."

Stung, Noel leveled a finger at his friend. "Ought to get yourself a woman."

McCameron's jaw tightened. "Tried that. She wanted someone else."

412

"Shit," Noel muttered as contrition tightened around him. "Was badly done of me, bringing her up. I didn't mean —"

"About the McGales," McCameron said, plowing doggedly ahead. "There was a fire —"

"I know about that," Noel mumbled.

"Her parents died about eight months before that fire. She had to take over running the operation, and then the fire happened. She took a position as a companion, most likely to save up enough to rebuild."

"Doesn't matter what her motivation was. She lied. The whole time, she lied. To further her own ambition."

He'd told himself that he would never be taken in by a liar. He'd never be hurt by someone's deceit.

But he had. He bloody well had.

"Aye, she did." McCameron nodded. "Can't help but wonder, if I was in her place, and stood to lose it all, what would I do? How far would I go to take care of the people I love?"

"Damn it." Noel tugged his hands through his hair. "I don't know. I don't know a fucking thing."

"Do any of us?"

"Curse you — I'm sobering up."

"Ah, now that's a shame," McCameron said.

"Always looking out for me," Noel accused. "Like you did back at Eton. All of you, setting me down a peg, opening my eyes, making me *think.*" He spat the last word as though it was a vile practice. "Why? Why'd you all do that? Could have left me to sink into the mire of my own pride — yet you didn't. Why'd any of you take the trouble?"

McCameron exhaled a tiny laugh. "Because, jackass, we saw that you had the potential to be something great. To this day, every single one of us believes it still."

"Amazing that four men could be so very wrong," Noel said after a moment.

"Amazing that you're still a prideful bastard," McCameron replied. "I'd suggest we go in search of a drink, but you're sotted enough as it is." He moved forward and once again slid his arm around Noel, then hauled him to his feet. "Time to drag you home. And when you pass out, I'll help myself to what's left of your cellar."

CHAPTER 28

"Mind where you step, Cyn," Jess cautioned, guiding her sister through the Bond Street throng. "You'll crash into one of the fine folk and make them drop their parcels, and that's no way to make an impression on Mr. Daley."

"Can't help it," Cynthia whispered. "There's so much. Have you ever seen such *hats,* Jess?" She stared as a woman in an enormous feathered bonnet glided past. "I think there's a whole forest of birds on that one. I want to feed her crackers."

"Gawking later." Holding on to her sister's elbow, Jess maneuvered them toward Daley's Emporium. She tried, without success, to navigate around her memories of meeting Noel here, but their spectral selves haunted the pavement, ghostly apparitions that only served to remind her of what had been lost. "Business first."

Bless her, Cynthia snapped to attention.

415

"Right you are. This is the place?" She stared at the sign proclaiming Mr. Daley's shop.

"It is." Jess drew in a steadying breath. "Remember what I told you."

"Don't touch anything and don't stare at the customers," Cynthia echoed, then rolled her eyes. "Remember what *I* told you. I'm not a child anymore."

Jess smiled ruefully. "Point taken. Ready?" She straightened the collar of her pelisse, though she fought the urge to perform the same service for her sister.

Cynthia hefted the satchel in her arms. "Ready."

"Here we go." Jess pushed open the door to Daley's Emporium. Inside was exactly the same as it had been weeks ago when she'd first visited here, with the same shelves and counters full of high-quality merchandise, the shop itself filled with elegant people.

"Mr. Daley," she said to the pale man watching the clerks with a sharp eye.

His expression brightened and he came out from behind the counter. "Ah, Miss McGale."

"This is my sister, Cynthia McGale."

Cyn curtsied. "Thank you for meeting us, Mr. Daley."

"I cannot tell you what a relief it is to have you here at last." The shop owner guided them toward a quiet corner. "The number of customers asking for your soap surpasses all expectations."

"We've three dozen bars of soap in here," Jess said, patting the satchel Cynthia carried. "There's a crate holding five dozen more back at the coaching inn, which we can bring if we come to a mutually agreeable arrangement."

Mr. Daley nodded. "My emporium wants exclusive rights to carry McGale & McGale soap."

"For how long?" Cynthia asked.

The shop owner blinked, clearly surprised at the question. "I imagine . . . a year to begin with."

Jess and Cynthia shared a look. "Three months to start," Jess said.

"Oh." Mr. Daley blinked again. "Six months."

"Four," Cynthia countered.

After a moment, the shop owner inclined his head. "Very good. Four months at the onset."

"At which point we will renegotiate," Jess said crisply. "We must be candid, Mr. Daley. The repairs to our operation still need to happen, especially if we're to meet your customers' demands. Surely we can revisit your decision regarding the provision of the necessary capital required to fund these repairs."

"It is quite unusual for the Emporium to enter into such an arrangement," Mr. Daley said uncertainly.

"Unusual, but possible," Cynthia said. "Consider what that investment will secure you — exclusive rights to sell McGale & McGale soap, and the possibility to gratify all of your customers' wishes." She nodded slowly.

"True, true." Mr. Daley mirrored Cynthia's nods. "I think we can supply the means to accomplish those repairs. I employ a bookkeeper — you can send him the estimate."

Jess had never been so proud of her sister than she was at that moment. Cynthia's negotiating skills were incomparable, and remorse pinched Jess to think of how much she'd underestimated her siblings.

The rest of the meeting went smoothly, with handshakes securing the partnership and wide smiles from Mr. Daley. When it was at last concluded, Jess and Cynthia emerged from the shop and walked half a block before ducking into an alleyway.

"We did it," Cynthia said in wonderment.

She grabbed hold of Jess's hands and swung them.

"We did."

"McGale & McGale, sold on Bond Street!" Cynthia let out a little scream of excitement.

"You were brilliant, my love. Had him agreeing to our terms and nodding along with you."

"Only following in the path blazed by my big sister." Cynthia peered at Jess. "Aren't you happy, Jessie? We've just rescued Mc-Gale & McGale, and you look positively dejected."

Jess made herself smile. "I'm happy. I *am*," she averred when Cynthia looked like she wanted to argue the point. "Only tired, and there's much to do, many things to consider."

Though Cynthia's brow furrowed with concern, she seemed to know better than to press a point when it was clear that Jess didn't want to discuss it. "We'll have to rush back to Honiton to get the wheels turning. There should be space on tomorrow's mail coach."

"You can have the rest of the day to explore London. I recommend Catton's, and Covent Garden Market." Two places Jess could never go again, not without drowning in bittersweet memories. She threaded her arm through her sister's and walked toward the street.

Cynthia halted. "Aren't you coming with me?"

"Before I return to Wiltshire, there are some things here in the city I need to take care of," Jess said sadly.

"I'll come with you," her sister offered.

"I've got to go on my own. But don't worry." She made herself smile. "I'll meet you at the coaching inn tonight and we can have supper together." It would be a rare treat to spend the evening with her sister away from home, but there was no chance Jess would enjoy her meal. She would eat and sleep and go on, of course, but she'd never again feel joy in anything. That was certain.

"You're telling me the truth?" Lady Farris studied Jess from the other side of the tea table. Like everything else in the countess's home, it was graceful and restrained — which contrasted with the bright buttercup-yellow wall in the drawing room, a color more exuberant than elegant.

"You deserve complete honesty," Jess answered. She looked down at her hands in her lap, then up again. "It was all my idea,

420

not Noel's — His Grace's. I deceived him, and you, and everyone at the Bazaar."

"That is . . . quite astounding." Lady Farris sat back, her expression dazed.

"And true."

The countess rose to her feet, and paced to the drawing room window, where she looked at the passing traffic. "If that's so . . ."

Jess braced herself for Lady Farris's condemnation. Though they hadn't known each other for long, she'd come to value the countess's camaraderie. Yet she had to be prepared to lose it.

"If that's so," Lady Farris said, turning to face Jess, "then it's even better."

Jess's mouth fell open. "I — What?"

"English society, especially the *ton,* is an ancient, crumbling castle that desperately needs leveling." Lady Farris took several steps forward. "And you, Miss McGale, are the incendiary device."

"But I *lied.*" Jess stood. "To Lord Trask. To you, the duke. To everyone."

"That's something that you'll have to live with," the countess said evenly. "Which won't be easy."

Jess could only stare at Lady Farris. She had planned for many outcomes, but this had not been one of them. "You aren't angry."

"I am. I don't enjoy being deceived." The countess raised an eyebrow. "But I admire you, Miss McGale. You were no one's pawn, which is no small feat for a woman in this world."

"You humble me," Jess murmured.

"Unfortunately, a small amount of humility is necessary. Even so," the countess went on, tapping a finger to her chin, "I must ask, everything you did, the falsehoods you told, the role you played — what was the cost?"

A small, forlorn smile touched Jess's lips. She touched the ha'penny in her reticule, which would, no doubt, become smooth and worn as a pebble from her constant handling of it.

"In the case of the duke, it cost me everything."

Noel turned the seashell over in his hand, its smooth surface cool against his palm. He set it back down in its cubby before moving on to the next object in his grandfather's cabinet of curiosities.

He hadn't been in this room since he was a child, when he used to find the collection of oddments and rarities fascinating. His grandfather once employed a man to travel in search of new additions to the cabinet, and as a boy, Noel had believed that line of work was far preferable to being a duke. To his young eyes, dukehood involved the dullest of tasks — interminable meetings with dust-dry men, tromping off to Parliament to hear and speak to more boring men. Nothing exciting like hunting down fragments of ancient pottery buried within the earth, or collecting jewel-bright butterflies from tropical latitudes.

This morning, he'd awakened — alone as usual, sober, less usual — and was seized by a powerful urge to visit his grandfather's cabinet once more. Perusing the shelves and drawers of curiosities was preferable to pacing and brooding and staring out of his study window, which was all he'd been good for since McCameron had hauled him out of the chophouse and told him the circumstances behind Jess's bid to save her family's business.

He'd thought of no one and nothing else. During daylight hours and in the evening, even in his dreams, where he still felt her touch and heard her sensual commands. When traveling around town, he directed his coachman to drive through Covent Garden, even if it was nowhere near his final destination. But he couldn't keep himself from that place, burning with anger and sadness and aching to hear her voice again.

"Forgive me for disturbing you, Your Grace," his butler intoned from the doorway. "A visitor is requesting a moment of your time."

"I said I'm not at home to callers, Symes," Noel said, an edge in his voice.

"Understood, Your Grace." The butler bowed. "I will tell her."

Noel stilled, though his heart thundered. "Her."

"Yes, Your Grace. Miss Jessica McGale. She asked to see you, and, barring that, she was to deliver a letter. Shall I accept the letter and send the young woman on her way?"

The shelves of the cabinet were crowded with things, so many things, all of them keen reminders that there was nothing that could withstand time. Eventually, all creatures, all civilizations, all beliefs — they all vanished. Leaving one with only the present moment.

"Show her into the green drawing room," he said.

"Yes, Your Grace." Symes retreated.

Noel picked up his coat, which he'd draped over a marble bust of a Roman senator, and tugged it on. His whole body was stiff and tight. He was a stranger in his own skin, but then, he'd been unknown to himself ever since the night of Ashford's ball.

Were he wise, he would send Jess away, and burn whatever letter she left behind without reading it. Perhaps that was the fault of being born a ducal heir — he was unused to denying his impulses, and right now, every impulse and instinct he had shouted that Jess was near, and he had to see her, regardless of the pain it caused him.

After three leisurely, unhurried steps toward the green drawing room, he all but ran down the corridor. He made himself pause outside the door to the chamber. He fussed with the cuffs of his shirt — it became vitally important that just the right hint of white appeared at the edge of his sleeves — and then, with one shaky exhalation, he entered the room.

She stood next to the portrait of Noel and his sisters, studying it, then whirled around at his entrance.

Concern dug into him to see the violet circles beneath her eyes, and the pale cast of her face. Her dress — the same one she'd worn when he first met her on Bond Street, the one she'd had on when they'd visited Covent Garden — was too loose now.

He imagined iron spikes hammered into

his boots to keep him from going to her and running a concerned hand across her forehead.

Silence stretched between them.

"You and your sisters?" She gestured to the portrait behind her.

"Painted when I was nine, Sophia was seven, and Elizabeth was four."

Her mouth curved slightly. "One of them loves harebells."

Of course Jess would remember that. Of course she had a mind as sharp and expansive as any scholar — because she was her.

"Thank you for agreeing to see me," she said when he'd gone mute once more.

"I shouldn't have."

She winced at his bluntness, and, like a fool, he wanted to comfort her from his own words.

"I will go," she said, her eyes bleak. "But I hope you'll allow me a minute more."

He crossed his arms over his chest. "Talk, then."

"Your anger is justified," she said after a moment. She did not fidget, or shuffle her feet. She was immobile, as if facing an inevitable fate. "I'll never contest that. Just as I won't contest your kindness at the Earl of Ashford's ball. You could have left me to be torn apart, but you didn't. For that, I'm

426

grateful."

He chopped his hand through the air. "It was instinct. I protect people I —" He bit back words he couldn't let himself speak.

"Whatever made you do it, I'm indebted." Her smile was melancholy. "Though I imagine you don't want anything from me."

"Perceptive as always." His words were acidic in his throat. Then, because he could not help himself, he said, "Lost your investors, I suppose."

"We did — all but Lady Farris. She pledged some capital to aid in our rebuilding. And," she added, "thanks to you, McGale & McGale soap has become a fiercely coveted item. As of today, Daley's Emporium will be the only shop in London to exclusively carry our soap. Mr. Daley has even agreed to finance part of the repairs to our operation in order to supply enough product to his customers, so between his funds and Lady Farris's, we have a chance after all."

"Jess, that's wonderful." The words were out of his mouth before he could stop them, and he clamped his lips together to silence any more felicitations or pleasure in her accomplishment.

She seemed to recognize that he regretted his praise, her expression dimming. "It will require trips to the city to supervise shipments. But you don't have to worry. I won't return to London. Cynthia will oversee everything."

He stared at her. "This must be the attainment of your ambition, why you infiltrated the Bazaar. Everything you wanted, you're getting. You should be the one to come to London and enjoy the fruits of your labors."

"It is." She lifted a shoulder. "But there's always a chance you and I would see each other, and" — her throat worked — "I know you wouldn't want that. It's better if I stay away — permanently."

His body locked to keep from staggering as her meaning hit him. She was giving up the realization of something that clearly meant everything to her — for his sake.

Yet she had been the one to lie. It had been her deceit that caused the chasm between them.

"I can't praise the medicine when you administered the poison," he said.

Her lids closed, and she shuddered once, as if trying to master agony. "It would be wrong and false to seek your forgiveness when I deserve none of it." She opened her eyes, shining with tears. "All I can say is, I'm so very sorry, Noel. So sorry I was not honest with you. It was never right, what I did. It was all wrong. I was on the verge of losing the family home. Without that home, I'd lose my siblings, too. I was desperate to keep that from happening, and acted desperately, though that's no excuse."

She ran the back of her hand across her eyes. "Whatever you think of me, I want you to know one true thing."

"Tell me."

Her lower lip trembled — he remembered how she hated to show signs of weakness, but here she was, vulnerable and raw.

"Everything between us," she went on, her words urgent, "was all true. Every moment we had together, I gave you my genuine self. There was no dissembling there, not in my words and never in my body." Her smile shook as tears tracked down her cheeks. "Being with you brought me a happiness I've never known, and will never know again. I do not regret knowing you, but for the rest of my life I'll regret the hurt I caused you."

His body ached with the need to hold her, yet he had to deny that need. He had to deny everything because of her, and what she'd done. Didn't he?

Goddamn this uncertainty. Goddamn *her,* and himself. Because he was flayed and had no idea how to heal.

"Your time is valuable, and I've squandered enough of it already." She rushed toward the door, tugging it open. "Goodbye, Noel."

He watched her go, his wounded heart following in her wake. The door closed and footsteps rushed away, growing fainter until they disappeared.

For several minutes he could do nothing but stare at the place where she'd stood. Her words rang within him — whispers that reverberated, growing and growing until they were as loud as screams. He'd never seen her so unprotected and exposed, but she'd had enough faith in him to be without defenses, knowing full well that he could have seized his advantage and torn her apart.

With her deception, she'd dealt him a blow that had proven nearly mortal. Certainly, it scarred.

But where did that leave him now? Where did that leave them?

He did not know if he could trust her again. But she'd trusted him, and that was something he could not cast aside.

A life without Jess . . . or a life with her. Damaged, yes, but wiser, and ready to move forward into an unknown but limitless future.

He wrenched the door open and raced down the corridor. Symes was in the entryway, making minute adjustments to a collection of porcelain vases.

"Where is she?" Noel demanded. If she was on foot, he could go after her, chase her down.

"The young woman looked distressed, Your Grace, so I took the liberty of putting her in a cab. She left several minutes ago."

"She must have given her destination to the driver."

"If she did, alas I did not hear it." The butler clasped his hands behind his back. "Shall I summon the carriage?"

To run all over London, searching for her. Perhaps the kindest thing would be to relinquish her, allow them both to get on with their lives, because he was not certain he could ever truly forgive her. He was not certain of anything anymore.

CHAPTER 29

Jess stood at a safe distance from the workmen, hands on her hips as she watched the rebuilding efforts. The afternoon air was dense with pollen and sawdust, creating thick beams of sunlight as timbers were hauled into place. They would serve as supports for the roof for the open-air structure. New equipment stood nearby in crates, ready to be unpacked when the final nail had been hammered into the building.

It could not come fast enough. Three new orders were tucked into her apron pocket from shops across the country — Manchester, Liverpool, Birmingham — eager to stock McGale & McGale soap. And with those orders had come a missive from Mr. Daley. The Emporium was nearing the end of their supply of soap, and currently had a list of customers eager to buy more when the next shipment came in.

"How much longer, do you reckon?" Fred

asked, coming to stand beside her.

"Mr. Troutte says by the end of the week nearly everything should be completed."

Her brother exhaled. "Can't keep 'em waiting long."

"We won't." She'd worked too hard, lost too much, to let anything stand in the way of McGale & McGale's progress.

Fred clapped his hands together, the same habitual gesture of excitement he'd been making all his life. He beamed at her. "It's truly happening, isn't it?"

"It is." For the past weeks, she'd done everything she could to secure the business's future, including hiring the workmen for repairs, ordering and receiving the needed equipment, and staying vigilant in her bookkeeping so that their costs and profits were well monitored.

This was supposed to be the most thrilling time of her life.

Yet she was sluggish and fatigued constantly. Her siblings' exhilaration seemed far away, barely glimpsed through a fog. She tried to join in on their eagerness, their good humor, and the sense of relief that at last McGale & McGale was no longer at death's door.

She was here in Wiltshire, but her thoughts, her heart, those were both in

London. In Mayfair, and that green-hued room that held the portrait of young Noel, his eyes playful but his arms wrapped protectively around his sisters' shoulders. That room was the last place she'd seen him, and she pinned it in her memory to return to again and again over the solitary years ahead.

Cynthia strode up. "Someone's here for you, Jess."

"The business is yours and Fred's now," she answered. "I'm just here to help you two. Whoever's come about McGale & McGale can speak to one of you."

"Aye, but I don't think this gent wants me or Fred," Cynthia said. "He's come a long way for *you.*"

Jess exhaled — she'd deliberately stepped back from being the figurehead of the business. She would help the operation grow and function, but it was no longer hers to steer. A month earlier, she'd wanted nothing more than to be in charge of McGale & McGale as it entered into a new stage of development. She hadn't merely exiled herself from London, she'd deliberately exiled herself from joy.

"Go see him, Jess," Cynthia said gently. "Only this once. He's waiting outside the house."

There was no harm in it this final time. "As you like."

She headed toward the house, footsteps leaden. Perhaps it was Mr. Daley, come to see how his investment was progressing. Lady Farris's capital had also assisted considerably, so there was a possibility that she'd sent her man of business to take a look at the construction.

Drawing nearer to the house, she saw a man waiting in the front garden. He was broad-shouldered and elegantly dressed and so spectacularly handsome that more than a few sighs went up — from men and women. There was only one man in the world like him, and a month ago, Jess had been fortunate enough to be sheltered in his embrace. She'd known his taste and his feel and, briefly, she'd known what it was like to have him care for her.

Joy and sorrow collided in her, leaving chaos in their wake.

There was caution in his dark gaze as she approached.

"Noel," Jess said breathlessly.

"Jess." He nodded at her, his expression giving away nothing.

Her heartbeat roared in her ears. She couldn't begin to guess why he'd come. Perhaps he was on his way to Carriford . . .

but no . . . that was in the other direction . . . so why . . . ?

Closer inspection of his face revealed a new gauntness, and there was dark stubble on his cheeks and chin.

"Are you well? Forgive me," she added, "I've no right to ask, only . . ."

"I'm not sleeping," he said, his eyes fixed on a point over her shoulder.

Pain on his behalf gripped her. "I'm sorry."

His gaze found her face. "Why should you be sorry?"

"I don't want you suffering in any way. You might not believe that, but it's true."

His look was piercing, going all the way into the deepest part of her. She tried to hold still for his perusal, yet she'd no idea what he looked for, or if he found it.

Agony twisted inside of her. She had this one chance with him before he turned and walked away from her forever, one chance to try to repair some of the damage she'd done.

"I *am* sorry, Noel," she said. "For all of it. And I know that you might never believe that, but I will go to my grave cherishing my time with you. I will breathe my last breath content that, for a very short time, I had the privilege of loving you."

Oh, damn. She'd said it.

His body jerked, as if she'd struck him. *"What?"*

"I didn't mean to say that," she whispered. "It's not fair of me to speak those words when I know that you —"

He closed the distance between them. At his sides, his hands flexed, as though he struggled not to hold her. He demanded, "You love me?"

She'd thought she had cried her final tear, but her cheeks were wet. "I do love you. But," she added hoarsely, "it doesn't signify anything. Love isn't a weapon. It's not a way to bind someone to you or make someone feel obligated. It should be a gift, a blessing."

His words gravelly, he said, "I went back and forth with myself for weeks, trying to decide what to do. Let you go, or go after you. Didn't eat, couldn't rest. Went nowhere and saw no one. Not even the Union. Because I had to understand it on my own.

"And I learned something." His voice was low and urgent. "Love is many things. It's a bullet and it's a balm. Some people fire it with the intention to wound or kill. And others ease the hurts we've suffered over the course of our lives. Sometimes, love is both. It brings you such pain and yet you want that pain because it proves that you're alive. It's so much better to be alive and hurting than dead and numb."

As he spoke, she felt her pulse speed faster and faster.

His gaze burned her. "Jess. You did hurt me. Terribly. But," he continued over her when she tried to apologize again, "I understand why you did what you did. The wound you gave me would not have been so deep if I hadn't loved you."

Her breath caught, yet she said, "*Loved.* Past tense."

"Present tense." He reached up and gently cupped her jaw. "I love you, Jess. I never stopped. You're courageous and you know your mind and you're the most intelligent person I know — and I know some damned brilliant people. And," he went on, his words so deep that they went right to the heart of her, "you see me not as a duke, but as a man."

He tipped her chin up as he stepped even closer, the distance between them shrinking to scant inches. "When I'm with you, I'm more myself than ever before. I know what I am with you. I know *who* I am."

"Who are you?" she breathed.

"I'm just Noel. You are just Jess." His voice thickened. "And I would be so honored, so very humbled, if you would be my duchess."

She stared at him. Surely she hadn't heard him properly. "I'm a commoner. I deceived you."

"Yes, and yes." Naked longing shone in his gaze. "And I want to move forward with you in my life. Be beside me, Jess. Always."

"I . . ." She couldn't find words, not a single one. Happiness rushed through her, so intense it verged on pain, but she leaned into that pain. Loving it. Loving him.

His brow furrowed. "Do you want me to kneel? Because I will do it. I'll kneel for you, Jess. Only you."

When he started to sink down, she gripped his arms tightly, trying to keep him on his feet. He looked up at her, a flare of fear in his eyes, as if she might refuse him.

Nothing could be further from the truth. "Not yet," she murmured. "The next time you kneel before me, by God, we will have the time and privacy to enjoy it." She went on, "I do love you on your knees. I love that you love me to command you. I will, you know. Command you."

Slowly, his expression brightened. "What will you command me to do?"

"So many wicked things. You do them so well." She lifted up on her toes to put her mouth to his.

He kissed her back, searing and urgent. Then he pulled away enough to ask, "That's a yes?"

She laughed. "It's a yes. But, Noel," she could not stop herself from saying, "all of what I said is true. I'm a commoner, a farmer's daughter. Surely if I become your duchess, you will shock Society. You'll lose friends."

"I might," he said. "And I don't give a goddamn about it. What Society believes doesn't matter to me. And my true friends will adore you, as I do."

"Not *exactly* as you do," she said with a grin.

"Not exactly." He looped his arms around her, drawing her as close as two clothed beings could be. "I vow to spend the remainder of my days serving you, giving you pleasure. Loving you." His gaze was dark and limitless and hot. "Will that satisfy you, Jess?"

"Oh, yes," she whispered against his lips. "That will satisfy me, indeed."

EPILOGUE
FOUR MONTHS LATER

The open window let in a faint trace of woodsmoke on the crisp autumn air. From her place at the kitchen table, with the ledgers open in front of her, Jess drew the fragrance deep into her lungs.

She sanded the pages now covered with her columns of numbers. Her work had taken her most of the morning and into the afternoon, but she didn't mind her labor. Not when the end result was so wonderful.

Jess stretched as she rose from the table, working out the stiffness that had collected in her bones from sitting for hours. Once she'd loosened her body, she headed outside, eager to tell everyone the good news.

McGale & McGale Honey Soap thrived. She had the figures to prove it.

The staff was busy making enough soap to fill the staggering number of orders that had come in now that the term of exclusivity with Daley's had ended. It seemed that having a duchess as part owner and operator of a business was enough of a novelty to attract customers, but the quality of the product kept them coming back for more.

Meeting the demand had been a struggle, since there simply hadn't been enough hands. But after sending out word that the operation was in the process of expansion and in need of help, people found their way to Honiton. Many of the McGale & McGale workers were veterans, as well as widows, and others seeking steady employment.

She headed toward the main barn. As she walked toward it, she passed Fred.

"Come with me," she said to him. "I've some information to share with you, Cynthia, and Noel."

"You'll find both of them in the shipping yard," Fred said. "Can't you tell me now?"

"No preferential treatment." Jess sniffed, but she likely punctured her faux annoyance by grinning. "About-face, sirrah."

Her brother grumbled, but he fell into step beside her as they walked toward the part of the farm where delivery drays were loaded. Several heavy wagons stood there now, and a line of workers passed crates of soap to each other, moving them from where they were boxed up to the drays themselves.

As Jess neared, her gaze moved down the line of workers. One man had his back to her as he accepted each box and stacked them in the bed of the wagon, working without a coat and waistcoat. No mistaking who it was — her husband.

The wild happiness she felt whenever she saw him struck her anew. It opened petals within her, blossoming.

"A duke stacking boxes of soap in a wagon is certainly not a typically aristocratic pastime," she said as she approached. "But you're anything from a typical aristocrat."

"That's because I've perfected what it means to be a toff," he said easily.

"I've some news," she said.

"Paul, will you take my place in line?" Noel asked the man standing beside him. When Paul nodded, Noel stepped away from his task. He grabbed his coat and waistcoat, which had been draped over one side of the wagon, and shrugged into both of them. A moment later, he stood next to Jess and took her hand in his.

At this rate, Jess would have a whole meadow full of happiness blooming inside her.

"Tell us!" Cynthia said, bouncing on the balls of her feet.

Jess looked at each of them — her sister, Fred, and Noel all looking at her expectantly — and couldn't contain her grin. "We've made a profit. Not a little one, either. Our net profit margin is twenty-three percent."

Cynthia let out a whoop, and Fred beamed.

Noel turned to her and cupped her jaw with one of his broad hands. Affection was warm in his gaze as he murmured, "By God, Jess, you're a wonder."

"It was a group effort," she said. "The credit belongs to all of us."

"But *you* were the one steering the ship. *You* brought us here."

"I like that." She ran her fingertip over his lips. "How you say *us.*"

"It's always *us,* Jess."

He bent to kiss her, but froze when Cynthia called, "Oof, have a care for your workers' delicate sensibilities."

Jess scowled at her sister. Before Jess could call back a rude reply, Noel lightly held her chin and moved her to face him once more.

He kissed her. In full view of all of their workers, uncaring what anyone might think of a duke seducing his duchess in plain sight, he kissed her deeply.

"For God's sake," Cynthia grumbled.

"Flaunt your undying love somewhere else."

"As you like, dearest little sister," Jess said, though her words were a little breathless.

"Meant to tell you," Noel said, weaving his fingers with hers and leading her away, "a letter came to Carriford this morning and I hadn't a chance to say. Lord Trask has already requested that we both attend next year's Bazaar."

"That's not for months and months."

Noel shrugged. "Suppose he wanted, and I quote, 'two of England's top financial minds' to give his event a little more polish. After the wild success of Catton's, and then the Graveses' fire-suppression system, he knew that we were both necessary components for the Bazaar."

"A wise man, that Lord Trask." She noticed that Noel guided her toward their waiting carriage. "Should we go back to Carriford now? They might need me here."

"They might," he agreed. "Did you want to remain?"

"That depends."

"On?"

"If *you* need me."

His gaze turned sultry and his voice dropped into a growl. "I need you, Jess. *Now.*"

Her whole body heated, and she slid her

445

hands up his solid chest. "That's something we haven't tried." She glanced meaningfully at the carriage.

"Today's the day we do." He helped her up into the vehicle, then climbed in beside her and shut the door. He pulled down the curtains in each of the windows, turning the interior of the carriage dim and intimate.

At once, he knelt between her legs, his hands gathering her skirts as they slid up her legs.

She tried for a laugh, but the sound came out more of a gasp. Arousal climbed higher with each of his caresses. "What have I done with the influential, urbane duke?"

"He's right here," Noel rumbled. "On his knees before you. Exactly where he wants to be."

ABOUT THE AUTHOR

Eva Leigh is a romance author who has always loved the Regency era. She writes novels chock-full of determined women and sexy men. She enjoys baking, spending too much time on the Internet, and listening to music from the '80s. Eva and her husband live in Central California.